THE LITTLE SAVAGE

Frederick Marryat

THE LITTLE SAVAGE

THIS IS FAIRY GOLD, BOY; AND 'T WILL
PROVE SO.

SHAKESPEARE

BIBLIOBAZAAR

THE LITTLE SAVAGE

INTRODUCTION

There is a reference, in *The Life and Letters of Captain Marryat* by his daughter Florence Marryat, to *"The Little Savage*, only two chapters of the second volume of which were written by himself."

This sentence may be variously interpreted, but most probably implies that Marryat wrote all Part I (of the first edition) and two chapters of Part II, that is—as far as the end of Chapter xxiv. The remaining pages may be the work of his son Frank S. Marryat, who edited the first edition, supplying a brief preface to Part II:—

> "I cannot publish this last work of my late father without some prefatory remarks, as, in justice to the public, as well as to himself, I should state, that his lamented decease prevented his concluding the second volume."
>
> "The present volume has been for some time at press, but the long-protracted illness of the author delayed its publication."

The Little Savage opens well. The picture of a lad, who was born on a desert island—though of English parents—and really deserves to be called a savage, growing up with no other companionship than that of his father's murderer, is boldly conceived and executed with some power. The man Jackson is a thoroughly human ruffian, who naturally detests the boy he has so terribly injured, and bullies him brutally. Under this treatment Frank's animal passions are inevitably aroused, and when the lightning had struck his tyrant blind, he turns upon him with a quiet savagery that is narrated with admirable detachment.

This original situation arrests the reader's attention and secures his interest in Frank Henniker's development towards civilisation and virtue. His experience of absolute solitude after Jackson's death serves to bring out his sympathies with animals and flowers; while, on the arrival of Mrs Reichardt, he proves himself a loyal comrade under kind treatment.

It is much to be regretted that Marryat did not live to finish his work.

R. B. J.

The Little Savage originally appeared in 1848-49. Marryat, who was born in 1792, died at Langham, Norfolk, August 9, 1848.

The following is the list of his published works:—

Suggestions for the Abolition of the Present System of Impressment in the Naval Service, 1822; The Naval Officer, or Scenes and Adventures in the Life of Frank Mildmay, 1829; The King's Own, 1830; Newton Forster (from the *Metropolitan Magazine*), 1832; Jacob Faithful (from the *Metropolitan Magazine*), 1834; Peter Simple, 1834; The Pacha of Many Tales, 1835; Midshipman Easy (from the *Metropolitan Magazine*), 1836; Japhet in Search of a Father (from the *Metropolitan Magazine*), 1836; The Pirate and The Three Cutters, 1836; A Code of Signals for the Use of Vessels employed in the Merchant Service, 1837; Snarleyyow, or The Dog Fiend, 1837; A Diary in America, with Remarks on its Institutions, 1839; The Phantom Ship, 1839; Poor Jack, 1840; Olla Podrida (articles from the *Metropolitan Magazine*), 1840; Joseph Rushbrook, or The Poacher, 1841; Masterman Ready, or The Wreck of the *Pacific*, 1841; Percival Keene, 1842; Narrative of the Travels and Adventures of Monsieur Violet in California, Sonora, and Western Texas, 1843; The Settlers in Canada, 1844; The Mission, or Scenes in Africa, 1845; The Privateer's Man, 1846; The Children of the New Forest, 1847; The Little Savage (posthumous), 1848-49; Valerie (posthumous), 1849; Life and Letters, Florence Marryat, 1872.

CHAPTER I

I am about to write a very curious history, as the reader will agree with me when he has read this book. We have more than one narrative of people being cast away upon desolate islands, and being left to their own resources, and no works are perhaps read with more interest; but I believe I am the first instance of a boy being left alone upon an uninhabited island. Such was, however, the case; and now I shall tell my own story.

My first recollections are, that I was in company with a man upon this island, and that we walked often along the sea-shore. It was rocky and difficult to climb in many parts, and the man used to drag or pull me over the dangerous places. He was very unkind to me, which may appear strange, as I was the only companion that he had; but he was of a morose and gloomy disposition. He would sit down squatted in the corner of our cabin, and sometimes not speak for hours—or he would remain the whole day looking out at the sea, as if watching for something, but what I never could tell; for if I spoke, he would not reply; and if near to him, I was sure to receive a cuff or a heavy blow. I should imagine that I was about five years old at the time that I first recollect clearly what passed. I may have been younger. I may as well here state what I gathered from him at different times, relative to our being left upon this desolate spot. It was with difficulty that I did so; for, generally speaking, he would throw a stone at me if I asked questions, that is, if I repeatedly asked them after he had refused to answer. It was on one occasion, when he was lying sick, that I gained the information, and that only by refusing to attend him or bring him food and water. He would be very angry, and say, that when he got well again, he would make me smart for it; but I cared not, for I was then getting strong, whilst he was getting weaker every day, and I had no love for him, for he had never shown any to me, but always treated me with great severity.

He told me, that about twelve years before (not that I knew what he meant by a year, for I had never heard the term used by him), an English ship (I did not know what a ship was) had been swamped near the island, in a heavy gale, and that seven men and one woman had been saved, and all the other people lost. That the ship had been broken into pieces, and that they had saved nothing—that they had picked up among the rocks pieces of the wood with which it had been made, and had built the cabin in which we lived. That one had died after another, and had been buried (what death or burial meant, I had no idea at the time), and that I had been born on the island; (How was I born? thought I)—that most of them had died before I was two years old; and that then, he and my mother were the only two left besides me. My mother had died a few months afterwards. I was obliged to ask him many questions to understand all this; indeed, I did not understand it till long afterwards, although I had an idea of what he would say. Had I been left with any other person, I should, of course, by conversation, have learnt much; but he never would converse, still less explain. He called me, Boy, and I called him, Master. His inveterate silence was the occasion of my language being composed of very few words; for, except to order me to do this or that, to procure what was required, he never would converse. He did however mutter to himself, and talk in his sleep, and I used to lie awake and listen, that I might gain information; not at first, but when I grew older. He used to cry out in his sleep constantly.—"A judgment, a judgment on me for my sins, my heavy sins—God be merciful!" But what judgment, or what sin was, or what was God, I did not then know, although I mused on words repeated so often.

I will now describe the island, and the way in which we lived. The island was very small, perhaps not three miles round; it was of rock, and there was no beach nor landing place, the sea washing its sides with deep water. It was, as I afterwards discovered, one of the group of islands to which the Peruvians despatch vessels every year to collect the guano, or refuse of the sea birds which resort to the islands; but the one on which we were was small, and detached some distance from the others, on which the guano was found in great profusion; so that hitherto it had been neglected, and no vessel had ever come near it. Indeed, the other islands were not to be seen from it except on a very clear day, when they appeared like a cloud or mist on the horizon. The shores of the island were, moreover, so precipitous, that there was no landing place, and the eternal wash of the ocean would have made it almost impossible for a vessel to have taken off a cargo. Such was the island upon which I found myself in company with this man. Our cabin was built of ship-plank and timber, under the shelter of a cliff, about fifty yards from the water; there was a flat of about thirty yards square in front of it, and from the cliff there trickled down a rill of water, which fell into a hole dug out to collect it, and then found its way over the flat to the rocks beneath. The cabin itself was large, and capable of holding many more people than had ever lived in it; but it was not too large, as we had to secure in it our provisions for many months. There were several bed-places level with the floor, which were rendered soft enough to lie on, by being filled with the feathers of birds. Furniture there was none, except two or three old axes, blunted with long use, a tin pannikin, a mess kid and some rude vessels to hold water, cut out of wood. On the summit of the island there was a forest of underwood, and the bushes extended some distance down the ravines which led from the summit to the shore. One of my most arduous tasks was to climb these ravines and collect wood, but fortunately a fire was not often required. The climate was warm all the year round, and there seldom was a fall of rain; when it did fall, it was generally expended on the summit of the island, and did not reach us. At a certain period of the year, the birds came to the island in numberless quantities to breed, and their chief resort was some tolerably level ground—indeed, in many places, it was quite level with the accumulation of guano—which ground was divided from the spot where our cabin was built by a deep ravine. On this spot, which might perhaps contain about twenty acres or more, the sea birds would sit upon their eggs, not four inches apart from each other, and the whole surface of this twenty acres would be completely covered with them. There they would remain from the time of the laying of the eggs, until the young ones were able to leave the nests and fly away with them. At the season when the birds were on the island, all was gaiety, bustle, and noise, but after their departure it was quiet and solitude. I used to long for their arrival, and was delighted with the animation which gladdened the island, the male birds diving in every direction after fish, wheeling and soaring in the air, and uttering loud cries, which were responded to by their mates on the nests.

But it was also our harvest time; we seldom touched the old birds, as they were not in flesh, but as soon as the young ones were within a few days of leaving the nests, we were then busy enough. In spite of the screaming and the flapping of their wings in our faces, and the darting their beaks at our eyes, of the old birds, as we robbed them of their progeny, we collected hundreds every day, and bore as heavy a load as we could carry across the ravine to the platform in front of our cabin, where we busied ourselves in skinning them, splitting them, and hanging them out to dry in the sun. The air of the island was so pure that no putrefaction ever took place, and during the last fortnight of the birds coming on the island, we had collected a sufficiency for our support until their return on the following year. As soon as they were quite dry they were packed up in a corner of the cabin for use.

These birds were, it may be said, the only produce of the island, with the exception of fish, and the eggs taken at the time of their first making their nests. Fish were to be taken in large quantities. It was sufficient to put a line over the rocks, and it had hardly time to go down a fathom before anything at the end of it was seized. Indeed, our means of taking them were as simple as their voracity was great. Our lines were composed of the sinews of the legs of the man-of-war birds, as I afterwards heard them named; and, as these were only about a foot long, it required a great many of them knotted together to make a line. At the end of the line was a bait fixed over a strong fish-bone, which was fastened to the line by the middle; a half-hitch of the line round one end kept the bone on a parallel with the line until the bait was seized, when the line being taughtened, the half-hitch slipped off and the bone remained crossways in the gullet of the fish, which was drawn up by it. Simple as this contrivance was, it answered as well as the best hook, of which I had never seen one at that time. The fish were so strong and large, that, when I was young, the man would not allow me to attempt to catch them, lest they should pull me into the water; but, as I grew bigger, I could master them. Such was our food from one year's end to the other; we had no variety, except when occasionally we broiled the dried birds or the fish upon the embers, instead of eating them dried by the sun. Our raiment, such as it was, we were also indebted to the feathered tribe for. The birds were skinned with the feathers on, and their skins sewn together with sinews, and a fish-bone by way of a needle. These garments were not very durable, but the climate was so fine that we did not suffer from the cold at any season of the year. I used to make myself a new dress every year when the birds came; but by the time that they returned, I had little left of my last year's suit, the fragments of which might be found among the rocky and steep parts of the ravine where we used to collect firing.

Living such a life, with so few wants, and those periodically and easily supplied, hardly varied from one year's end to another, it may easily be imagined that I had but few ideas. I might have had more, if my companion had not been of such a taciturn and morose habit; as it was, I looked at the wide ocean, and the sky, and the sun, moon, and stars, wondering, puzzled, afraid to ask questions, and ending all by sleeping away a large portion of my existence. We had no tools except the old ones, which were useless—no employment of any kind. There was a book, and I asked what it was for and what it was, but I got no answer. It remained upon the shelf, for if I looked at it I was ordered away, and at last I regarded it with a sort of fear, as if it were a kind of incomprehensible animal. The day was passed in idleness and almost silence; perhaps not a dozen sentences were exchanged in the twenty-four hours. My companion always the same, brooding over something which appeared ever to occupy his thoughts, and angry if roused up from his reverie.

CHAPTER II

The reader must understand that the foregoing remarks are to be considered as referring to my position and amount of knowledge when I was seven or eight years old. My master, as I called him, was a short square-built man, about sixty years of age, as I afterwards estimated from recollection and comparison. His hair fell down his back in thick clusters and was still of a dark color, and his beard was full two feet long and very bushy; indeed, he was covered with hair, wherever his person was exposed. He was, I should say, very powerful had he had occasion to exert his strength, but with the exception of the time at which we collected the birds, and occasionally going up the ravine to bring down faggots of wood, he seldom moved out of the cabin unless it was to bathe. There was a pool of salt water of about twenty yards square, near the sea, but separated from it by a low ridge of rocks, over which the waves only beat when the sea was rough and the wind on that side of the island. Every morning almost we went down to bathe in that pool, as it was secure from the sharks, which were very numerous. I could swim like a fish as early as I can recollect, but whether I was taught, or learnt myself, I cannot tell. Thus was my life passed away; my duties were trifling; I had little or nothing to employ myself about, for I had no means of employment. I seldom heard the human voice, and became as taciturn as my companion. My amusements were equally confined—looking down into the depths of the ocean, as I lay over the rocky wall which girded the major portion of the island, and watching the motions of the finny tribes below, wondering at the stars during the night season, eating, and sleeping. Thus did I pass away an existence without pleasure and without pain. As for what my thoughts were I can hardly say, my knowledge and my ideas were too confined for me to have any food for thought. I was little better than a beast of the field, that lies down on the pasture after he is filled. There was one great source of interest however, which was, to listen to the sleeping talk of my companion, and I always looked forward to the time when the night fell and we repaired to our beds. I would lie awake for hours, listening to his ejaculations and murmured speech, trying in vain to find out some meaning in what he would say—but I gained little; he talked of "that woman"—appearing to be constantly with other men, and muttering about something he had hidden away. One night, when the moon was shining bright, he sat up in his bed, which, as I have before said, was on the floor of the cabin, and throwing aside the feathers upon which he had been lying, scratched the mould away below them and lifted up a piece of board. After a minute he replaced everything, and lay down again. He evidently was sleeping during the whole time. Here, at last, was something to feed my thoughts with. I had heard him say in his sleep that he had hidden something—this must be the hiding place. What was it? Perhaps I ought here to observe that my feelings towards this man were those of positive dislike, if not hatred; I never had received one kind word or deed from him, that I could recollect. Harsh and unfeeling towards me, evidently looking upon me with ill-will, and only suffering me because I saved him some trouble, and perhaps because he wished to have a living thing for his companion,—his feelings towards me were reciprocated by mine towards him. What age I was at the time my mother died, I know not, but I had some faint recollection of one who treated me with kindness and caresses, and these recollections became more forcible in my dreams, when I saw a figure very different from that of my companion (a female figure) hanging over me or leading me by the hand. How I used to try to continue those dreams, by closing my eyes again after I had woke up! And yet I knew not that they had been brought about by the dim recollection of my infancy; I knew not that the figure that appeared to me was the shadow of my mother; but I loved the dreams because I was treated kindly in them.

But a change took place by the hand of Providence. One day, after we had just laid in our yearly provision of sea birds, I was busy arranging the skins of the old birds, on the flat rock, for my annual garment, which was joined together something like a sack, with holes for the head and arms to pass through; when, as I looked to seaward, I saw a large white object on the water.

"Look, master," said I, pointing towards it.

"A ship, a ship!" cried my companion.

"Oh," thought I, "that is a ship; I recollect that he said they came here in a ship." I kept my eyes on her, and she rounded to.

"Is she alive?" inquired I.

"You're a fool," said the man; "come and help me to pile up this wood that we may make a signal to her. Go and fetch some water and throw on it, that there may be plenty of smoke. Thank God, I may leave this cursed hole at last!"

I hardly understood him, but I went for the water and brought it in the mess kid.

"I want more wood yet," said he. "Her head is this way, and she will come nearer."

"Then she is alive," said I.

"Away, fool!" said he, giving me a cuff on the head; "get some more water and throw on the wood."

He then went into the cabin to strike a light, which he obtained by a piece of iron and flint, with some fine dry moss for tinder. While he was so employed, my eyes were fixed on the vessel, wondering what it could be. It moved through the water, turned this way and that. "It must be alive," thought I; "is it a fish or a bird?" As I watched the vessel, the sun was going down and there was not more than an hour's daylight. The wind was very light and variable, which accounted for the vessel so often altering her course. My companion came out with his hands full of smoking tinder, and putting it under the wood, was busy blowing it into a flame. The wood was soon set fire to, and the smoke ascended several feet into the air.

"They'll see that," said he.

"What then, it has eyes? it must be alive. Does it mind the wind?" inquired I, having no answer to my first remark, "for look there, the little clouds are coming up fast," and I pointed to the horizon, where some small clouds were rising up and which were, as I knew from experience and constantly watching the sky, a sign of a short but violent gale, or tornado, of which we usually had one, if not two, at this season of the year.

"Yes; confound it," replied my companion, grinding his teeth, "it will blow her off! That's my luck."

In the meantime, the smoke ascended in the air and the vessel approached nearer and nearer, until she was within, I suppose, two miles of the island, and then it fell quite calm. My companion threw more water on to increase the smoke, and the vessel now hauling up her courses, I perceived that there were people on board, and while I was arranging my ideas as to what the vessel might be, my companion cried out—"They see us, they see us! there's hope now. Confound it, I've been here long enough. Hurrah for old England!" and he commenced dancing and capering about like a madman. At last he said,

"Look out and see if she sends a boat, while I go into the cabin."

"What's a boat?" said I.

"Out, you fool! tell me if you see anything,"

"Yes, I do see something," replied I. "Look at the squall coming along the water, it will be here very soon; and see how thick the clouds are getting up: we shall have as much wind and rain as we had the time before last, when the birds came."

"Confound it," replied he, "I wish they'd lower a boat, at all events;" and so saying, he went into the cabin, and I perceived that he was busy at his bed-place.

My eyes were still fixed upon the squall, as I watched it advancing at a furious speed on the surface of the water; at first it was a deep black line on the horizon, but as it approached the vessel, it changed to white; the surface of the water was still smooth. The clouds were not more than ten degrees above the horizon, although they were thick and opaque—but at this season of the year, these tornadoes, as I may call them, visited us; sometimes we had one, sometimes more, and it was only when these gusts came on that we had any rain below. On board of the vessel—I speak now from my after knowledge—they did not appear to be aware of the danger; the sails were all set and flapping against the masts. At last, I perceived a small object close to the vessel; this I presumed was the boat which my companion looked for. It was like a young vessel close to the old one, but I said nothing; as I was watching and wondering what effect the rising wind would have upon her, for the observations of my companion had made me feel that it was important. After a time, I perceived that the white sails were disappearing, and that the forms of men were very busy, and moving on board, and the boat went back to the side of the vessel. The fact is, they had not perceived the squall until it was too late, for in another moment almost, I saw that the vessel bowed down to the fury of the gale, and after that, the mist was so great that I couldn't see her any more.

"Is she sending a boat, boy?" cried my companion.

"I can't see her," replied I; "for she is hidden by the wind."

As I said this, the tornado reached to where we stood, and threw me off my legs to the entrance of the cabin; and with the wind came down a torrent of rain, which drenched us, and the clouds covered the whole of the firmament, which became dark; the lightning darted in every direction, with peals of thunder which were deafening. I crawled into the cabin, into which the rain beat in great fury and flowed out again in a small river.

My companion sat near me, lowering and silent. For two hours the tornado lasted without interruption; the sun had set, and the darkness was opaque. It was impossible to move against the force of the wind and the deluge of water which descended. Speak, we did not, but shut our eyes against the lightning, and held our fingers to our ears to deaden the noise of the thunder, which burst upon us in the most awful manner. My companion groaned at intervals, whether from fear, I know not; I had no fear, for I did not know the danger, or that there was a God to judge the earth.

Gradually the fury of the gale abated, the rain was only heavy at intervals, and we could now hear the beating of the waves, as they dashed against the rocks beneath us. The sky also cleared up a little, and we could dimly discern the white foam of the breakers. I crawled out of the cabin, and stood upon the platform in front, straining my eyes to see the vessel. A flash of lightning, for a second, revealed her to me; she was dismasted, rolling in the awful breakers, which bore her down upon the high rocks, not a quarter of a mile from her.

"There it is," exclaimed I, as the disappearance of the lightning left me in darkness, more opaque than ever.

"She's done for," growled my companion, who, I was not till then aware, stood by my side. "No hopes this time, confound it!" Then he continued for some time to curse and swear awfully, as I afterwards discovered, for I did not then know what was cursing and swearing.

"There she is again," said I, as another flash of lightning revealed the position of the vessel.

"Yes, and she won't be there long; in five minutes she'll be dashed to atoms, and every soul perish."

"What are souls?" inquired I.

My companion gave me no reply.

"I will go down to the rocks," said I, "and see what goes on."

"Go," said he, "and share their fate."

CHAPTER III

I left him, and commenced a careful descent of the precipices by which we were surrounded, but, before I had gone fifty paces, another flash of lightning was followed up by a loud shriek, which arrested my steps. Where the noise came from, I could not tell, but I heard my companion calling to me to come back. I obeyed him, and found him standing where I had left him.

"You called me, master?"

"Yes, I did; take my hand, and lead me to the cabin."

I obeyed him, wondering why he asked me so to do. He gained his bed-place, and threw himself down on it.

"Bring the kid full of water," said he—"quick!"

I brought it, and he bathed his head and face. After a time, he threw himself back upon the bed-place, and groaned heavily.

"O God! it's all over with me," said he at last. "I shall live and die in this cursed hole."

"What's the matter, master?" said I.

He gave me no answer, but lay groaning and occasionally cursing. After a time, he was still, and then I went out again. The tornado was now over, and the stars were to be seen here and there, but still the wind was strong and the wild clouds flew fast. The shores of the island were one mass of foam, which was dashed high in the air and fell upon the black rocks. I looked for the vessel, and could see nothing—the day was evidently dawning, and I sat down and waited its coming. My companion was apparently asleep, for he lay without motion or noise. That some misfortune had happened, I was convinced, but what, I knew not, and I passed a long time in conjecture, dividing my thoughts between him and the vessel. At last the daylight appeared—the weather was moderating fast, although the waves still beat furiously against the rocky shore. I could see nothing of the vessel, and I descended the path, now slippery and insecure from the heavy fall of rain, and went as near to the edge of the rocks as the breaking billows would permit. I walked along, occasionally drenched by the spray, until I arrived where I had last seen the vessel. The waves were dashing and tossing about, as if in sport, fragments of timber, casks, and spars; but that was all I could see, except a mast and rigging, which lay alongside of the rocks, sometimes appearing above them on the summit of the waves, then descending far out of my sight, for I dared not venture near enough to the edge to look over. "Then the vessel is dashed to pieces, as my companion said," thought I. "I wonder how she was made." I remained about an hour on the rocks, and then turned back to the cabin. I found my companion awake, and groaning heavily.

"There is no ship," said I, "nothing but pieces of wood floating about."

"I know that," replied he; "but what do I care now?"

"I thought by your making a smoke, that you did care."

"Yes, I did then, but now I am blind, I shall never see a ship or anything else again. God help me! I shall die and rot on this cursed island."

"Blind, what is blind?" inquired I.

"The lightning has burned out my eyes, and I can see nothing— I cannot help myself—I cannot walk about—I cannot do anything, and I suppose you will leave me here to die like a dog."

"Can't you see me?"

"No, all is dark, dark as night, and will be as long as I live." And he turned on his bed-place and groaned. "I had hope, I lived in hope—it has kept me alive for many weary years, but now hope is gone, and I care not if I die to-morrow."

And then he started up and turned his face towards me, and I saw that there was no light in his eyes.

"Bring me some more water, do you hear?" said he, angrily. "Be quick, or I'll make you."

But I now fully comprehended his condition, and how powerless he was. My feelings, as I have before said, were anything but cordial towards him, and this renewed violence and threatening manner had its effect. I was now, I suppose, about twelve or thirteen years old—strong and active. I had more than once felt inclined to rebel, and measure my strength against his. Irritated, therefore, at his angry language, I replied—

"Go for the water yourself."

"Ah!" sighed he, after a pause of some seconds, "that I might have expected. But let me once get you into my hands, I'll make you remember it."

"I care not if I were in your hands," replied I; "I am as strong as you." For I had thought so many a day, and meant to prove it.

"Indeed! well, come here, and let us try."

"No, no," replied I; "I'm not such a fool as you say I am—not that I'm afraid of you; for I shall have an axe in my hand always ready, and you will not find another."

"I wish that I had tossed you over the cliffs when you were a child," said he, bitterly, "instead of nursing you and bringing you up."

"Then why have you not been kind to me? As far back as I can remember you have always treated me ill; you have made me work for you; and yet never even spoken kindly to me. I have wanted to know things, and you have never answered my questions, but called me a fool, and told me to hold my tongue. You have made me hate you, and you have often told me how you hated me—you know you have."

"It's true, quite true," replied he, as if talking to himself. "I have done all that he says, and I have hated him. But I have had cause. Come here, boy."

"No," replied I; "do you come here. You have been master, and I have been boy, long enough. Now I am master and you are boy, and you shall find it so."

Having said this, I walked out of the cabin and left him. He cried out, "Don't leave me," but I heeded him not, and sat down at the edge of the flat ledge of the rock before the cabin. Looking at the white dancing waves, and deep in my own thoughts, I considered a long while how I should behave towards him. I did not wish him to die, as I knew he must if I left him. He could not obtain water from the rill without a great chance of falling over the cliff. In fact, I was now fully aware of his helpless state; to prove it to myself, I rose and shut my own eyes; tried if I could venture to move on such dangerous ground, and I felt sure that I could not. He was then in my power; he could do nothing; he must trust to me for almost everything. I had said, let what would follow, I would be master and he boy; but that could not be, as I must still attend upon him, or he would die. At last the thought came suddenly upon me—I will be master, nevertheless, for now he shall answer me all my questions, tell me all he knows, or he shall starve. He is in my power. He shall now do what I have ever tried to make him do, and he has ever refused. Having thus arranged my plans, I returned to the cabin, and said to him:

"Hear what I say—I will be kind to you, and not leave you to starve, if you will do what I ask."

"And what is that?" replied he.

"For a long while I have asked you many questions, and you have refused to answer them. Instead of telling me what I would know, you have beaten or thrown stones at me, called me names, and threatened me. I now give you your choice—either you shall promise to answer every question that I put to you, or you may live how you can, for I shall leave you to help yourself. If you do as I wish, I will do all I can to help you, but if you will not, thank yourself for what may happen. Recollect, I am master now; so take your choice."

"Well," replied he slowly, "it's a judgment upon me, and I must agree to it. I will do what you wish."

"Well, then, to begin," said I, "I have often asked you what your name was, and what was mine. I must call you something, and Master I will not, for I am master now. What is your name?"

He groaned, ground his teeth, and then said, "Edward Jackson."

"Edward Jackson! very well; and my name?"

"No, I cannot bear the name. I cannot say it," replied he, angrily.

"Be it so," replied I. "Then I leave you."

"Will you bring me some water for my eyes? they burn," said he.

"No, I will not, nor anything else, unless you tell me my name."

"Frank Henniker—and curses on it."

"Frank Henniker. Well, now you shall have the water."

I went out, filled a kid, and put it by his side,

"There is the water, Jackson; if you want anything, call me. I shall be outside."

"I have gained the mastery," thought I,—"it will be my turn now. He don't like to answer, but he shall, or he shall starve. Why does he feel so angry at my name? Henniker! what is the meaning of Henniker, I wonder? I will make him tell me. Yes, he shall tell me everything." I may here observe, that as for pity and compassion, I did not know such feelings. I had been so ill-treated, that I only felt that might was right; and this right I determined upon exercising to the utmost. I felt an inconceivable pleasure at the idea of my being the master, and he the boy. I felt the love of power, the pride of superiority. I then revolved in my mind the daily task which I would set him, before he should receive his daily sustenance. He should talk now as much as I pleased, for I was the master. I had been treated as a slave, and I was now fully prepared to play the tyrant. Mercy and compassion I knew not. I had never seen them called forth, and I felt them not. I sat down on the flat rock for some time, and then it occurred to me that I would turn the course of the water which fell into the hole at the edge of the cliff; so that if he crawled there, he would not be able to obtain any. I did so, and emptied the hole. The water was now only to be obtained by climbing up, and it was out of his power to obtain a drop. Food, of course, he could obtain, as the dried birds were all piled up at the farther end of the cabin, and I could not well remove them; but what was food without water? I was turning in my mind what should be the first question to put to him; and I had decided that I would have a full and particular account of how the vessel had been wrecked on the island, and who were my father and mother, and why I was named Henniker—when I was roused by hearing Jackson (as I shall in future call him) crying out, "Boy, boy!" "Boy, indeed," thought I—"no longer boy," and I gave no reply. Again he called, and at last he cried out, "Henniker," but I had been ruffled by his calling me boy, and I would not answer him. At last he fairly screamed my name, and then was silent. After a moment, I perceived that he crawled out of his bed-place, and feeling by the sides of the cabin, contrived on his hands and knees to crawl in the direction of the hole into which the water had previously been received; and I smiled at what I knew would be his disappointment when he arrived there. He did so at last: put his hand to feel the edge of the hole, and then down into it to feel for the water; and when he found that there was none, he cursed bitterly, and I laughed at his vexation. He then felt all the way down where the water had fallen, and found that the course of it had been stopped, and he dared not attempt anything further. He dashed his clenched hand against the rock. "Oh! that I had him in this grasp—if it were but for one moment. I would not care if I died the next."

"I do not doubt you," replied I to him, above, "but you have not got me in your hands, and you will not. Go in to bed directly—quick," cried I, throwing a piece of rock at him, which hit him on the head. "Crawl back as fast as you can, you fool, or I'll send another at your head directly. I'll tame you, as you used to say to me."

The blow on the head appeared to have confused him; but after a time he crawled back to his bed-place, and threw himself down with a heavy groan.

CHAPTER IV

I then went down to the water's edge to see if I could find anything from the wreck, for the water was smooth, and no longer washed over the rocks of the island. Except fragments of wood, I perceived nothing until I arrived at the pool where we were accustomed to bathe; and I found that the sea had thrown into it two articles of large dimensions—one was a cask of the size of a puncheon, which lay in about a foot of water farthest from the seaward; and the other was a seaman's chest. What these things were I did not then know, and I wish the reader to recollect that a great portion of this narrative is compiled from after knowledge. The cask was firm in the sand, and I could not move it. The chest was floating; I hauled it on the rocks without difficulty, and then proceeded to open it. It was some time before I could discover how, for I had never seen a lock, or a hinge in my life; but at last, finding that the lid was the only portion of the chest which yielded, I contrived, with a piece of rock, to break it open. I found in it a quantity of seamen's clothes, upon which I put no value; but some of the articles I immediately comprehended the use of, and they filled me with delight. There were two new tin pannikins, and those would hold water. There were three empty wine bottles, a hammer, a chisel, gimlet, and some other tools, also three or four fishing-lines many fathoms long. But what pleased me most were two knives, one shutting up, with a lanyard sheath to wear round the waist; and the other an American long knife, in a sheath, which is usually worn by them in the belt. Now, three or four years back, Jackson had the remains of a clasp knife—that is, there was about an inch of the blade remaining—and this, as may be supposed, he valued very much; indeed, miserable as the article was, in our destitute state it was invaluable.

This knife he had laid on the rock when fishing, and it had been dragged into the sea as his line ran out; and he was for many days inconsolable for its loss. We had used it for cutting open the birds when we skinned them, and, indeed this remains of a knife had been always in request. Since the loss of it, we had had hard work to get the skins off the birds; I therefore well knew the value of these knives, which I immediately secured. The remainder of the articles in the chest, which was quite full, I laid upon the rocks, with the clothes, to dry; of most of them I did not know the use, and consequently did not prize them at the time. It was not until afterwards, when I had taken them to my companion, that I learned their value. I may as well here observe, that amongst these articles were two books, and, from the positive commands of my companion, not to touch the book in the cabin, I looked upon them with a degree of awe, and hesitated upon taking them in my hand; but, at last, I put them out to dry on the rocks, with the rest of the contents of the chest.

I felt the knives, the blades were sharp; I put the lanyard of the clasp knife round my neck; the sheath knife, which was a formidable weapon, I made fast round my waist, with a piece of the fishing lines, which I cut off; and I then turned my steps towards the cabin, as night was coming on, though the moon was high in the heavens, and shining brightly. On my return, I found Jackson in his bed-place; he heard me come in, and asked me, in a quiet tone, whether I would bring him some water? I answered,

"No, that I would not, for what he had said about me, and what he would do, if he got me into his power. I'll tame you," cried I. "I'm master now, as you shall find."

"You may be," replied he, quickly, "but still, that is no reason why you should not let me have some water. Did I ever prevent you from having water?"

"You never had to fetch it for me," I rejoined, "or you would not have taken the trouble. What trouble would you take for me, if I were blind now, and not you? I should become of no use to you, and you would leave me to die. You only let me live that you might make me work for you, and beat me cruelly. It's my turn now—you're the boy, and I'm the master."

The reader must remember that I did not know the meaning of the word "boy"; my idea of it was, that it was in opposition to "master," and boy, with me, had the same idea as the word "slave."

"Be it so," replied he, calmly. "I shall not want water long."

There was a quietness about Jackson which made me suspect him, and the consequence was, that although I turned into my bed-place, which was on the ground at the side of the cabin opposite to his, I did not feel inclined to go to sleep, but remained awake, thinking of what had passed. It was towards morning when I heard him move; my face being turned that way, I had no occasion to stir to watch his motions. He crept very softly out of his bed-place towards me, listening, and advancing on his knees, not more than a foot every ten seconds. "You want me in your grasp," thought I, "come along," and I drew my American knife from its sheath, without noise, and awaited his approach, smiling at the surprise he would meet with. I allowed him to come right up to me; he felt the side of my bed, and then passed his right hand over to seize me. I caught his right hand with my left, and passing the knife across his wrist, more than half divided it from his arm. He gave a shriek of surprise and pain, and fell back.

"He has a knife," exclaimed he, with surprise, holding his severed wrist with the other hand.

"Yes, he has a knife, and more than one," replied I, "and you see that he knows how to use it. Will you come again? or will you believe that I'm master?"

"If you have any charity or mercy, kill me at once," said he, as he sat up in the moonlight, in the centre of the floor of the cabin.

"Charity and mercy," said I, "what are they? I never heard of them."

"Alas! no," replied he, "I have shewed none—it's a judgment on me—a judgment on me for my many sins; Lord, forgive me! First my eyes, now my right hand useless. What next, O Lord of Heaven?"

"Why, your other hand next," replied I, "if you try it again."

Jackson made no reply. He attempted to crawl back to his bed, but, faint with loss of blood, he dropped senseless on the floor of the cabin. I looked at him, and satisfied that he would make no more attempts upon me, I turned away, and fell fast asleep. In about two hours, I awoke, and looking round, perceived him lying on the floor, where he had fallen the night before. I went to him and examined him—was he asleep, or was he dead? He lay in a pool of blood. I felt him, and he was quite warm. It was a ghastly cut on his wrist, and I thought, if he is dead, he will never tell me what I want to know. I knew that he bound up cuts to stop the blood. I took some feathers from the bed, and put a handful on the wound. After I had done it, I bound his wrist up with a piece of fishing-line I had taken to secure the sheath knife round my waist, and then I went for some water. I poured some down his throat; this revived him, and he opened his eyes.

"Where am I?" said he faintly.

"Where are you?—why, in the cabin," said I.

"Give me some more water."

I did so, for I did not wish to kill him. I wanted him to live, and to be in my power. After drinking the water he roused himself, and crawled back to his bed-place. I left him then, and went down to bathe.

The reader may exclaim—What a horrid tyrant this boy is— why, he is as bad as his companion. Exactly—I was so—but let the reader reflect that I was made so by education. From the time that I could first remember, I had been tyrannised over; cuffed, kicked, abused and ill-treated. I had never known kindness. Most truly was the question put by me, "Charity and mercy—what are they?" I never heard of them. An American Indian has kind feelings—he is hospitable and generous—yet, educated to inflict, and receive, the severest tortures to and from, his enemies, he does the first with the most savage and vindictive feelings, and submits to the latter with indifference and stoicism. He has, indeed, the kindlier feelings of his nature exercised; still, this changes him not. He has been from earliest infancy brought up to cruelty, and he cannot feel that it is wrong. Now, my position was worse. I had never seen the softer feelings of our nature called into play; I knew nothing but tyranny and oppression, hatred and vengeance. It was therefore not surprising that, when my turn came, I did to others as I had been done by. Jackson had no excuse for his treatment of me, whereas, I had every excuse for retaliation. He did know better, I did not. I followed the ways of the world in the petty microcosm in which I had been placed. I knew not of mercy, of forgiveness, charity, or goodwill. I knew not that there was a God; I only knew that might was right, and the most pleasurable sensation which I felt, was that of anxiety for vengeance, combined with the consciousness of power.

After I had bathed, I again examined the chest and its contents. I looked at the books without touching them. "I must know what these mean," thought I, "and I will know." My thirst for knowledge was certainly most remarkable, in a boy of my age; I presume for the simple reason, that we want most what we cannot obtain; and Jackson having invariably refused to enlighten me on any subject, I became most anxious and impatient to satisfy the longing which increased with my growth.

CHAPTER V

For three days did Jackson lie on his bed; I supplied him with water, but he did not eat anything. He groaned heavily at times, and talked much to himself, and I heard him ask forgiveness of God, and pardon for his sins. I noted this down for an explanation. On the third day, he said to me,

"Henniker, I am very ill. I have a fever coming on, from the wound you have given me. I do not say that I did not deserve it, for I did, and I know that I have treated you ill, and that you must hate me, but the question is, do you wish me to die?"

"No," replied I; "I want you to live, and answer all my questions, and you shall do so."

"I will do so," replied he. "I have done wrong, and I will make amends. Do you understand me? I mean to say, that I have been very cruel to you, and now I will do all you wish, and answer every question you may put to me, as well as I can."

"That is what I want," replied I.

"I know it is, but my wound is festering and must be washed and dressed. The feathers make it worse. Will you do this for me?"

I thought a little, and recollected that he was still in my power, as he could not obtain water. I replied, "Yes, I will."

"The cord hurts it, you must take it off."

I fetched the kid of water, and untied the cord, and took away the feathers, which had matted together with the flow of blood, and then I washed the wound carefully. Looking into the wound, my desire of information induced me to say, "What are these little white cords, which are cut through?"

"They are the sinews and tendons," replied he, "by which we are enabled to move our hands and fingers; now these are cut through, I shall not have the use of my hand again."

"Stop a moment," said I, rising up, "I have just thought of something." I ran down to the point where the chest lay, took a shirt from the rock, and brought it back with me, and tearing it into strips, I bandaged the wound.

"Where did you get that linen?" said Jackson.

I told him.

"And you got the knife there, too," said he, with a sigh. I replied in the affirmative.

As soon as I had finished, he told me he was much easier, and said,

"I thank you."

"What is I thank you?" replied I.

"It means that I am grateful for what you have done."

"And what is grateful?" inquired I again. "You never said those words to me before."

"Alas, no," replied he; "it had been better if I had. I mean that I feel kindly towards you, for having bound up my wound, and would do anything for you if I had the power. It means, that if I had my eyesight, as I had a week ago, and was master, as I then was, that I would not kick nor beat you, but be kind to you. Do you understand me?"

"Yes," replied I, "I think I do; and if you tell me all I want to know I shall believe you."

"That I will as soon as I am well enough; but now I am too ill—you must wait a day or two, till the fever has left me."

Satisfied with Jackson's promise, I tended him carefully, and washed and dressed his wound for the two following days. He said that he felt himself much better, and his language to me was so kind and conciliatory, that I hardly knew what to make of it; but this is certain, that it had a good effect upon me, and gradually the hatred and ill-will that I bore to him wore off, and I found myself handling him tenderly, and anxious not to give him more pain than was necessary, yet without being aware that I was prompted by better feelings. It was on the third morning that he said,—

"I can talk to you now; what do you want to know?"

"I want to know the whole story of how we came to this island, who my father and mother were, and why you said that you hated me and my name?"

"That," said Jackson, after a silence of a few minutes, "will take some time. I could soon tell it you if it were not for the last question,—why I hated your name? But the history of your father is so mixed up with mine, that I cannot well tell one without the other. I may as well begin with my own history, and that will be telling you both."

"Then tell it me," replied I, "and do not tell me what is not true."

"No; I will tell you exactly what it was," replied Jackson; "you may as well know it as not.—Your father and I were both born in England, which you know is your country by birth, and you also know that the language we talk is English."

"I did not know it. Tell me something about England before you say any more."

I will not trouble the reader with Jackson's description of England, or the many questions which I put to him. It was night-fall before he had finished answering, and before I was satisfied with the information imparted. I believe that he was very glad to hold his tongue, for he complained of being tired, and I dressed his wound and wetted the bandage with cold water for him before he went to sleep.

I can hardly describe to the reader the effect which this uninterrupted flow of language had upon me; I was excited in a very strange way, and for many nights after could not sleep for hours. I may say here, I did not understand a great proportion of the meaning of the words used by Jackson; but I gathered it from the context, as I could not always be interrupting him.

It is astonishing how fast ideas breed ideas, and how a word, the meaning of which I did not understand when it was first used, became by repetition clear and intelligible; not that I always put the right construction on it, but if I did not find it answer when used at another time to my former interpretation of it, I would then ask and obtain an explanation. This did not however occur very often. As for this first night, I was positively almost drunk with words, and remained nearly the whole of it arranging and fixing the new ideas that I had acquired. My feelings towards Jackson also were changed—that is, I no longer felt hatred or ill-will against him. These were swallowed up in the pleasure which he had afforded me, and I looked upon him as a treasure beyond all price,—not but that many old feelings towards him returned at intervals, for they were not so easily disposed of, but still I would not for the world have lost him until I had obtained from him all possible knowledge; and if his wound did not look well when I removed the bandage, I was much more distressed than he was. Indeed, there was every prospect of our ultimately being friends, from our mutual dependence on each other. It was useless on his part, in his present destitute condition, to nourish feelings of animosity against one on whose good offices he was now so wholly dependant, or on my part, against one who was creating for me, I may say, new worlds for imagination and thought to dwell on. On the following morning, Jackson narrated in substance (as near as I can recollect) as follows:—

"I was not intended for a sailor. I was taught at a good school, and when I was ten years old, I was put into a house of business as a clerk, where I remained at the desk all day long, copying into ledgers and day-books, in fact, writing what was required of me. This house was connected with the South American trade."

"Where is South America?" said I.

"You had better let me tell my story," replied Jackson, "and after I have done, you can ask any questions you like, but if you stop me, it will take a week to finish it; yesterday we lost the whole day."

"That's very true," replied I, "then I will do so."

"There were two other clerks in the counting-house—the head clerk, whose name was Manvers, and your father, who was in the counting-house but a few months before me. Our master, whose name was Evelyn, was very particular with both your father and myself, scanning our work daily, and finding fault when we deserved it. This occasioned a rivalry between us, which made us both very active, and I received praise quite as often as he did. On Sunday, Mr Evelyn used to ask your father and me to spend the day. We went to church in the forenoon and dined with him. He had a daughter a little younger than we were. She was your mother. Both of us, as we grew up, were very attentive to her, and anxious to be in her good graces. I cannot say which was preferred at first, but I rather think that if anything I was the favourite, during the first two years of our being acquainted with her. I was more lively and a better companion than your father, who was inclined to be grave and thoughtful. We had been about four years in the counting-house, when my mother died—my father had been dead some time before I went into it—and at her death I found my share of her property to amount to about L2500. But I was not yet twenty-one years of age. I could not receive it for another year. Mr Evelyn, who had till then every reason to be satisfied with my conduct, used to joke with me, and say that as soon as I was of age, he would allow me, if I chose it, to put the money in the business, and thus obtain a small share in it—and such was my intention, and I looked forward to bright prospects and the hope of one day being married to your mother, and I have no doubt but such would have been the case, had I still conducted myself properly. But, before I was of age, I made some very bad acquaintances, and soon ran into expenses which I could not afford—and the worst was, that I contracted a habit of sitting up late at night, and drinking to excess, which I never have since got over, which proved my ruin then, and has proved my ruin through life. This little fortune of mine not only gave me consequence, but was the cause of my thinking very highly of myself. I now was more particular in my attentions to Miss Evelyn, and was graciously received by her father; neither had I any reason to complain of my treatment from the young lady. As for your father, he was quite thrown into the back-ground. He had no property nor hope of any, except what he might hereafter secure by his diligence and good conduct; and the attention I received from Mr Evelyn, and also the head clerk, who had an idea that I was to be a partner and consequently would become his superior, made him very melancholy and unhappy—for I believe that then he was quite as much in love with Miss Evelyn as I was myself; and I must tell you, that my love for her was unbounded, and she well deserved it. But all these happy prospects were overthrown by my own folly. As soon as it was known that I had property left to me, I was surrounded by many others who requested to be introduced to me, and my evenings were passed in what I considered very good company, but which proved the very reverse. By degrees I took to gambling, and after a time, lost more money than I could afford to pay. This caused me to have recourse to a Jew, who advanced me loans at a large interest to be repaid at my coming of age. Trying to win back my money, I at last found myself indebted to the Jew for the sum of nearly L1000. The more that I became involved, the more reckless I became. Mr Evelyn perceived that I kept late hours, and looked haggard, as I well might; indeed, my position had now become very awkward. Mr Evelyn knew well the sum that had been left me, and how was I to account to him for the deficiency, if he proposed that I should put it into the business? I should be ruined in his opinion, and he never, I was convinced, would entrust the happiness of his daughter to a young man who had been guilty of such irregularities. At the same time, my love for her nearly amounted to adoration. Never was there a more miserable being than I was for the last six months previous to my coming of age, and to drown my misery I plunged into every excess, and seldom, if ever, went to bed but in a state of intoxication. Scheme after scheme did I propose to enable me to conceal my fault, but I could hit upon nothing. The time approached; I was within a few days of coming of age, when Mr Evelyn sent for me and then spoke to me seriously, saying, that out of regard to the memory of my father, with whom he had been very intimate, he was willing to allow me to embark my little capital in the business, and that he hoped that by my good conduct and application I might soon become a useful partner. I stammered some reply which surprised him; and he asked me to be more explicit. I stated that I considered my capital too small to be of much use in such a business as his, and that I preferred trying some quick method of doubling it; that as soon as I had so done I would accept his offer with gratitude. 'As you please,' replied he coolly; 'but take care, that in risking all, you do not lose all. Of course, you are your own master,' and so saying, he left me, apparently much displeased and mortified. But circumstances occurred, which exposed the whole affair. When in company with my evening companions, I stated my intentions of trying my fortune in the East Indies, not seriously, but talking at random. This came to the ears of the Jew of whom I had borrowed the money; he thought that I intended to leave the kingdom without taking up my bonds, and immediately repaired to Mr Evelyn's counting-house, to communicate with the head clerk, and ascertain if the report was correct, stating also the sums I was indebted to him. The head clerk informed Mr Evelyn, and on the day upon which I became twenty-one years of age, he sent for me into his private room, and, after some remonstrances, to which I replied very haughtily, it ended in my being dismissed. The fact was, that Mr Evelyn had, since his last interview with me, made inquiries, and finding out I had been living a very riotous life, he had determined upon my leaving his service. As soon as my first burst of indignation was over, I felt what I had lost; my attachment to Miss Evelyn was stronger than ever, and I bitterly deplored my folly, but after a time, as usual, I had recourse to the bottle, and to drowning my cares in intemperance. I tried very hard to obtain an interview with Miss Evelyn previous to my quitting the house, but this Mr Evelyn would not permit, and a few days after, sent his daughter away, to reside, for a time with a relation in the country. I embarked my capital in the wine trade, and, could I have restrained myself from drinking, should have been successful, and in a short time might have doubled my property, as I stated to Mr Evelyn; but now, I had become an irreclaimable drunkard, and when that is the case, all hope is over. My affairs soon became deranged, and, at the request of my partner, they were wound up, and I found myself with my capital of L1500 reduced to L1000. With this, I resolved to try my fortune in shipping; I procured a share in a brig, and sailed in her myself. After a time, I was sufficiently expert to take the command of her, and might have succeeded, had not my habit of drinking been so confirmed. When at Ceylon, I fell sick, and was left behind. The brig was lost, and as I had forgotten to insure my portion of her, I was ruined. I struggled long, but in vain—intemperance was my curse, my bane, the millstone at my neck, which dragged me down: I had education, talents, and energy, and at one time, capital, but all were useless; and thus did I sink down, from captain of a vessel to mate, from mate to second mate, until I at last found myself a drunken sailor before the mast. Such is my general history; to-morrow, I will let you know how, and in what way, your father and I met again, and what occurred, up to this present time."

But I was too much bewildered and confused with what he had told me, to allow him to proceed, as he proposed.

"No, no," replied I. "I now recollect all you have said, although I do not understand. You must first answer my questions, as to the meaning of words I never heard of before. I cannot understand what money is, what gaming is, and a great many more things you have talked about, but I recollect, and can repeat every word that you have said. To-morrow, I will recall it all over, and you shall tell me what I cannot make out; after that, you can go on again."

"Very well," replied he, "I don't care how long it takes me to answer your questions, for I am not very anxious to tell all about your father and myself."

CHAPTER VI

I can hardly describe to the reader the effect which these conversations with Jackson had upon me at first. If a prisoner were removed from a dark cell, and all at once introduced into a garden full of fruit and flowers, which he never before had an idea were in existence, he could not have been more filled with wonder, surprise, and pleasure. All was novelty and excitement, but, at the same time, to a great degree, above my comprehension. I had neither language nor ideas to meet it, and yet, I did, to a certain degree, comprehend. I saw not clearly, but sometimes as through a mist, at others through a dark fog, and I could discern little. Every day, however, my increased knowledge of language and terms gave me an increased knowledge of ideas. I gained more by context than I did by any other means, and as I was by degrees enlightened, so my thirst for information and knowledge became every day more insatiable.

That much that I considered I understood was erroneous, is certain, for mine was a knowledge, as yet, of theory only. I could imagine to myself, as far as the explanation I received, what such an object might be, and, having made up my ideas on the matter, I was content; further knowledge, would however incline me to think, and occasionally to decide, that the idea I had formed was incorrect, and I would alter it. Thus did I flounder about in a sea of uncertainty, but still of exciting interest.

If any one who has been educated, and has used his eyes in a civilised country, reads an account of people and things hitherto unknown to him, he can, from the description and from his own general knowledge, form a very correct idea of what the country contains. But then he has used his eyes—he has seen those objects, between which the parallel or the difference has been pointed out. Now I had not that advantage. I had seen nothing but the sea, rocks, and sea-birds, and had but one companion. Here was my great difficulty, which, I may say, was never surmounted, until I had visited and mixed with civilisation and men. The difficulty, however, only increased my ardour. I was naturally of an ingenious mind, I had a remarkable memory, and every increase of knowledge was to me a source of delight. In fact, I had now something to live for, before I had not; and I verily believe, that if Jackson had been by any chance removed from me at this particular time, I should soon have become a lunatic, from the sudden drying up of the well which supplied my inordinate thirst for knowledge.

Some days passed before I asked Jackson to continue his narrative, during which we lived in great harmony. Whether it was that he was deceiving me, and commanding his temper till he had an opportunity of revenge, or whether it was that his forlorn and helpless condition had softened him down, I could not say, but he appeared gradually to be forming an attachment to me; I was however on my guard at all times. His wounded wrist had now healed up, but his hand was quite useless, as all the tendons had been severed. I had therefore less to fear from him than before. At my request that he would continue his history, Jackson related as follows:—

"After sailing in vessel after vessel, and generally dismissed after the voyage for my failing of intemperance, I embarked on board a ship bound to Chili, and after having been on the coast for nearly a year, we were about to proceed home with a cargo, when we anchored at Valdivia, previous to our homeward voyage, as we had some few articles to ship at that port. We were again ready for sea, when we heard from the captain, that he had agreed to take two passengers, a gentleman and his wife, who wished to proceed to England. The cabin was cleared out, and every preparation made to receive them on board, and in the evening the boat was sent on shore for the luggage. I went in the boat, as I thought it likely that the gentleman would give the boat's crew something to drink; nor was I wrong—he gave us four dollars, which we spent immediately in one of the ventas, and were all more or less intoxicated. It had been arranged that the luggage should first be carried on board, and after that, we were to return for the passengers, as we were to sail early in the morning. We pulled off with the luggage, but on our arrival on board, I was so drunk, that the captain would not allow me to return in the boat, and I knew nothing of what had passed until I was roused up the next morning to assist in getting the ship under weigh. We had been under weigh two or three hours, and were clearing the land fast, when the gentleman passenger came on neck; I was then coiling down a rope on the quarter-deck, and as he passed by me, I looked at him, and I recognised him immediately as your father. Years had passed—from a stripling he had grown a man, but his face was not to be mistaken. There he was, apparently a gentlemen of property and consideration; and I, what was I? a drunken sailor. All I hoped was, that he would not recognise me. Shortly afterwards he went down again, and returned escorting his wife on deck. Again I took a furtive curious glance, and perceived at once that she was that Miss Evelyn whom I had once so loved, and by my folly had lost. This was madness. As they stood on the deck enjoying the cool sea breeze, for the weather was delightfully fine, the captain came up and joined them. I was so confused at my discovery, that I knew not what I was about, and I presume was doing something very awkwardly; for the captain said to me— 'Jackson, what are you about, you drunken hound? I suppose you are not sober yet.' At the mention of my name, your father and mother looked at me, and as I lifted up my head to reply to the captain, they eyed me earnestly, and then spoke to each other in a low tone; after which they interrogated the captain. I could not hear what they said, but I was certain they were talking about me, and that they had suspected, if they had not recognised me. I was ready to sink to the deck, and, at the same time, I felt a hatred of your father enter my heart, of which, during his life, I never could divest myself. It was as I supposed; your father had recognised me, and the following morning he came up to me as I was leaning over the gunwale amidships, and addressed me,—'Jackson,' said he, 'I am sorry to find you in this situation. You must have been very unfortunate to have become so reduced. If you will confide your history to me, perhaps I may, when we arrive in England, be able to assist you, and it really will give me great pleasure.' I cannot say that I replied very cordially. 'Mr Henniker,' said I, 'you have been fortunate by all appearances, and can therefore afford compassion to those who have not been so; but, sir, in our positions, I feel as if pity was in reality a sort of triumph, and an offer of assistance an insult. I am content with my present position, and will at all events not change it by your interference. I earn my bread honestly. You can do no more. Times may change yet. It's a long road that has no turning to it. I wish you a good morning.' So saying, I turned from him, and walked away forward, with my heart full of bitterness and anger. From that hour he never spoke to me or noticed me again, but the captain was more severe upon me, and I ascribed his severity most unjustly to your father. We were about to go round Cape Horn, when the gale from the S.E. came on, which ended in the loss of the vessel. For several days we strove up against it, but at last the vessel, which was old, leaked so much from straining, that we were obliged to bear up and run before it, which we did for several days, the wind and sea continuing without intermission. At last we found ourselves among these islands, and were compelled occasionally to haul to the wind to clear them. This made her leak more and more, until at last she became water logged, and we were forced to abandon her in haste during the night, having no time to take anything with us; we left three men on board, who were down below. By the mercy of Heaven we ran the boat into the opening below, which was the only spot where we could have landed. I think I had better stop now, as I have a good deal to tell you yet."

"Do then," replied I; "and now I think of it, I will bring up the chest and all the things which were in it, and you shall tell me what they are."

I went down and returned with the clothes and linen. There were eight pair of trousers, nine shirts, besides the one I had torn up to bandage his wounds with, two pair of blue trousers, and two jackets, four white duck frocks, some shoes, and stockings. Jackson felt them one by one with his hands, and told me what they were, and how worn.

"Why don't you wear some of them?" inquired I.

"If you will give me leave, I will," replied he. "Let me have a duck frock and a pair of trousers."

I handed the articles to him, and then went back for the rest which I had left on the rocks.

When I returned, with my arms full, I found that he had put them on, and his other clothes were beside him. "I feel more like a Christian now," said he.

"A Christian," said I, "what is that?"

"I will tell you by-and-bye. It is what I have not been for a long, long while," replied he. "Now, what have you brought this time?"

"Here," said I, "what is this?"

"This is a roll of duck, to make into frocks and trousers," replied he. "That is bees'-wax." He then explained to me all the tools, sailing-needles, fish-hooks, and fishing-lines, some sheets of writing-paper, and two pens, I had brought up with me. "All these are very valuable," said he, after a pause, "and would have added much to our comfort, if I had not been blind."

"There are more things yet," said I; "I will go and fetch them."

This time I replaced the remaining articles, and brought up the chest. It was a heavy load to carry up the rocks, and I was out of breath when I arrived and set it down on the cabin-floor.

"Now, I have the whole of them," said I. "Now, what is this?"

"That is a spy-glass—but, alas! I am blind—but I will show you how to use it, at all events."

"Here are two books," said I.

"Give them to me," said he, "and let me feel them. This one is a Bible, I am quite sure by its shape, and the other is, I think, a Prayer-book."

"What is a Bible, and what is a Prayer-book?" replied I.

"The Bible is the Word of God, and the Prayer-book teaches us how to pray to him."

"But who is God? I have often heard you say, 'O God!' and 'God damn'—but who is he?"

"I will tell you to-night before we go to sleep," replied Jackson, gravely.

"Very well, I shall remind you. I have found a little box inside the chest, and it is full of all manner of little things—strings and sinews."

"Let me feel them?"

I put a bundle into his hand.

"These are needles and thread for making and mending clothes—they will be useful bye-and-bye."

At last the whole contents of the chest were overhauled and explained: I could not well comprehend the glass bottles, or how they were made, but I put them with the pannikins, and everything else, very carefully into the chest again, and hauled the chest to the farther end of the cabin, out of the way. Before we went to bed that night, Jackson had to explain to me who God was, but as it was only the commencement of several conversations on the subject, I shall not at present trouble the reader with what passed between us. Jackson appeared to be very melancholy after the conversation we had had on religious matters, and was frequently agitated and muttering to himself.

CHAPTER VII

I did not on the following day ask him to resume his narrative relative to my father and mother, as I perceived that he avoided it, and I already had so far changed as to have consideration for his feelings. Another point had now taken possession of my mind, which was, whether it were possible to learn to read those books which I had found in the chest, and this was the first question that I put to Jackson when we arose on that morning.

"How is it possible?" replied he. "Am I not blind—how can I teach you?"

"Is there no way?" replied I, mournfully.

"Let me think.—Yes, perhaps there is a way—at all events we will try. You know which book I told you was the Prayer-book?"

"Oh yes! the small, thin one."

"Yes—fetch it here. Now," said he, when I put it into his hand, "tell me; is there a straight line down the middle of the page of the book, so that the words and letters are on both sides of it?"

"Yes, there is," replied I; "in every page, as you call it, there is a black line down the middle, and words and letters (I suppose they are) on both sides."

"And among the letters, there are some larger than others, especially at the side nearest to the margin."

"I don't know what margin is."

"I mean here," replied he, pointing to the margin of the page.

"Yes, there are."

"Well then, I will open the book as near as I can guess at the Morning service, and you tell me if you can find any part of the writing which appears to begin with a large round letter, like—what shall I say?—the bottom of a pannikin."

"There is one on this leaf, quite round."

"Very well—now get me a small piece of stick, and make a point to it."

I did so, and Jackson swept away a small place on the floor of the cabin.

"Now," said he, "there are many other prayers which begin with a round O, as the letter is called; so I must first ascertain if this one is the one I require. If it is, I know it by heart, and by that shall be able to teach you all the letters of the alphabet."

"What's an alphabet?"

"The alphabet is the number of letters invented to enable us to read and write. There are twenty-six of them. Now look, Frank; is the next letter to O the shape of this?" and he drew with the pointed stick the letter U on the ground.

"Yes, it is," replied I.

"And the next is like this," continued he, drawing the letter R, after he had smoothed the ground and effaced the U.

"Yes," replied I.

"Well then, to make sure, I had better go on. OUR is one word, and then there is a little space between; and next you come to an F."

"Yes," replied I, looking at what he had drawn and comparing it with the letter in the book.

"Then I believe that we are all right, but to make sure, we will go on for a little longer."

Jackson then completed the word "Father," and "which art," that followed it, and then he was satisfied.

"Now," said he, "out of that prayer I can teach you all the letters, and if you pay attention, you will learn to read."

The whole morning was passed in my telling him the different letters, and I very soon knew them all. During the day, the Lord's Prayer was gone through, and as I learnt the words as well as the letters, I could repeat it before night; I read it over to him twenty or thirty times, spelling every word, letter by letter, until I was perfect. This was my first lesson.

"Why is it called the Lord's Prayer?" said I.

"Because, when our Lord Jesus Christ was asked by His followers in what way they ought to address God, He gave them this prayer to repeat, as being the most proper that they could use."

"But who was Jesus Christ?"

"He was the Son of God, as I told you yesterday, and at the same time equal with God."

"How could he be equal with God, if, as you said yesterday, God sent him down to be killed?"

"It was with his own consent that he suffered death; but all this is a mystery which you cannot understand at present."

"What's a mystery?"

"That which you cannot understand."

"Do you understand it yourself?"

"No, I do not; I only know that such is the fact, but it is above not only mine, but all men's comprehension. But I tell you honestly that, on these points, I am but a bad teacher; I have paid little attention to them during my life, and as far as religion is concerned, I can only give you the outlines, for I know no more."

"But I thought you said, that people were to be punished or rewarded when they died, according as they had lived a bad or good life; and that to live a good life, people must be religious, and obey God's commands."

"I did tell you so, and I told you the truth; but I did not tell you that I had led a bad life, as I have done, and that I have neglected to pay obedience to God's word and command."

"Then you will be punished when you die, will you not?"

"Alas! I fear so, child," replied Jackson, putting his hands up to his forehead and hiding his face. "But there is still time," continued he, after a pause, and "O God of mercy!" exclaimed he, "how shall I escape?"

I was about to continue the conversation, but Jackson requested that I would leave him alone for a time. I went out and sat on a rock, watching the stars.

"And those, he says, were all made by God,"—"and God made everything," thought I, "and God lives up beyond those stars." I thought for a long while, and was much perplexed. I had never heard anything of God till the night before, and what Jackson had told me was just enough to make me more anxious and curious; but he evidently did not like to talk on the subject. I tried after a time, if I could repeat the Lord's Prayer, and I found that I could, so I knelt down on the rock, and looking up to a bright star, as if I would imagine it was God, I repeated the Lord's Prayer to it, and then I rose up and went to bed.

This was the first time that I had ever prayed.

I had learnt so much from Jackson, latterly, that I could hardly retain what I had learnt; at all events, I had a very confused recollection in my brain, and my thoughts turned from one subject to another, till there was, for a time, a perfect chaos; by degrees things unravelled themselves, and my ideas became more clear; but still I laboured under that half-comprehension of things, which, in my position, was unavoidable.

But now my mind was occupied with one leading object and wish, which was to learn to read. I thought no more of Jackson's history and the account he might give me of my father and mother, and was as willing as he was that it should be deferred for a time. What I required now was to be able to read the books, and to this object my whole mind and attention were given. Three or four hours in the earlier portion of the day, and the same time in the latter, were dedicated to this pursuit, and my attention never tired or flagged. In the course of, I think, about six weeks, I could read, without hesitation, almost any portion of the Bible or Prayer-Book. I required no more teaching from Jackson, who now became an attentive hearer, as I read to him every morning and evening a portion of the Gospel or Liturgy. But I cannot say that I understood many portions which I read, and the questions which I put to Jackson puzzled him not a little, and very often he acknowledged that he could not answer them. As I afterwards discovered this arose from his own imperfect knowledge of the nature of the Christian religion, which, according to his statement to me, might be considered to have been comprised in the following sentence: "If you do good on earth, you will go to heaven and be happy; if you do ill, you will go to hell and be tormented. Christ came down from heaven to teach us what to do, and how to follow his example; and all that we read in the Bible we must believe." This may be considered as the creed imparted to me at that time. I believe that Jackson, like many others, knew no better, and candidly told me what he himself had been taught to believe.

But the season for the return of the birds arrived, and our stock of provender was getting low. I was therefore soon obliged to leave my books, and work hard for Jackson and myself. As soon as the young birds were old enough, I set to my task. And now I found how valuable were the knives which I had obtained from the seaman's chest; indeed, in many points I could work much faster. By tying the neck and sleeves of a duck frock, I made a bag, which enabled me to carry the birds more conveniently, and in greater quantities at a time, and with the knives I could skin and prepare a bird in one quarter of the time. With my fishing-lines also, I could hang up more to dry at one time, so that, though without assistance, I had more birds cured in the same time than when Jackson and I were both employed in the labour. The whole affair, however, occupied me from morning to evening for more than three weeks, by which time the major portion of my provender was piled up at the back of the cabin. I did not, however, lose what I had gained in reading, as Jackson would not let me go away in the morning, or retire to my bed in the evening, without my reading to him a portion of the Bible. Indeed, he appeared to be uncomfortable if I did not do so.

At last, the work was ended, and then I felt a strong desire return to hear that portion of Jackson's history connected with my father and mother, and I told him so. He did not appear to be pleased with my communication, or at all willing to proceed, but as I pressed him hard and showed some symptoms of resolution and rebellion, he reluctantly resumed his narrative.

CHAPTER VIII

"I wish you to understand," said he, "that my unwillingness to go on with my history, proceeds from my being obliged to make known to you the hatred that subsisted between your father and me; but if you will recollect, that we both had, in our early days, been striving to gain the same object—I mean your mother—and also that he had taken, as it were, what I considered to have been my place, in other points—that he had been successful in life, and I had been unfortunate, you must not then be surprised at my hating him as I did."

"I understand nothing about your feelings," replied I; "and why he injured you by marrying my mother, I cannot see."

"Why I loved her."

"Well, suppose you did, I don't know what love is, and therefore cannot understand it, so tell me the story."

"Well then, when I left off, I told you that we had ventured to land upon this island by running the boat into the bathing-pond, but in so doing, the boat was beaten to pieces, and was of no use afterwards. We landed, eight persons in all—that is, the captain, your father, the carpenter, mate, and three seamen, besides your mother. We had literally nothing in the boat except three axes, two kids, and the two pannikins, which we have indeed now, but as for provisions or even water we had none of either. Our first object, therefore, was to search the island to obtain water, and this we soon found at the rill which now runs down by the side of the cabin. It was very fortunate for us that we arrived exactly at the time that the birds had come on the island, and had just laid their eggs; if not, we must have perished with hunger, for we had not a fish-hook with us or even a fathom of line.

"We collected a quantity of eggs, and made a good meal, although we devoured them raw. While we were running about, or rather climbing about, over the rocks, to find out what chance of subsistence we might have on the island, the captain and your father remained with your mother, who sat down in a sheltered spot near to the bathing-pool. On our return in the evening, the captain called us all together that he might speak to us, and he said that if we would do well we must all act in concert; that it also would be necessary that one should have the command and control of the others; that without such was the case, nothing would go on well;—and he asked us if we did not consider that what he said was true. We all agreed, although I, for one, felt little inclination to do so, but as all the rest said so, I raised no objections. The captain then told us that as we were all of one opinion, the next point, was to decide as to who should have the command—he said, that if it had been on ship-board, he of course would have taken it himself, but now we were on shore he thought that Mr Henniker was a much more competent person than he was, and he therefore proposed that the command should be given to him, and he, for one, would willingly be under his orders. To this proposal, the carpenter and mate immediately agreed, and at last two of the seamen. I was left alone, but I resisted, saying, that I was not going to be ordered about by a landsman, and that if I were to obey orders, it must be from a thorough-bred seaman. The other two sailors were of my way of thinking, I was sure, although they had given their consent, and I hoped that they would join me, which they appeared very much inclined to do. Your father spoke very coolly, modestly, and prudently. He pointed out that he had no wish to take the command, and that he would cheerfully serve under the captain of the vessel, if it would be more satisfactory to all parties that such should be the case. But the captain and the others were positive, saying that they would not have their choice disputed by such a drunken vagabond as I was, and that if I did not like to remain with them, I might go to any part of the island that I chose. This conference ended by my getting in a passion, and saying that I would not be under your father's orders; and I was seizing one of the axes to go off with it, when the captain caught my arm and wrested it from me, stating that the axe was his property, and then telling me that I was welcome to go where I pleased.

"I left them, therefore, and went away by myself to where the birds were hatching, as I wished to secure a supply of eggs. When the night closed in, I lay down upon the guano, and felt no cold, for the gale was now over, and the weather was very mild.

"The next morning, when I awoke, I found that the sun had been up some time. I looked for the rest of my companions whom I had quitted, and perceived that they were all busily at work. The sea was quite calm; and, when the vessel went down after we left, many articles had floated, and had been washed to the island. Some of the men were busy collecting spars and planks, which were near the rocks, and pushing them along with the boat-hooks to the direction of the bathing pond, where they hauled them over the ridge, and secured them. Your father and mother, with the carpenter, were on this ledge where we now are, having selected it as a proper place for building a shelter, and were apparently very busy. The captain and one of the seamen were carrying up what spars and timber could be collected to where your father was standing with the carpenter. All appeared to be active, and working into each others hands; and I confess that, as I looked on, I envied them, and wished that I had been along with them; but I could not bear the idea of obeying any orders given by your father; and this alone prevented my joining them, and making my excuses for what I had done and said the previous night. I therefore swallowed some more birds' eggs raw, and sat down in the sun, looking at them as they worked.

"I soon perceived that the carpenter had commenced operations. The frame of this cabin was, with the assistance of your father, before it was noon, quite complete and put up; and then they all went down to the bathing place, where the boat was lying with her bottom beaten out. They commenced taking her to pieces and saving all the nails; the other men carried up the portions of the boat as they were ripped off, to where the frame of the cabin had been raised. I saw your mother go up with a load in her hand, which I believed to be the nails taken from the boat. In a couple of hours the boat was in pieces and carried up, and then your father and most of the men went up to assist the carpenter. I hardly need tell what they did, as you have the cabin before you. The roof, you see, is mostly built out of the timbers of the boat; and the lower part out of heavier wood; and a very good job they made of it. Before the morning closed in, one of the sides of the cabin was finished; and I saw them light a fire with the chips that had been cut off with the axes, and they then dressed the eggs and birds which they had collected the first day.

"There was one thing which I had quite forgotten when I mutinied and left my companions, which was, the necessity of water to drink; and I now perceived that they had taken possession of the spot where the only water had as yet been found. I was suffering very much from thirst towards the close of the day, and I set off up the ravine to ascertain if there was none to be found in that direction. Before night I succeeded in finding some, as you know, for you have often drunk from the spring when you have gone up for firewood. This gave me great encouragement, for I was afraid that the want of water would have driven me to submission. By way of bravado, I tore off, and cut with my knife, as many boughs of the underwood on the ravine as I well could carry, and the next morning I built a sort of wigwam for myself on the guano, to show them that I had a house over my head as well as they had; but I built it farther up to the edge of the cliff, above the guano plain, so that I need not have any communication with those who I knew would come for eggs and birds for their daily sustenance.

"Before the night of the following day set in, the cabin was quite finished.

"The weather became warmer every day, and I found it very fatiguing to have to climb the ravine two or three times a day to procure a drink of water, for I had nothing to hold water in, and I thought that it would be better that I should take up my quarters in the ravine, and build myself a wigwam among the brushwood close to the water, instead of having to make so many journeys for so necessary an article. I knew that I could carry eggs in my hat and pocket-handkerchief sufficient for two or three days at one trip; so I determined that I would do so; and the next morning I went up the ravine, loaded with eggs, to take up my residence there. In a day or two I had built my hut of boughs, and made it very comfortable. I returned for a fresh supply of eggs on the third day, with a basket I had constructed out of young boughs, and which enabled me to carry a whole week's sustenance. Then I felt quite satisfied, and made up my mind that I would live as a hermit during my sojourn on the island, however long it might be; for I preferred anything to obeying the orders of one whom I detested as I did your father.

"It soon was evident, however, how well they had done in selecting your father as their leader. They had fancied that the birds would remain on the island, and that thus they would always be able to procure a supply. Your father, who had lived so long in Chili, knew better, and that in a few weeks they would quit their nesting place. He pointed this out to them, showing them what a mercy it was that they had been cast away just at this time, and how necessary it was to make a provision for the year. But this they could not imagine that it was possible to do without salt to cure the birds with; but he knew how beef was preserved without salt on the continent, and showed them how to dry the birds in the sun. While therefore I was up in the ravine, they were busy collecting and drying them in large quantities, and before the time of the birds leaving they had laid up a sufficient supply. It was he also that invented the fishing lines out of the sinews of the legs of the birds, and your mother who knotted them together. At first, they caught fish with some hooks made of nails, but your father showed them the way to take them without a hook, as you have learnt from me, and which he had been shown by some of the Indians on the continent. Owing to your father, they were well prepared when the birds flew away with their young ones, while I was destitute. Previous to the flight, I had fared but badly, for the eggs contained the young birds half formed, and latterly so completely formed that I could not eat them, and as I had no fire and did not understand drying them, I had no alternative but eating the young birds raw, which was anything but pleasant. I consoled myself, however, with the idea that your father and mother and the rest were faring just as badly as myself, and I looked forward to the time when the birds would begin to lay eggs again, when I resolved to hoard up a much larger supply while they were fresh. But my schemes were all put an end to, for in two days, after a great deal of noise and flying about in circles, all the birds, young and old, took wing, and left me without any means of future subsistence.

"This was a horrid discovery, and I was put to my wits' ends. I wandered over the guano place, and, after the third day of their departure, was glad to pick up even a dead bird with which to appease my hunger. At the same time, I wondered how my former companions got on, for I considered that they must be as badly off as I was. I watched them from behind the rocks, but I could perceive no signs of uneasiness. There was your mother sitting quietly on the level by the cabin, and your father or the captain talking with her. I perceived, however, that two of the party were employed fishing off the rocks, and I wondered where they got their fishing-lines, and at last I concluded that it was by catching fish that they supported themselves. This, however, did not help me—I was starving, and starvation will bring down the pride of any man. On the fifth day, I walked down to the rocks, to where one of the seamen was fishing, and having greeted him, I told him that I was starving, and asked for something to eat.

"'I cannot help you,' replied he; 'I have no power to give anything away; it is more than I dare do. You must apply to Mr Henniker, who is the governor now. What a foolish fellow you were to mutiny, as you did; see what it has brought you to.'

"'Why,' replied I, 'if it were not for fishing, you would not be better off than I am.'

"'Oh yes we should be; but we have to thank him for that— without him, I grant, we should not have been. We have plenty of provisions, although we fish to help them out.'

"This puzzled me amazingly, but there was no help for it. I could starve no longer, so up I went to the level where your father was standing with the captain, and in a swaggering sort of tone, said that I had come back, and wanted to join my comrades. The captain looked at me, and referred me to your father, who said that he would consult with the rest when they came to dinner, as without their permission he could do nothing, and then they both turned away. In the meantime I was ravenous with hunger, and was made more so by perceiving that two large fish were slowly baking on the embers of the fire, and that your mother was watching them; however, there was no help for it, and I sat down at some little distance, anxiously waiting for the return of the rest of the party, when my fate would be decided. My pride was now brought down so low that I could have submitted to any terms which might have been dictated. In about two hours they were all assembled to dinner, and I remained envying every morsel that they ate, until the repast was finished; when after some consultation, I was ordered to approach—which I did—and your father addressed me: 'Jackson, you deserted us when you might have been very useful, and when our labour was severe; now that we have worked hard, and made ourselves tolerably comfortable, you request to join us, and partake with us of the fruits of our labour and foresight. You have provided nothing, we have—the consequence is that we are in comparative plenty, while you are starving. Now I have taken the opinion of my companions, and they are all agreed, that as you have not assisted when you are wanted, should we now allow you to join us, you will have to work more than the others to make up an equivalent. It is therefore proposed that you shall join us on one condition, which is, that during the year till the birds again visit the island, it will be your task to go up to the ravine every day, and procure the firewood which is required. If you choose to accept these terms, you are permitted to join, always supposing that to all the other rules and regulations which we have laid down for our guidance, you will be subject as well as we are. These are our terms, and you may decide as you think proper.' I hardly need say, that I gladly accepted them, and was still more glad when the remnants of the dinner were placed before me; I was nearly choked, I devoured with such haste until my appetite was appeased.

"When this was done, I thought over the conditions which I had accepted, and my blood boiled at the idea that I was to be in a manner the slave to the rest, as I should have to work hard every day. I forgot that it was but justice, and that I was only earning my share of the years' provisions, which I had not assisted to collect. My heart was still more bitter against your father, and I vowed vengeance if ever I had an opportunity, but there was no help for it. Every day I went up with a piece of cord and an axe, cut a large faggot of wood, and brought it down to the cabin. It was hard work, and occupied me from breakfast to dinner-time, and I had no time to lose if I wanted to be back for dinner. The captain always examined the faggot, and ascertained that I had brought down a sufficient supply for the day's consumption."

CHAPTER IX

"A year passed away, during which I was thus employed. At last, the birds made their appearance, and after we had laid up our annual provision, I was freed from my task, and had only to share the labour with others. It was now a great source of speculation how long we were likely to remain on the island; every day did we anxiously look out for a vessel, but we could see none, or if seen, they were too far off from the island to permit us to make signals to them. At last we began to give up all hope, and, as hope was abandoned, a settled gloom was perceptible on most of our faces. I believe that others would have now mutinied as well as myself, if they had known what to mutiny about. Your father and mother were the life and soul of the party, inventing amusements, or narrating a touching story in the evenings, so as to beguile the weary time; great respect was paid to your mother, which she certainly deserved; I seldom approached her; she had taken a decided dislike to me, arising, I presume, from my behaviour towards her husband, for now that I was again on a footing with the others, I was as insolent to him as I dared to be, without incurring the penalty attached to insubordination, and I opposed him as much as I could in every proposal that he brought forward—but your father kept his temper, although I lost mine but too often. The first incident which occurred of any consequence, was the loss of two of the men, who had, with your father's permission, taken a week's provisions, with the intention of making a tour round the island, and ascertaining whether any valuable information could be brought back; they were the carpenter and one of the seamen. It appears that during their return, as they were crossing the highest ridge, they, feeling very thirsty, and not finding water, attempted to refresh themselves by eating some berries which they found on a plant. These berries proved to be strong poison, and they returned very ill—after languishing a few days, they both died.

"This was an event which roused us up, and broke the monotony of our life; but it was one which was not very agreeable to dwell upon, and yet, at the same time, I felt rather pleasure than annoyance at it—I felt that I was of more consequence, and many other thoughts entered my mind which I shall not now dwell upon. We buried them in the guano, under the first high rock, where, indeed, the others were all subsequently buried. Three more months passed away, when the other seaman was missing. After a search, his trousers were found at the edge of the rock. He had evidently been bathing in the sea, for the day on which he was missed, the water was as smooth as glass. Whether he had seen something floating, which he wished to bring to land, or whether he had ventured for his own amusement, for he was an excellent swimmer, could never be ascertained—any more than whether he had sunk with the cramp, or had been taken down by a shark. He never appeared again, and his real fate is a mystery to this day, and must ever remain so. Thus were we reduced to four men—your father, the captain, the mate, and me. But you must be tired—I will stop now, and tell you the remainder some other time."

Although I was not tired, yet, as Jackson appeared to be so, I made no objection to his proposal, and we both went to sleep.

While I had read the Bible to Jackson, I had often been puzzled by numbers being mentioned, and never could understand what was meant, that is, I could form no of the quantity represented by seventy or sixty, or whatever it might be. Jackson's answer was, "Oh! it means a great many; I'll explain to you bye-and-bye, but we have nothing to count with, and as I am blind, I must have something in my hand to teach you." I recollected that at the bathing pool there were a great many small shells on the rocks, about the size of a pea; there were live fish in them, and they appeared to crawl on the rocks. I collected a great quantity of these, and brought them up to the cabin, and requested Jackson would teach me to count. This he did, until he came to a thousand, which he said was sufficient. For many days I continued to count up to a hundred, until I was quite perfect, and then Jackson taught me addition and subtraction to a certain degree, by making me add and take away from the shells, and count the accumulation, or the remainder. At last, I could remember what I had gained by manipulation, if I may use the term, but further, I could not go, although addition had, to a degree, made me master of multiplication, and subtraction gave me a good idea of division.

This was a new delight to me, and occupied me for three or four weeks. At last I had, as I thought, learned all that he could teach me in his blind state, and I threw away the shells, and sighed for something more.

Of a sudden it occurred to me, that I had never looked into the book which still lay upon the shelf in the cabin, and I saw no reason now that I should not; so I mentioned it to Jackson, and asked him why I might not have that book?

"To be sure you may," replied he; "but you never asked for it, and I quite forgot it."

"But when I asked you before, you were so particular that I should not open it. What was your reason then?"

Jackson replied—"I had no reason except that I then disliked you, and I thought that looking into the book would give you pleasure. It belonged to that poor fellow that was drowned; he had left it in the stern-sheets of the boat when we were at Valdivia, and had forgotten it, and we found it there when we landed on the island. Take it down, it will amuse you."

I took down the book, and opened it. It was, if I recollect right, called "Mavor's Natural History." At all events, it was a Natural History of Beasts and Birds, with a plate representing each, and a description annexed. It would be impossible for me to convey to the reader my astonishment and delight. I had never seen a picture or drawing in my life. I did not know that such things existed. I was in an ecstasy of delight as I turned over the pages, hardly taking sufficient time to see one object before I hastened on to another. For two or three hours did I thus turn over leaves, without settling upon any one animal; at last my pulse beat more regularly, and I commenced with the Lion. But now what a source of amusement, and what a multitude of questions had to be answered by my companion. He had to tell me all about the countries in which the animals were found; and the description of the animals, with the anecdotes, were a source of much conversation; and, what was more, the foregrounds and backgrounds of the landscapes with which the animals were surrounded produced new ideas. There was a palm-tree, which I explained to Jackson, and inquired about it. This led to more inquiries. The lion himself occupied him and me for a whole afternoon, and it was getting dark when I lay down, with my new treasure by my side. I had read of the lion in the Scriptures, and now I recalled all the passages; and before I slept I thought of the bear which destroyed the children who had mocked Elisha the prophet, and I determined that the first animal I would read about the next morning should be the bear.

I think that this book lasted me nearly two months, during which time, except reading a portion every night and morning to Jackson, the Bible and Prayer-book were neglected. Sometimes I thought that the book could not be true; but when I came to the birds, I found those which frequented the island so correctly described, that I had no longer any doubt on the subject. Perhaps what interested me most were the plates in which the barn-door fowls and the peacock were described, as in the background of the first were a cottage and figures, representing the rural scenery of England, my own country; and in the second there was a splendid mansion, and a carriage and four horses driving up to the door. In short, it is impossible to convey to the reader the new ideas which I received from these slight efforts of the draftsman to give effect to his drawing. The engraving was also a matter of much wonder, and required a great deal of explanation from Jackson. This book became my treasure, and it was not till I had read it through and through, so as almost to know it by heart, that at length I returned to my Bible. All this time I had never asked Jackson to go on with his narrative; but now that my curiosity was appeased, I made the request. He appeared, as before, very unwilling; but I was pertinacious, and he was worried into it.

"There were but four of us left and your mother, and the mate was in a very bad state of health; he fretted very much, poor fellow, for he had left a young wife in England, and what he appeared to fear most was, that she would be married again before he could get home. It ended in a confirmed liver complaint, which carried him off nine months afterwards; and thus was one more of our companions disposed of. He died very quietly, and gave me his sleeve-buttons and watch to deliver to his wife, if ever I should escape from the island. I fear there is little chance of her ever receiving them."

"Where are they?" said I, recollecting how I had seen him lift up the board under his bed-place.

"I have them safe," replied Jackson, "and if necessary, will tell you where to find them."

This reply satisfied me, and I allowed him to proceed.

"We buried him in the guano, by the side of the two others, and now we were but three. It was at this time that your mother was confined and you were born; that is about three months after the death of the mate. We had just finished laying in our stock of birds for the year when she was taken ill, sooner than was expected, and it was supposed that it was occasioned by over-exertion at the time. However, she got up very well without any medical assistance, and your father was much pleased at having a son, for he had been married five years without any prospect of a family. I ought to observe that the loss of our companions, one after another, had had the effect of bringing those that remained much closer together; I was treated with more kindness by both your father and mother, and the captain, and I returned it as well as my feelings would permit me, for I could not altogether get rid of my animosity to your father. However, we became much more confidential, that is certain, and I was now treated as an equal.

"Six months passed away and you had become a thriving child, when a melancholy occurrence"—here Jackson covered up his face with his hands and remained for some time silent.

"Go on," said I, "Jackson, I know that they all died somehow or another."

"Very true," replied he, recovering himself. "Well, your father disappeared. He had gone to the rocks to fish, and when I was sent to bring him home to dinner, he was nowhere to be found. It was supposed that a larger fish than usual had been fast to his line, and that he had been jerked off the rocks into the water and the sharks had taken him. It was a dreadful affair," continued Jackson, again covering his face.

"I think," replied I, "that any man in his senses would have allowed the fish to have taken the line rather than have been dragged into the water. I don't think that the supposed manner of his death is at all satisfactory."

"Perhaps not," replied Jackson; "his foot may have slipped, who knows? we only could guess; the line was gone as well as he, which made us think what I said. Still we searched everywhere, but without hope; and our search—that is the captain's and mine, for your poor mother remained with you in her arms distracted— was the cause of another disaster—no less than the death of the captain. They say misfortunes never come single, and surely this was an instance of the truth of the proverb."

"How did he die?" replied I, gravely, for somehow or other I felt doubts as to the truth of what he was saying. Jackson did not reply till after a pause, when he said—

"He was out with me up the ravine collecting firewood, and he fell over the high cliff. He was so injured that he died in half an hour."

"What did you do?"

"What did I do—what could I do but go back and break the news to your mother, who was distracted when she heard it; for the captain was her friend, and she could not bear me."

"Well go on, pray," said I.

"I did all that I could to make your mother comfortable, as there now were but her, you, and I, left on the island. You were then about three years old; but your mother always hated me, and appeared now to hate me more and more. She never recovered the loss of your father to whom she was devotedly attached; she pined away, and after six months she died, leaving you and me only on the island. Now you know the whole history, and pray do not ask me any more about it."

CHAPTER X

Jackson threw himself back in his bed-place and was silent. So was I, for I was recalling all that he had told me, and my doubts were raised as to the truth of it. I did not like his hurrying over the latter portion of his narrative in the way which he had done. What he had said about my mother was not satisfactory. I had for some time been gradually drawing towards him, not only shewing, but feeling, for him a great increase of goodwill; but suspicion had entered my mind, and I now began to feel my former animosity towards him renewed. A night's sleep, however, and more reflection, induced me to think that possibly I was judging him too harshly, and as I could not afford to quarrel with him, our intercourse remained as amicable as before, particularly as he became more and more amiable towards me and did everything in his power to interest and amuse me.

I was one day reading to him the account of a monkey given in the book of Natural History, in which it is said that that animal is fond of spirits and will intoxicate itself, and Jackson was telling me many anecdotes of monkeys on board of the vessel he had sailed in, when it occurred to me that I had never thought of mentioning to him or of ascertaining the contents of the cask which had been thrown into the bathing-pool with the seaman's chest, and I did so then to Jackson, wondering at its contents and how they were to be got at.

Jackson entered into the question warmly, explaining to me how and where to bore holes with a gimlet, and making two spiles for me to stop the holes with. As soon as he had done so, curiosity induced me to go down to the pool where the cask had been lying so long, in about a foot-and-half water. By Jackson's directions I took a pannikin with me, that I might bring him a specimen of the contents of the cask, if they should prove not to be water. I soon bored the hole above and below, following Jackson's directions, and the liquor, which poured out in a small stream into the pannikin, was of a brown colour and very strong in odour, so strong, indeed, as to make me reel as I walked back to the rocks with the pannikin full of it. I then sat down, and after a time tasted it. I thought I had swallowed fire, for I had taken a good mouthful of it. "This cannot be what Jackson called spirits," said I. "No one can drink this—what can it be?" Although I had not swallowed more than a table-spoonful of it, yet, combined with the fumes of the liquor which I had inhaled when drawing it off into the pannikin, the effect was to make my head swim, and I lay down on the rock and shut my eyes to recover myself. It ended in my falling asleep for many hours, for it was not much after noon when I went to the cask, and it was near sunset when I awoke, with an intense pain in my head. It was some time before I could recollect where I was, or what had passed, but the pannikin full of liquor by my side first reminded me; and then perceiving how late it was, and how long I must have slept, I rose up, and taking the pannikin in my hand, I hastened to return to the cabin.

As I approached, I heard the voice of Jackson, whose hearing, since his blindness, I had observed, had become peculiarly acute.

"Is that you, Frank?"

"Yes," replied I.

"And what has kept you so long—how you have frightened me. God forgive me, but I thought that I was to be left and abandoned to starvation."

"Why should you have thought that?" replied I.

"Because I thought that some way or another you must have been killed, and then I must have died, of course. I never was so frightened in my life, the idea of dying here all alone—it was terrible."

It occurred to me at the time that the alarm was all for himself, for he did not say a word about how sorry he should have been at any accident happening to me, but I made no remark, simply stating what had occurred, and my conviction that the contents of the cask were not drinkable.

"Have you brought any with you?" inquired he, sharply.

"Yes, here it is," said I, giving him the pannikin.

He smelt it, and raised it to his lips—took about a wine-glassful of it, and then drew his breath.

"This is delightful," said he; "the best of old rum, I never tasted so good. How big did you say that the cask was?"

I described it as well as I could.

"Indeed, then it must be a whole puncheon—that will last a long while."

"But do you mean to say that you really like to drink that stuff?" inquired I.

"Do I like to drink it? yes, it is good for men, but it's death to little boys. It will kill you. Don't you get fond of it. Now promise me that you will never drink a drop of it. You must not get fond of it, or some sad accident will happen to you."

"I don't think you need fear my drinking it," replied I. "I have had one taste, as I told you, and it nearly burnt my mouth. I shan't touch it again."

"That's right," replied Jackson, taking another quantity into his mouth. "You are not old enough for it; bye-and-bye, when you are as old as I am, you may drink it, then it will do you good. Now, I'll go to bed, it's time for bed. Bring the pannikin after me and put it by my side. Take care you don't spill any of it."

Jackson crawled to his bed, and I followed him with the pannikin, and put it by his side, as he requested, and I returned to my own resting-place, without however having the least inclination to sleep, having slept so long during the day.

At first Jackson was quiet, but I heard him occasionally applying to the pannikin, which held, I should say, about three half-pints of liquor. At last he commenced singing a sea song; I was much surprised, as I had never heard him sing before; but I was also much pleased, as it was the first time that I had ever heard anything like melody, for he had a good voice and sang in good tune. As soon as he had finished, I begged him to go on.

"Ah!" replied he, with a gay tone I had never heard from him before. "You like songs, do you? my little chap. Well, I'll give you plenty of them. 'Tis a long while since I have sung, but it's a 'poor heart that never rejoiceth.' The time was when no one in company could sing a song as I could, and so I can again, now that I have something to cheer my heart. Yes, here's another for you. I shall rouse them all out by-and-bye, as I get the grog in—no fear of that—you find the stuff, and I'll find songs."

I was surprised at first at this unusual mirth; but recollecting what Jackson had told me about his intemperance, I presumed that this mirth which it produced was the cause why he indulged so much in it; and I felt less inclined to blame him. At all events, I was much pleased with the songs that he sang to me one after another for three or four hours, when his voice became thick, and, after some muttering and swearing, he was quite silent, and soon afterwards snored loudly. I remained awake some time longer, and then I also sank into forgetfulness.

When I awoke the next morning, I found Jackson still fast asleep. I waited for him for our morning meal; but, as he did not wake, I took mine by myself, and then I walked out to the rock, where I usually sat, and looked round the horizon to see if there was anything in sight. The spy-glass, from having been in sea water, was of no use, and I did not know what to do with it; nor could Jackson instruct me. After I had been out about an hour I returned, and found Jackson still snoring, and I determined to wake him up. I pushed him for some time without success; but, at last he opened his eyes, and said:

"My watch already?"

"No," said I; "but you have slept so long, that I have waked you up."

He paused, as if he did not know my voice, and then said:

"But I can't see anything; how's this?"

"Why, don't you know that you're blind, Jackson?" replied I, with amazement.

"Yes, yes; I recollect now. Is there anything in the pannikin?"

"Not a drop," replied I; "why, you must have drunk it all."

"Yes, I recollect now. Get me some water, my good boy; for I am dying with thirst."

I went for the water; he drank the whole pannikin, and asked for more.

"Won't you have something to eat?" said I.

"Eat? oh no; I can't eat anything. Give me drink;" and he held out his hand for the pannikin. I perceived how it trembled and shook, and I observed it to him.

"Yes," replied he, "that's always the case after a carouse, and I had a good one last night—the first for many a year. But there's plenty more of it. I wish you would get me a little more now, Frank, just to steady me; just about two or three mouthfuls, no more; that is, no more till night-time. Did I make much noise last night?"

"You sang several songs," replied I, "with which I was much amused."

"I'm glad that you liked them. I used to be considered a good singer in my day; indeed, if I had not been such good company, as they term it, I had not become so fond of drinking. Just go and fetch me about half an inch high of the pannikin, my good fellow, that's all I want now."

I went down to the cask, drew of the quantity that he requested, and brought it to him. He drank it off; and, in a few moments, appeared to be quite himself again. He then asked for something to eat, and commenced telling me a variety of stories relative to what he termed jolly parties in his former days; so that the day passed very agreeably. As the night closed in, he said:

"Now, Frank, I know you want to hear some more songs; so go down and bring me up a full pannikin, and I will sing you plenty."

I complied with his request, for I was anxious to be again amused as I was the night before. The consequence was that this night was, in the early portion of it, but a repetition of the previous one. Jackson took the precaution to get into his bed-place before he commenced drinking; and, as soon as he had taken his second dose, he asked me what sort of songs I liked. My reply naturally was, that I had never heard any one sing but him, and therefore could not say.

"What did I sing to you last night?" said he.

I replied as well as I could.

"Ah," said he, "they were all sea songs; but now I will give you something better."

After a little thought, he commenced singing a very beautiful and plaintive one, and certainly much better than he had sung the night before; for he now was sober. The consequence was, that I was still more delighted; and, at my request, he sang several others; but at last his speech became rapid and thick, and he would not sing any more, using some very coarse expressions to me when I asked him. For a time he was silent, and I thought that he was going to sleep, and I was reflecting upon the various effects which the liquor appeared to have upon him, when I heard him talking and muttering, and I listened.

"Never mind how I got them," said he; "quite as honestly as other people, Old Moshes. There they are, do you choose to buy them?" Then there was a pause, after which he commenced: "They're as pure diamonds as ever came out of a mine. I know that, so none of your lies, you old Jew. Where did I come by them? that's no concern of yours. The question is, will you give me the price, or will you not? Well, then, I'm off. No, I won't come back, you old thief." Here he swore terribly, and then was silent.

After a while he recommenced—

"Who can ever prove that they were Henniker's diamonds?"

I started up at the mention of my father's name; I rested with my hands on the floor of the cabin, breathless as to what would come next.

"No, no," continued Jackson, "he's dead, and food for fishes—dead men tell no tales—and she's dead, and the captain's dead, all dead—yes, all;" and he gave a bitter groan and was silent.

The day was breaking, and I could just see him as he lay; but he said no more, and appeared to breathe heavily. As the sun rose, I got out of my bed-place; and, now that it was broad daylight, I looked at Jackson. He was lying on his back; his brow was covered with large drops of perspiration, and his hands were clenched together. Although asleep, he appeared, by the convulsive twitching of the muscles of his face, to be suffering and in great agony. Occasionally he groaned deeply, and his lips appeared to move, but no sound proceeded from them. I perceived that the pannikin of liquor was not finished, one-third at least having been left.

CHAPTER XI

I then went out of the cabin and took my usual seat, and began to reflect upon what I had heard. He had talked about diamonds; now I knew what diamonds were, so far as they were of great value, for I had read of them in the Bible, and Jackson had explained the value of precious stones to me, and had told me of diamonds of very great value indeed. Then he said that they were Henniker's diamonds—he must have meant my father, that was positive. And that no one could prove they were his—this implied that Jackson had no right to them; indeed how could he have? And then I recalled to mind his having a secret hiding place under his bed, where I presumed the diamonds were deposited. I then turned over in my mind what he had told me relative to the death of my father, the captain, and my mother, how confused he was, and how glad he was to get rid of the subject, and how unsatisfactory I thought his account was at the time. After much cogitation, I made up my mind that Jackson had not told me the truth, and that there was a mystery yet to be explained; but how was I to get at it? There was but one way. The liquor made him talk. I would supply him with liquor, and by degrees I would get the truth out of him. At the same time I would not allow him to suppose that he had said anything to commit himself, or that I had any suspicions.

How naturally do we fall into treachery and deceit, from the evil in our own hearts, without any assistance or example from the world. How could I have learnt deceit? Isolated as I had been, must it not have been innate?

I returned to the cabin, and woke Jackson without much difficulty, since he had not drunk so much as on the previous night.

"How are you this morning?" said I.

"Not very well; I have had some bad dreams."

"Well you sang me some beautiful songs," replied I.

"Yes, I recollect," said he; "but I fell asleep at last."

"Yes, you refused to sing any more, and went off in a loud snore."

Jackson got out of his bed-place, and I gave him his meal. We talked during the whole day about singing, and I hummed the air which had pleased me most.

"You have got the air pretty correct," said he; "you must have an ear for music. Have you ever tried to sing?"

"No, never; you know I have not."

"You might have tried when I was not with you. Try now. I will sing a tune, and then do you repeat it after me."

He did so, and I repeated it.

"Very good," said he. "Let's try the compass of your voice."

He ran up the gamut, and I followed him.

"I think you can go higher than I can," said he, "however you go quite high enough, so now I'll give you a singing lesson."

Thus were we occupied at intervals during the whole day, for Jackson would not allow me to try my voice too much at first. As the evening fell, he again asked me to fetch some liquor, and as I had three quart wine bottles, as I before mentioned, which I had found in the chest, I took them down to fill, as it would save me many trips, and be more convenient in every respect.

I brought them up full, and Jackson stopped them up with some of the rags which I had torn to bind round his wrist, and put them all three in his bed-place.

"That will be a much better arrangement," said he, "as now I can pour out the liquor into the pannikin as I want it; besides, I mean to take a little water with it in future. It's not quite so good with water, but it lasts longer, and one don't go to sleep so soon. Well, I little thought that I should have such a comfort sent me after all my sufferings. I don't so much care now about staying here. Go and fetch some water in the pannikin."

That night was a repetition of the first. Jackson sang till he was intoxicated, and then fell fast asleep, not talking or saying a word, and I was disappointed, for I remained awake to catch anything he might say. It would be tedious to repeat what took place for about a month;—suffice it to say it was very rarely, during that time, that Jackson said anything in his sleep, or drunken state, and what he did say I could make nothing of. He continued, in the daytime, to give me lessons in singing, and I could now sing several songs very correctly. At night, he returned to his usual habit, and was more or less intoxicated before the night was over. I perceived, however, that this excess had a great effect upon his constitution, and that he had become very pale and haggard. Impatient as I felt to find out the truth, I concealed my feelings towards him (which had certainly very much changed again since the discovery I had made and the suspicions I had formed) and I remained on the best of terms with him, resolving to wait patiently. He had spoken once, and therefore I argued that he would speak again, nor was I wrong in my calculations.

One night, after he had finished his usual allowance of liquor, and had composed himself for sleep, I observed that he was unusually restless, changing his position in his bed-place every few minutes, and, at last, he muttered, "Captain James. Well, what of Captain James, eh?"

A thought struck me that he might reply to a question.

"How did he die?" said I, in a low clear voice.

"Die?" replied Jackson, "he fell down the cliff. Yes, he did. You can't say I killed him. No—never put my finger on him."

After that, he was silent for some time, and then he recommenced.

"She always said that I destroyed them both, but I did not—only one—yes, one, I grant—but I hated him—no, not for his diamonds—no, no—if you said his wife indeed—love and hate."

"Then you killed him for love of his wife, and hate of himself?"

"Yes, I did. Who are you that have guessed that? Who are you? I'll have your life."

As he said this, he started up in his bed-place, awakened by his dream, and probably by my voice, which he had replied to.

"Who spoke?" said he. "Frank Henniker, did you speak?"

I made no reply, but pretended to be sound asleep, as he still sat up, as if watching me. I feigned a snore.

"It could not have been him," muttered Jackson, "he's quite fast. Mercy, what a dream!"

He then sank down in his bed-place, and I heard the gurgling noise which told me that he had put the bottle of liquor to his mouth, and was drinking out of it. From the time that the gurgling lasted, he must have taken a great deal. At last, all was quiet again.

"So I have discovered it at last," said I, as my blood boiled at what I had heard. "He did murder my father. Shall I kill him while he sleeps?" was the first thought that came into my troubled mind. "No, I won't do that. What then, shall I tax him with it when he is awake, and then kill him?" but I thought, that, as he was blind, and unable to defend himself, it would be cowardly, and I could not do that. What then was I to do? and as I cooled down, I thought of the words of the Bible, that we were to return good for evil; for Jackson, of whom, when I read it, I asked why we were told to do so, had explained it to me, and afterwards when I came to the part which said, "Vengeance is mine, saith the Lord," he had told me that there was punishment for the wicked hereafter, and that was the reason why we were not to obey the Jewish law of "an eye for an eye, and a tooth for a tooth," which I had referred to. This portion of the Bible he had well explained, and certain it is that it prevented my raising my hand against him that night. Still, I remained in a state of great excitement; I felt that it would be impossible for me to be any longer on good terms with him, and I revolved the question in my mind, till at last, worn out by excitement, I fell fast asleep.

A short time before daylight, I started up at what I thought was a faint cry, but I listened, and hearing nothing more, I again fell asleep, and it was broad daylight when I arose; my first thoughts were naturally of Jackson, and I looked at where he lay, but he was no longer there—his bed-place was empty. I was astonished, and after a moment's thought, I recollected the cry I had heard in the night, and I ran out of the cabin and looked around me, but I could see nothing of him. I then went to the edge of the flat rock upon which the cabin was built and looked over it; it was about thirty feet from this rock to the one below, and nearly perpendicular. I thought that he must have gone out in the night, when intoxicated with liquor, and have fallen down the precipice; but I did not see him as I peered over. "He must have gone for water," thought I, and I ran to the corner of the rock, where the precipice was much deeper, and looking over, I perceived him lying down below without motion or apparent life. I had, then, judged rightly. I sat down by the side of the pool of water quite overpowered; last night I had been planning how I should destroy him, and now he lay dead before me without my being guilty of the crime. "Vengeance is mine, saith the Lord," were the words that first escaped my lips; and I remained many minutes in deep thought. At last it occurred to me that he might not yet be dead; I ran down the cliff, and, clambering over the rocks, arrived breathless at the spot where Jackson lay. He groaned heavily as I stood by him.

"Jackson," said I, kneeling down by him, "are you much hurt?" for all my feelings of animosity had vanished when I perceived his unhappy condition. His lips moved, but he did not utter any sound. At last he said, in a low voice, "Water." I hastened back as fast as I could to the cabin, got a pannikin half full of water, and poured a little rum in it out of the bottle. This journey and my return to him occupied some ten minutes. I put it to his lips, and he seemed to revive. He was a dreadful object to look at. The blood from a cut on his head had poured over his face and beard, which were clotted with gore. How to remove him to the cabin I knew not. It would be hardly possible for me to carry him over the broken rocks which I had climbed to arrive at where he lay; and there was no other way but what was longer, and just as difficult. By degrees he appeared to recover; I gave him more of the contents of the pannikin, and at last he could speak, although with great pain and difficulty. As he did so he put his hand to his side. He was indeed a ghastly object, with his sightless eyeballs, his livid lips, and his face and beard matted with blood.

"Do you think you could get to the cabin, if I helped you?" said I.

"I shall never get there—let me die where I am," said he.

"But the cut on your head is not very deep," replied I.

"No, I don't feel it;—but—my side—I bleed inwardly—I am—broken to pieces," said he, pausing and gasping between each word.

I looked at his side, and perceived that it was already black and much swollen. I offered him more drink, which he took eagerly, and I then returned for a further supply. I filled two of the wine-bottles with water and a small drop of spirits as before, and went back to where he lay. I found him more recovered, and I had hopes that he might still do well, and I told him so.

"No, no," replied he; "I have but a few hours to live—I feel that. Let me die here, and die in peace."

He then sank into a sort of stupor, occasioned, I presume, by what I had given him to drink, and remained quite quiet, and breathing heavily. I sat by him waiting till he should rouse up again; for more than an hour I was in a very confused state of mind, as may well be imagined, after what had passed in the night.

CHAPTER XII

What I most thought of was obtaining from him, now that he was dying, the full truth as to the deaths of my father and mother.

Jackson remained so long in this state of stupor, I feared that he would die before I could interrogate him; but this, as it proved, was not to be the case. I waited another hour, very impatiently I must acknowledge, and then I went to him and asked him how he felt. He replied immediately, and without that difficulty which he appeared before to have experienced.

"I am better now—the inward bleeding has stopped; but still I cannot live—my side is broken in, I do not think there is a rib that is not fractured into pieces, and my spine is injured, for I cannot move or feel my legs; but I may live many hours yet, and I thank God for His mercy in allowing me so much time—short indeed to make reparation for so bad a life, but still nothing is impossible with God."

"Well, then," replied I, "if you can speak, I wish you would tell me the truth relative to my father's death, and also about the death of others; as for my father I know that you murdered him—for you said so last night in your sleep."

After a pause, Jackson replied—"I am glad that I did, and that you have told me so—I wished to make a full confession even to you, for confession is a proof of repentance. I know that you must hate me, and will hate my memory, and I cannot be surprised at it; but look at me now, Frank, and ask your own heart whether I am not more an object of pity than of hatred. 'Vengeance is mine, saith the Lord!' and has not His vengeance fallen upon me even in this world? Look at me; here I am, separated from the world that I loved so much, with no chance of ever joining it—possessed of wealth which would but a few months ago have made me happy— now blind, crushed to pieces by an avenging God, in whose presence I must shortly appear to answer for all my wickedness—all my expectations overthrown, all my hopes destroyed, and all my accumulated sins procuring me nothing, but, it may be, eternal condemnation. I ask you again, am I not an object of pity and commiseration?"

I could but assent to this, and he proceeded.

"I will now tell you the truth. I did tell the truth up to the time of your father and mother's embarkation on board of the brig, up to when the gale of wind came on which occasioned eventually the loss of the ship. Now give me a little drink.

"The vessel was so tossed by the storm, and the waves broke over her so continually, that the between-decks were full of water, and as the hatches were kept down, the heat was most oppressive. When it was not my watch I remained below, and looked out for another berth to sleep in. Before the cabin bulkheads on the starboard side, the captain had fitted up a sort of sail-room to contain the spare sails in case we should require them. It was about eight feet square, and the sails were piled up in it, so as to reach within two feet of the deck overhead; though the lower ones were wetted with the water, above they were dry, and I took this berth on the top of the sails as my sleeping place. Now the state-room in which your father and mother slept was on the other side of the cabin bulkhead, and the straining and rolling of the vessel had opened the chinks between the planks, so that I could see a great deal of what was done in the state-room, and could hear every word almost that was spoken by them. I was not aware of this when I selected this place as my berth, but I found it out on the first night, the light of the candle shining through the chinks into the darkness by which I was surrounded outside. Of course, it is when a man is alone with his wife that he talks on confidential subjects; that I knew well, and hoped by listening to be able to make some discovery;—what, I had no idea of; but, with the bad feelings which stimulated me, I determined not to lose an opportunity. It was not till about a week after I had selected this berth, that I made any discovery. I had had the watch from six to eight o'clock, and had gone to bed early. About nine o'clock your father came into the state-room. Your mother was already in bed. As your father undressed, your mother said, 'Does not that belt worry you a great deal, my dear?'

"'No,' replied your father, 'I am used to it now; it did when I first put it on, but now I have had it on four days, I do not feel it. I shall keep it on as long as this weather lasts; there is no saying what may happen, and it will not do to be looking for the belt at a moment's warning.'

"'Do you think then that we are in danger?'

"'No, not particularly so, but the storm is very fierce, and the vessel is old and weak. We may have fine weather in a day or two, or we may not; at all events, when property of value is at stake, and that property not my own, I should feel myself very culpable, if I did not take every precaution.'

"'Well—I wish we were safe home again, my dear, and that my father had his diamonds, but we are in the hands of God.'

"'Yes, I must trust to Him,' replied your father.

"This circumstance induced me to look through one of the chinks of the bulkhead, so that I could see your father, and I perceived that he was unbuckling a belt which was round his body, and which no doubt contained the diamonds referred to. It was of soft leather, and about eight inches wide, sewed lengthways and breadthways in small squares, in which I presumed the diamonds were deposited. After a time your mother spoke again.

"'I really think, Henniker, that I ought to wear the belt.'

"'Why so, my dear?'

"'Because it might be the means of my preservation in case of accident. Suppose now, we were obliged to abandon the vessel and take to the boats; a husband, in his hurry, might forget his wife, but he would not forget his diamonds. If I wore the belt, you would be certain to put me in the boat.'

"'That observation of yours would have force with some husbands, and some wives,' retorted your father; 'but as I have a firm belief in the Scriptures, it does not affect me. What do the Proverbs say? "The price of a virtuous woman is far above rubies;" and a good ruby is worth even more in the market than a diamond of the same size.'

"'Well, I must comfort myself with that idea,' replied your mother, laughing.

"'Supposing we be thrown upon some out-of-the-way place,' said your father, 'I shall then commit the belt to your charge. It might soon be discovered on my person, whereas, on yours, it would stand every chance of being long concealed. I say this because, even in a desert, it would be dangerous to have it known by unscrupulous and unprincipled men that anyone had so much wealth about him.'

"'Well,' replied your mother, 'that is also comfortable for me to hear, for you will not leave me behind, because I shall be necessary to conceal your treasure.'

"'Yes,' replied your father, laughing, 'there is another chance for you, you see.'

"Your father then extinguished the light, and the conversation was not renewed; but I had heard enough. Your father carried a great treasure about his person—wealth, I took it for granted, that if I once could obtain, and return to England, would save me from my present position. My avarice was hereby excited, and thus another passion equally powerful, and equally inciting to evil deeds, was added to the hate which I already had imbibed for your father. But I must leave off now."

Jackson drank a little more, and then remained quiet, and as I had had no food that day, I took the opportunity of returning to the cabin, with the promise that I would be back very soon. In half an hour I returned, bringing with me the Bible and Prayer-book, as I thought that he would ask me to read to him after he had made his confession. I found him breathing heavily, and apparently asleep, so I did not wake him. As I looked at him, and recalled to mind his words, "Am not I an object of pity?" I confessed that he was, and then I asked myself the question, Can you forgive him who was the murderer of your father? After some reflection, I thought that I could. Was he not already punished? Had not the murder been already avenged? It was not possible to retain animosity against one so stricken, so broken to pieces, and my heart smote me when I looked at his disabled hand, and felt that I, boy as I was, had had a share in his marring. At last he spoke.

"Are you there, Frank?"

"Yes," replied I.

"I have had a little sleep," said he.

"Do you feel easier?" inquired I kindly.

"Yes, I feel my side more numbed, and so it will remain till mortification takes place. But let me finish my confession; I wish to relieve my mind, not that I shall die to-night, or perhaps to-morrow, but still I wish it over. Come nearer to me, that I may speak in a lower voice, and then I shall be able to speak longer."

I did so, and he proceeded.

"You know how we were cast upon this island, and how I behaved at first. When I afterwards took my place with the others, my evil thoughts gradually quitted me, and I gave up all idea of any injury to your father. But this did not last long. The deaths of so many, and at last the captain your father and your mother being the only ones left on the island besides myself, once more excited my cupidity. I thought again of the belt of diamonds, and by what means I should gain possession of it; and the devil suggested to me the murders of the captain and of your father. I had ascertained that your father no longer carried the belt on his person when we all used to bathe at the bathing-pool; it was, therefore, as your father had proposed, in your mother's keeping. Having once made up my mind, I watched every opportunity to put my intentions into execution. It was the custom for one of us to fish every morning, as your mother would not eat the dried birds, if fish could be procured, and I considered that the only chance I had of executing my horrible wish was when your father went to fish off the rocks. We usually did so off the ledge of rocks which divide the bathing-pool from the sea, but I found out another place, where more fish, and of a better quality, were to be taken, which is off the high wall of rocks just below. You know where I mean, I have often sent you to fish there, but I never could go myself since your father's death. Your father took his lines there, and was hauling in a large fish, when I, who had concealed myself close to where he stood, watched the opportunity as he looked over the rock to see if the fish was clear of the water, to come behind him and throw him off into the sea. He could not swim, I knew, and after waiting a minute or two, I looked over and saw his body, just as it sank, after his last struggles. I then hastened away, and my guilty conscience induced me to ascend the ravine, and collect a faggot of firewood to bring home, that no suspicions might be entertained; but my so doing was the very cause of suspicion, as you will afterwards perceive. I returned with the wood, and the captain observed, when I came up to the cabin:

"'Why, it's something new for you to collect wood out of your turn, Jackson. Wonders will never cease.'

79

"'The fact is, that I am becoming very amiable,' replied I, hardly knowing what to say, and afraid to look either of them in the face, for your mother, with you on her lap, was standing close by.

"'Has my husband caught any fish, do you know, Jackson?' said your mother, 'for it is high time that he came home.'

"'How can I tell?' replied I. 'I have been up the ravine for wood.'

"'But you were down on the rock two hours ago,' replied your mother, 'for Captain James saw you coming away.'

"'That I certainly did,' replied the captain. 'Had he caught any fish when you were with him?'

"They must have perceived my confusion when I said, 'Yes, I was on the rocks, but I never went near Henniker, that I'll swear.'

"'You must have been near him, even when I saw you,' replied the captain.

"'I never looked at him, if I was,' replied I.

"'Well, then, one of us had better go down and see what he is about,' said the captain. 'Shall I leave Jackson with you?'

"'Yes, yes,' replied your mother, much agitated, 'for I have my forebodings; better leave him here.'

"The captain hastened down to the rocks, and in a quarter of an hour returned very much heated, saying, 'He is not there!'

"'Not there?' replied I, getting up, for I had seated myself in silence on the rock during the captain's absence: 'that's very odd.'

"'It is,' replied the captain. 'Jackson, go and try if you see anything of him, while I attend to Mrs Henniker.'

"Your mother, on the captain's return, had bowed her head down to her knees, and covered her face with her hands. I was glad of an excuse to be away, for my heart smote me as I witnessed her condition.

"I remained away half-an-hour, and then returned, saying that I could see nothing of your father.

"Your mother was in the cabin, and the captain went in to her, while I remained outside with all the feelings of Cain upon my brow.

"That was a dreadful day for all parties—no food was taken. Your mother and the captain remained in the cabin, and I dared not, as usual, go in to my own bed-place. I lay all night upon the rocks—sleep I could not; every moment I saw your father's body sinking, as I had seen it in the morning. The next morning the captain came out to me. He was very grave and stern, but he could not accuse me, whatever his suspicions might have been. It was a week before I saw your mother again, for I dared not intrude into her presence; but, finding there was no accusation against me, I recovered my spirits, and returned to the cabin, and things went on as before."

CHAPTER XIII

"One thing, however, was evident, that your mother had an aversion—I may say a horror—of me, which she could not conceal. She said nothing, but she never could look at me; and to any question I put, would seldom make reply. Strange to say this treatment of hers produced quite a different effect from what might have been anticipated, and I felt my former love for her revive. Her shrinking from me made me more familiar towards her, and increased her disgust. I assumed a jocose air with her, and at times Captain James considered it his duty to interfere and check me. He was a very powerful man, and in a contest would have proved my master; this I knew, and this knowledge compelled me to be more respectful to your mother in his presence, but when his back was turned I became so disgustingly familiar, that at last your mother requested that whether fishing or collecting wood, instead of going out by turns we should both go, and leave her alone. This I could not well refuse, as Captain James would in all probability have used force if I had not consented, but my hatred to him was in consequence most unbounded. However, an event took place which relieved me from the subjection which I was under, and left me alone with you and your mother. Now I must rest a little. Wait another hour, and you shall know the rest."

It was now late in the evening, but there was a bright moon which shone over head, and the broad light and shadow made the rocks around us appear peculiarly wild and rugged. They towered up one above the other till they met the dark blue of the sky in which the stars twinkled but faintly, while the moon sailed through the ether, without a cloud to obscure her radiance. And in this majestic scenery were found but two living beings—a poor boy and a mangled wretch—a murderer—soon to breathe his last, and be summoned before an offended God. As I remained motionless by his side, I felt, as I looked up, a sensation of awe, but not of fear; I thought to myself—"And God made all this and all the world besides, and me and him. The Bible said so:" and my speculation then was as to what God must be, for although I had read the Bible, I had but a confused idea, and had it been asked me, as it was of the man in the chariot by Philip, "Understandest thou what thou readest?" I most certainly should have answered, No. I remained for nearly two hours in this reverie, and at last fell asleep with my back against the rock. I was, however, wakened up by Jackson's voice, when he asked in a low tone for water.

"There it is," said I, handing it to him. "Have you called long?"

"No," replied he; "I asked but once."

"I have been asleep," said I.

As soon as he had drunk, he said—

"I will finish now; my side begins to burn."

He then proceeded—

"It was about four months after your father's death that Captain James and I went together to the ravine to collect firewood. We passed under the wall of rock, which you know so well, and went through the gap, as we call it, when Captain James left the water-course and walked along the edge of the wall. I followed him; we both of us had our pieces of rope in our hands with which we tied the faggots. Of a sudden his foot slipped, and he rolled down to the edge of the rock, but catching hold of a small bush which had fixed its roots in the rocks, he saved himself when his body was hanging half over the precipice.

"'Give me the end of your rope,' said he to me, perfectly collected, although in such danger.

"'Yes,' replied I, and I intended so to do, as I perceived that if I refused he could still have saved himself by the bush to which he clung.

"But the bush began to loosen and give way, and Captain James perceiving it cried out—

"'Quick, quick, the bush is giving way!'

"This assertion of his determined me not to give him the rope. I pretended to be in a great hurry to do so, but entangled it about my legs, and then appeared occupied in clearing it, when he cried again—

"'Quick!'—and hardly had he said the word when the root of the bush snapped, and down he fell below.

"I heard the crash as he came to the rock beneath. See the judgment of God—am I not now precisely in his position, lying battered and crushed as he was? After a time I went down to where he lay, and found him expiring. He had just strength to say 'God forgive you,' and then he died. It was murder, for I could have saved him and would not, and yet he prayed to God to forgive me. How much happier should I have felt if he had not said that. His 'God forgive you' rang in my ears for months afterwards. I returned to the cabin, and with a bold air stated to your mother what had happened, for I felt I could say, this time, I did not do the deed. She burst out into frantic exclamations, accusing me of being not only his murderer but the murderer of her husband. I tried all I could do to appease her, but in vain. For many weeks she was in a state of melancholy and despondency, that made me fear for her life; but she had you still to bestow her affections upon, and for your sake she lived. I soon made this discovery. She was now wholly in my power, but I was awed by her looks even, for a time. At last I became bolder, and spoke to her of our becoming man and wife; she turned from me with abhorrence. I then resorted to other means. I prevented her from obtaining food; she would have starved with pleasure, but she could not bear to see you suffer. I will not detail my cruelty and barbarity towards her; suffice to say, it was such that she pined away, and about six months after the death of the captain she died, exhorting me not to injure you, but if ever I had an opportunity, to take you to your grandfather. I could not refuse this demand, made by a woman whom I as certainly killed by slow means as I had your father by a more sudden death. I buried her in the guano, by the side of the others. After her death my life was a torture to me for a long while. I dared not kill you, but I hated you. I had only one consolation, one hope, which occasionally gave me satisfaction; the consolation, if so it could be called, was—that I had possession of the diamonds; the hope—that I should one day see England again. You see me now—are they not all avenged?"

I could not but feel the truth of Jackson's last sentence. They were indeed avenged.

After a short pause, he said to me—

"Now, Frank, I feel that the mortification in my side is making great progress, and, in a short time I shall be in too great pain to talk to you. I have made a full confession of my crimes; it is all the reparation I can make to you. Now, can you forgive me? for I shall die very miserable if you do not. Just look at me. Can you feel resentment against one in my wretched state? Recollect that you pray to be forgiven as you forgive others. Give me your answer."

"I think—yes, I feel that I can forgive you, Jackson," replied I. "I shall soon be left alone on this island, and I am sure I should be much more miserable than I shall be, if I do not forgive you. I do forgive you."

"Thanks; you are a good boy, and may God bless you. Is it not nearly daylight?"

"Yes, it is. I shall soon be able to read the Bible or Prayer-book to you. I have them both here."

"The pain is too severe, and becomes worse every minute. I shall not be able to listen to you now; but I shall have some moments of quiet before I die; and then—"

Jackson groaned heavily, and ceased speaking.

For many hours he appeared to suffer much agony, which he vented in low groans; the perspiration hung on his forehead in large beads, and his breathing became laborious. The sun rose and had nearly set again before Jackson spoke; at last he asked for some drink.

"It is over now," said he faintly. "The pain is subsiding, and death is near at hand. You may read to me now; but, first, while I think of it, let me tell you where you will find your father's property."

"I know," replied I; "in your bed-place under the board. I saw you remove it when you did not see me."

"True. I have no more to say; it will all be over soon. Read the burial service over me after I am dead; and now, while still above, read me what you think I shall like best; for I cannot collect myself sufficiently to tell you what is most proper. Indeed I hardly know. But I can pray at times. Read on."

I did so, and came upon the parable of the prodigal son.

"That suits me," said Jackson. "Now let me pray. Pray for me, Frank."

"I don't know how," replied I; "you never taught me."

"Alas, no!"

Jackson was then silent. I saw his pale lips move for some time. I turned away for a few moments; when I came back to him, he was no more! His jaw had fallen; and this being the first time that I had ever faced death, I looked upon the corpse with horror and dismay.

After a few minutes I left the body, and sat down on a rock at some distance from it, for I was somewhat afraid to be near to it. On this rock I remained till the sun was sinking below the horizon; when, alarmed at the idea of being there when it was dark, I took up my books and hastened back to the cabin. I was giddy from excitement, and not having tasted food for many hours. As soon as I had eaten, I lay down in my bed-place, intending to reflect upon what I was to do, now that I was alone; but I was in a few moments fast asleep, and did not wake until the sun was high. I arose much refreshed, and, seeing my Bible and Prayer-book close to my bed-place, I recollected my promise to Jackson that I would read the burial service over his body. I found the place in the Prayer-book, for I had read it more than once before; and, having just looked over it, I went with my book to where the body lay. It presented a yet more hideous spectacle than it had the night before. I read the service and closed the book. "What can I do?" thought I. "I cannot bury him in the guano. It will be impossible to carry the body over these rocks." Indeed, if it had been possible, I do not think I could have touched it. I was afraid of it. At last I determined that I would cover it up with the fragments of rocks which lay about in all directions, and I did so. This occupied me about two hours, and then, carrying the bottles with me, I gladly hastened away from the spot, with a resolution never to revisit it. I felt quite a relief when I was once more in the cabin. I was alone, it was true, but I was no longer in contact with the dead. I could not collect my thoughts or analyse my feelings during the remainder of the day. I sat with my head resting on my hand, in the attitude of one thinking; but at the same time my mind was vacant. I once more lay down to sleep, and the following morning I found myself invigorated, and capable of acting as well as thinking. I had a weight upon my spirits which I could not at first account for; but it arose from the feeling that I was now alone, without a soul to speak to or communicate with; my lips must now be closed till I again fell in with some of my fellow-creatures—and was that likely? We had seen some of them perish not far from us, and that was all, during a period of many years.

CHAPTER XIV

I was now, by Jackson's account, nearly fourteen years old. During fourteen years but one vessel had been seen by us. It might be fourteen more, or double that time might elapse, before I should again fall in with any of my fellow-creatures. As these thoughts saddened me, I felt how much I would have sacrificed if Jackson had remained alive, were it only for his company; I would have forgiven him anything. I even then felt as if, in the murderer of my father, I had lost a friend.

That day I was so unsettled I could not do anything; I tried to read, but I could not; I tried to eat, but my appetite was gone, I sat looking at the ocean as it rolled wave after wave, sometimes wondering whether it would ever bring a fellow-creature to join me; at others I sat, and for hours, in perfect vacuity of thought. The evening closed in; it was dark, and I still remained seated where I was. At last I returned to my bed, almost brokenhearted; but fortunately I was soon asleep, and my sorrows were forgotten.

Another morning was gladdened with a brilliant sun, the dark blue ocean was scarcely ruffled by the breeze that swept over it, and I felt my spirits much revived, and my appetite returned. After taking a meal, I remembered what Jackson had told me about the belt with the diamonds, and I went up to his bed-place, and turning out the bird's skins and feathers, I raked up the gravel, which was not more than two inches deep, and came to the board. I lifted it up, and found underneath a hole, about a foot deep, full of various articles. There were the watch and sleeve buttons of the mate, some dollars wrapped in old rags, a tobacco-box, an old pipe, a brooch with hair forming initials, some letters which were signed J. Evelyn, and which I perceived were from my grandfather, and probably taken by Jackson after my mother's death. I say letters, because they were such, as I afterwards found out, but I had not then ever seen a letter, and my first attempt to decipher written hand was useless, although I did manage to make out the signature. There was in the tobacco-box a plain gold wedding-ring, probably my mother's; and there was also a lock of long dark hair, which I presumed was hers also. There were three or four specimens of what I afterwards found out to be gold and silver ores, a silver pencil-case, and a pair of small gold ear-rings. At the bottom of the hole was the belt; it was of soft leather, and I could feel a hard substance in it sewed in every square, which of course I presumed were the diamonds, but I did not cut one of the divisions open to see what was in them. It had on the upper part of it, in very plain writing, "The property of Mr J. Evelyn, 33, Minories, London." I examined all these articles one after another, and having satisfied my curiosity, I replaced them in the hole for a future survey. I covered the hole with the board, and put back the gravel and the feathers into the bed-place. This occupied me about two hours, and then I again took my former position on the rocks, and remained in a state of listless inactivity of body and mind the remainder of that day.

This state of prostration lasted for many days—I may say for weeks, before it was altogether removed. I could find no pleasure in my books, which were taken up, and after a few moments laid aside. It was now within a month of the time that the birds should come to the island. I was in no want of them for sustenance; there were plenty left, but I almost loathed the sight of food. The reader may inquire how it was that I knew the exact time of the arrival of the birds? I reply that the only reckoning ever kept by Jackson and me was the arrival of the full moons, and we also made a mark on the rock every time that the moon was at the full. Thirteen moons were the quantity which we reckoned from the time of the birds appearing on the island one year, until their re-appearance the next; and twelve moons had now passed. At length, tired with everything, tired of myself, and I may say, almost tired of life, I one day took it into my head that I would take some provisions with me and a bottle to hold water, and go up the ravine, and cut firewood which should last me a long while; and that I would remain up there for several days, for I hated the sight of the cabin and of all that was near to it. The next day I acted upon this resolution, and slinging my dry provisions on my shoulder, I set off for the ravine. In an hour I had gained it; but not being in a hurry to cut wood,

I resolved upon climbing higher up, to see if I could reach the opposite side of the island; that is, at least, get over the brow of the hill, to have a good view of it. I continued to climb until I had gained a smooth grassy spot, which was clear of brushwood; and as I sat down to rest myself, I observed some blue flowers which I had never seen before, indeed I did not know that there was a flower on the island. As I afterwards discovered, they were one of the varieties of Gentianellas. I looked at them, admired them, and felt quite an affection for them; they were very pretty, and they were, as well as myself, alone. Jackson, when I was pointing out the English cottages in the landscapes of "Mavor's Natural History," had told me a great deal about gardening in England, and how wild flowers and trees were transplanted and improved by culture; how roses and other plants were nailed up the walls, as I had observed in the engravings, and how they were watered and kept; and as I sat down looking at the flower, the thought occurred to me, Why should I not take it with me, and keep it for myself? I can water it, and take care of it. I resolved that I would do so, for I already looked upon the plant as a treasure. I took it up carefully with my American knife, leaving sufficient mould about the roots, and then I proceeded to ascend the hill; but before I had gone another hundred yards, I found at least a dozen more of these plants in flower, all finer than the one I had dug up, and three or four others very different from these, which were also quite new to me. I was puzzled what to do; I put down the plants I had dug up and continued my ascent, not having made up my mind. After half-an-hour's climbing, I gained the summit, and could perceive the ocean on the other side, and the other half of the island lying beneath me. It was very grand from the height I stood on, but I observed little difference between one side of the island and the other; all was rugged barren rock as on my side, with the exception of the portion close to me; this had brushwood in the ravine, which appeared to be a sort of cleft through the island. All was silent and solitary; not a bird was to be seen, and nothing that had life could I discover. I was about to return, when I thought I might as well go down the ravine facing me for a little way, and see what there was in it. I did so, and discovered some other plants that I had not seen on my side of the island. There were also some fern trees, and some twining plants running up them, and I thought to myself, Why, these plants are what I saw in the picture of the English cottages, or very like them. I wonder if they would run up my cabin? and then all at once the idea came to me that I would plant some of them round the cabin, and that I would make a garden of flowers, and have plants of my own. The reader can hardly imagine the pleasure that this idea gave me; I sat down to ruminate upon it, and felt quite happy for the time. I now recollected, however, that the cabin was built on the rock, and that plants would only grow in the earth. At first this idea chilled me, as it seemed to destroy all my schemes, but I resolved that I would bring some earth to the rock, and make my garden in that way. I at first thought of the guano, but Jackson had told me that it was only used in small proportions to enrich the soil, and would kill plants if used by itself. After an hour's consideration, during which I called to mind all that Jackson had told me on the subject, I made up my mind I would return to the cabin, and on my return ascertain how low down the ravine I could obtain earth for my garden; I would then carry the earth to the cabin, make a soil ready for the plants and flowers, and then, when all was ready, I would go up the ravine, collect what I could, and make my garden. I did so. I found that I could get soil about one-third of the way up the ravine, a quarter of a mile below where the brushwood grew; and having ascertained that, I returned to the cabin, threw down my provisions which were to have lasted me a week, and as it was late, I decided that I would not commence operations until the following day.

I took out of the chest a duck frock, and tying up the sleeves and collar, so as to form a bag of the body of the frock, I set off the next morning to begin my task. That day I contrived to carry to the cabin ten or twelve bags of mould, which I put round it in a border about four feet wide, and about a foot deep. It occupied me a whole week to obtain the quantity of earth necessary to make the bed on each side of the cabin; it was hard work, but it made me cheerful and happy to what I had been before. I found that the best cure for melancholy and solitude was employment, so I thus obtained valuable knowledge as well as the making of my garden. When I had finished carrying the mould, I started off for the ravine with two bags to hold the plants which I might collect, and after a day's toil, I returned with my bags full of small shrubs, besides a bundle of creepers to plant against the sides of the cabin. The following day was occupied in planting everything I had procured.

I was sorry to see that the leaves and flowers hung down, but I watered them all before I went to bed. The next morning I was delighted to perceive that they had all recovered and were looking quite fresh. But my garden was not full enough to please me, and I once more went up the ravine, selecting other plants which had no flowers on them, and one or two other shrubs, which I had not before observed. When these were planted and watered, my garden looked very gay and full of plants, and then I discovered the mould came down for want of support at the edges; I therefore went and picked up pieces of rock of sufficient size to make a border and hold up the mould, and now all was complete, and I had nothing to do but to go on watering them daily. This I did, and recollecting what Jackson had said about the guano, I got a bag of it, and put some to each plant. The good effect of this was soon observable, and before the birds came, my garden was in a very flourishing condition.

I cannot express to the reader the pleasure I derived from this little garden. I knew every plant and every shrub, and talked to them as if they were companions, while I watered and tended them, which I did every night and morning, and their rapid growth was my delight. I no longer felt my solitude so irksome as I had done. I had something to look after, to interest me, and to love; they were alive as well as I was; they grew, and threw out leaves and flowers; they were grateful for the care I bestowed upon them, and became my companions and friends.

I mentioned before that during the latter portion of the time I was with Jackson, he had taught me to sing several songs. Feeling tired, in my solitude, of not hearing the human voice, I found myself at first humming over, and afterwards singing aloud, the various airs I had collected from him. This afforded me much pleasure, and I used to sing half the day. I had no one to listen to me, it is true, but as my fondness for my garden increased, I used to sit down and sing to the flowers and shrubs, and fancy that they listened to me. But my stock of songs was not very large, and at last I had repeated them so often that I became tired of the words. It occurred to me that the Prayer-book had the Psalms of David at the end of it, set to music. I got the book, and as far as the airs that I knew would suit, I sang them all; never were Psalms, probably, sung to such tunes before, but it amused me, and there was no want of variety of language.

Every three or four days I would go up the ravine, and search carefully for any new flower or shrub which I had not yet planted in my garden, and when I found one, as I often did, it was a source of great delight.

CHAPTER XV

At last the birds came, and I procured some of their eggs, which were a very agreeable change, after living so long upon dried meat. My want of occupation occasioned me also to employ some of my time in fishing, which I seldom had done while Jackson was alive; and this created a variety in my food, to which, for a long while, I had been a stranger. Jackson did not care for fish, as to cook it we were obliged to go up the ravine for wood, and he did not like the trouble. When the birds came, I had recourse to my book on Natural History, to read over again the accounts of the Man-of-War birds, Gannets, and other birds mentioned in it; and there was a vignette of a Chinaman with tame cormorants on a pole, and in the letter-press an account of how they were trained and employed to catch fish for their masters. This gave me the idea that I would have some birds tame, as companions, and, if possible, teach them to catch fish for me; but I knew that I must wait till the young birds were fit to be taken from the nest.

I now resolved that during the time the birds were mating, I would go to the ravine and remain there several days, to collect bundles of firewood. The firewood was chiefly cut from a sort of low bush, like the sallow or willow, fit for making baskets, indeed fit for anything better than firewood; however, there were some bushes which were of a harder texture, and which burnt well. It was Jackson who told me that the former were called willow and used for making baskets, and he also shewed me how to tie the faggots up by twisting the sallows together. They were not, however, what Jackson said they were—from after knowledge, I should say that they were a species of Oleander or something of the kind.

Having roasted several dozen of eggs quite hard, by way of provision, I set off one morning, and went to the ravine. As Jackson had said before, I had to walk under a wall of rock thirty feet high, and then pass through a water-course to get up to the ravine, which increased the distance to where the shrubs grew, at least half a mile. It was over this wall that the captain fell and was killed, because Jackson would not assist him. I gained the thicket where the bushes grew, and for three days I worked very hard, and had cut down and tied about fifty large faggots, when I thought that I had collected enough to last me for a long while; but I had still to carry them down, and this was a heavy task, as I could not carry more than one at a time. It occurred to me that if I threw my faggots over the wall opposite to where they had been cut down, I should save myself nearly a mile of carriage, as otherwise I had to walk all the way to the water-course which divided the wall of rock, and then walk back again. Indeed, where I cut down the wood was not more than a quarter of a mile from the bathing-pool, and all down hill. I was delighted at this idea, which I wondered had never occurred to Jackson, and I commenced putting it into execution. The top of the wall of rock was slippery from the constant trickling of the water over the surface, but this was only in some places. I carried my faggots down one by one, and threw them over, being careful not to lose my footing in so doing. I had carried all but three or four, and had become careless, when, on heaving one over, my heels were thrown up, and before I could recover myself I slid down the remainder of the ledge and was precipitated down below, a distance of more than thirty feet. I must have remained there many hours insensible, but at last I recovered and found myself lying on the faggots which I had thrown down. It was my falling on the faggots, instead of the hard rock, which had saved my life. I rose as soon as I could collect my scattered senses. I felt very sore and very much shaken, and the blood was running out of my mouth, but there were no bones broken. I was, however, too ill to attempt anything more that day. I walked home at a very slow pace and went to bed. A sound sleep restored me, and in a day or two I was quite recovered. I watered my plants, which I found drooping, as if they had grieved at my being so long away from them, and then I returned to where my faggots had been left; and to lighten my labour I resolved to carry them down to the bathing-pool and stack them up there on the rocks near to it. I mention this for reasons that the reader will comprehend bye-and-bye. This occupied me two days, for I was not inclined, after my fall, to work hard; and very glad was I when the labour was over.

The young birds were now hatched, but I had to wait four or five weeks before they were fit to be taken. I began again to find solitude tedious. The flowers in my garden had all bloomed and withered, and there was not so much to interest me. I recommenced reading the Bible, and the narratives in the Old and New Testaments again afforded me pleasure. I hardly need say to the reader that I read the Bible as I would have read any other book—for amusement, and not for instruction. I had learnt little from Jackson—indeed, as regards the true nature of the Christian religion, I may say, nothing at all. I do not believe that he knew anything about it himself. It is true that the precepts in the New Testament struck me, and that I was more interested about Our Saviour than anybody else; but I could not comprehend him, or his mission. In short, I read in darkness; and I may say that I almost knew the Bible by heart without understanding it.—How could I? How many thousands are there who do the same, without having an excuse to offer for their blindness!

At last the time for taking the birds arrived, and I had then sufficient employment to keep me from being melancholy. I collected quite as many as we had done when Jackson and I had to be provided for; and with my new knives my labour was comparatively easy. As soon as I had completed my provision, I went back to take the young birds which already I had selected and left for that purpose. It was high time, for I found that when I went to take them they were ready to fly. However, after a good battle with the old birds (for I had taken six young ones—two from each nest, which arrayed a force of six old ones against me, who fought very valiantly in defence of their offspring), I succeeded in carrying them off, but followed by the old birds, who now screamed and darted close to me as they came pursuing me to the cabin. As soon as I got safe back, I took the young birds into the cabin, tying each of them by the leg with a piece of fishing line, and the other end of the line I fastened to some pieces of rock which I had collected ready on the platform outside of the cabin. The old birds continued to persecute me till it was dark, and then they went away, and I, tired with my day's labour, was not sorry to go to sleep.

When I woke up the next morning, I found the old birds on the platform, in company with the young ones, I presume trying to persuade them to fly away with them; but the lines on their legs prevented that. They did not leave at my approach for some little while; at last they all took wing, and went off to sea; but in the course of a few minutes they returned with some small fish in their mouths, with which they fed their young ones. They continued to do this for the two following days, when there was a general break up, announcing the departure of the main body, which, after much soaring and wheeling in the air, flew off in a northerly direction. The six parent birds, who were with their young ones at the cabin, appeared for some time very uneasy, flying round and round and screaming wildly; at last they soared in the air with loud shrieks, and flew away after the main body, which was still in sight—their love for their young overpowered by their instinctive habits. I was not sorry when they were gone, as I wanted to have my new family all to myself. I went down to the rocks and caught a fish, which was large enough to supply them for three or four days. I fed them with the inside of the fish, and they ate it very heartily. For several days they appeared very uneasy; but gradually they settled, and not only appeared to know me, but to welcome my coming, which was to me a source of great pleasure.

I now neglected my flowers for the birds, which were the more animated of the two; and I sat down for hours on the platform with my six companions, who I must own were not over-lively and intelligent, but they were alive, and had eyes. They seldom roused up, unless I brought them fish, of which they had a supply four times a day, and then they would stand on their legs and open their beaks far apart, each waiting for its share. They were a great happiness to me, and I watched their gradual increase of plumage and of size, which was very rapid. I gave them all names out of my Natural History book. One was Lion, then Tiger, Panther, Bear, Horse, and Jackass (at the time that I named them, the last would have been very appropriate to them all); and as I always called them by their names as I fed them, I soon found, to my great joy, that they knew them well enough. This delighted me. I read my books to them by way of amusement; I sang my songs to them; I talked to them; I would even narrate the various histories out of the Bible to them, such as that of Joseph and his brethren, &c., and the stolid air with which the communications were received made me almost imagine they were listened to.

After a time, I took the line off the legs of two of them, with the precaution of first cutting their wings, and these two became much more lively, following me into the cabin and generally staying there during the night. As I found that no attempt was made to escape, I let them all loose, after having cut their wings, and they all behaved equally well with the two first to which I had given their liberty.

The perfect obedience and good behaviour of my new companions again gave me leisure that was not altogether desirable, as it left a vacuum to fill up. But I returned to my garden. I could do no more at present but water my plants and look at the increased daily growth of the climbers, as they now boldly ascended the sides of the cabin; but I thought it was high time to go up into the ravine and about the island, to see if I could not add to my collection.

One morning I set off up the ravine. I was not successful, so I contented myself with carrying, by the long road, those faggots which I had left behind me on the day when I fell over the precipice. This labour I finished, and then returned to the cabin, where I was met by my birds with half-extended wings and open mouths, as if they were very glad to see me, and very hungry into the bargain. I ought to observe that my birds appeared now to separate into pairs, male and female, as their difference of plumage denoted. Lion and Horse were always side by side, as were Jackass and Bear, and Tiger and Panther. I now fed them one by one, calling them by name, to which they immediately responded, and if anyone came who was not called, it was switched for its trouble.

The next morning I set off on another voyage of discovery after plants, and this time I resolved upon trying what I could find among the crevices of the rocks, for I had seen at a distance what appeared to me to be a very pretty flower on the ledge of one of the clefts. I did not go up the ravine this time, but commenced climbing the rocks behind where the cabin was built. It was hard work, but I was not easily discouraged, and after a couple of hours I arrived at a level which I had in view when I commenced my labour, and here I was amply rewarded, for I found several plants quite new to me, and a variety of ferns, which I thought very beautiful, although they had no flowers. The scene, from where

I stood, was awful and beautiful. I looked down upon the rocks below, and the cabin, which appeared very small, and I thought that I could see my birds like dots upon the platform. It was a bright day and smooth water, I could clearly distinguish the other islands in the distance, and I thought that I saw something like a white speck close to them—perhaps it was a vessel. This made me melancholy, and I could not help asking myself whether I was to remain all my life upon the island, alone, or if there were any chance of my ever being taken off it. As I looked down upon the cabin, I was surprised at the steepness of the rocks which I had climbed, and felt alarmed, as if I never should be able to get back again. But these thoughts were soon chased away. I turned from the seaward, and looked inland. I found that on one side of me there was a chasm between the rocks, the bottom of which was so far down that I could not see it; and on the other side the rock rose up as straight as a wall. My attention was soon diverted by discovering another plant, and I now commenced my task of digging them all up. I obtained, with the ferns, about twenty new varieties, which I made up in a bundle ready for carrying down slung round my neck, for I knew that I should require both hands to descend with. Then I sat down to rest myself a little before I commenced my return, and after I had been seated a few minutes, I thought I would sing a song by way of amusement.

CHAPTER XVI

I have before said that, tired of repeating the words of the songs which Jackson had taught me, I had taken those of Psalms in metre, at the end of the Prayer-book, by way of variety; and, as far as metre went, they answered very well, although people would have been surprised to have heard Psalms sung to such quick and varied measure. The Psalm I chose this time was the first—"How blest is he who ne'er consents;" and I began accordingly; but when I came to the end of the line, to my astonishment I heard a plaintive voice, at a distance, repeat after me "con-sents." I looked round. I thought I must have been deceived, so I continued—"By ill advice to walk." This time I could not be mistaken—"to walk" was repeated by the same voice as plainly as possible. I stopped singing, lost in wonder. There must be somebody on the island as well as myself, thought I; for I never had heard an echo before, except when it thundered, and such echoes I had put down as a portion of the thunder. "Who's there?" cried I. "Who's there?" replied the voice. "It's me!" "It's me!" was the answer. I did not know what to make of it. I cried out again and again, and again and again I heard what I said repeated, but no answer to my questions. I thought I was insulted by somebody, and yet, when I listened, the voice that spoke came from the face of the rock on the other side of the chasm, and no one could be there without my seeing them. This made me think that I was mistaken, and that there could not be anybody, but still I could not solve the mystery. At last I became frightened, and as the sun was now setting, I determined to get back to the cabin. I did so, and went down much faster than I had gone up, for as it grew dark I became the more alarmed. The only thing that re-assured me was the softness and plaintiveness of the voice—not like Jackson's, but as of someone who would not think of injuring me.

Although I was, generally speaking, quiet and content with my isolated position, yet it was only when I was employed or amused with my favourites. At times, I could not find anything to do, and was overcome by weariness. I would then throw away my books, and remain for hours thinking upon the probability of my ever again seeing a fellow creature; and a fit of melancholy would come over me, which would last many days. I was in one of these moods, when it occurred to me, that, although I had seen the other side of the island from the summit, I had not gone down to the beach to explore it; and I resolved that I would do so, making a trip of three or four days. When my knives had become blunt, Jackson had told me how to sharpen them, by rubbing the blades upon a hard flat piece of rock, wetted with water. This I had found to answer very well, and I now determined I would try and sharpen one of the old axes in the same way, so as to make it serviceable, for I was very much afraid of breaking my knives in cutting down the brushwood, and I knew how much more rapidly it could be done with an axe. I picked out a large stone, suitable for the purpose, and with a kid of water at hand, I set-to to sharpen the axe. It was a long job, but in a day or two I had succeeded admirably, and the axe was in good order. I then thought how I could leave my birds for so many days, as they would require food. At last, I considered that if I caught two large fish and cut them up, they would be sufficient for their sustenance. I did so, and provided with a packet of dried birds for food, tied up in a duck frock, with my Natural History book for amusement, a pannikin to get water in, my axe on my shoulder, and my knives by my side—I first kissed all the birds, and told them to remain quiet and good till I came back—I set off on a bright clear morning on my tour of examination.

In a couple of hours I had gained the summit of the island, and prepared for my descent, by sitting down and eating my dinner. I observed that, as before, the water on the other side of the island was quite smooth, compared to what it was on the side where I resided. It was, in fact, from the prevailing winds during the year, the lee side of the island. Having rested myself sufficiently, I commenced my descent, which I accomplished in little less time than it took me to ascend from the other side. As I neared the rocks by the shore, I thought I perceived something occasionally moving about on them. I was not mistaken, for as I came closer, I found that there were several large animals lying on the rocks, and occasionally dropping into the sea close to them.

The sight of anything living was to me of great interest. I determined to get nearer, and ascertain what animals they were. At last, by creeping along from rock to rock, I arrived to within forty yards of them. I recollected some animals of the same shape in my book of Natural History, which, fortunately, I had with me in the duck frock, and sitting down behind the rock, I pulled it out, and turned over the pages until I came to a print which exactly answered to their appearance. It was the Seal. Having satisfied myself on that point, I read the history of the animal, and found that it was easily tamed, and very affectionate when taken young, and also might be easily killed by a blow on the nose. These, at least, were for me the two most important pieces of information. It occurred to me that it would be very pleasant to have a young seal for a playmate (for the Gannets, after all, were not very intelligent), and I resolved to obtain one if I could. I put down my duck frock with my provisions behind the rock, and taking my axe in my hand, I cautiously advanced to where the animals lay. There were about twenty of them all together on one rock, but they were all large, and seemed to be about five or six feet long. I could not see a small one anywhere, so I walked in behind the rocks farther to the right, towards another rock, where I saw another batch of them lying. As I neared them, I saw by herself a seal with a young one by her side, not more than two feet long. This was what I wanted. They lay at some distance from the water, upon a low rock. I watched them for some time, and was much amused at the prattling which passed between the old and the young one. I thought that to obtain the young one, I must of course kill the old one, for I perceived that it had large teeth. I considered it advisable to get between them and the water, that they might not escape me, and I contrived so to do before I made my appearance. As soon as the old one perceived me running to them, it gave a shrill cry, and then floundered towards the water; as we came close together, it showed its teeth, and rose upon its flappers to defend itself and its young one, which kept close to its side; but a blow on its nose with the axe rendered it motionless, and apparently dead. Delighted with my success, I seized hold of the young one and took it in my arms, and was carrying it away, when I found myself confronted with the male seal, which, alarmed by the cry of the female, had come to her assistance. It was much larger than the female, with more shaggy hair about the neck and shoulders, and apparently very fierce. I could not pass it, as it was in shore of me, and I had just time to drop the young seal, and leap behind a rock on one side, with my axe all ready. The animal reared itself on the rock to pass over to me, when I saluted it with a blow the head, which staggered it. I had lost my presence of mind by the creature coming upon me so unexpectedly, and my blow was not well aimed, but before it could recover the first blow, another on its nose tumbled it over, to all appearance lifeless. I then hastened to gain the other side of the rock, where I had left the young seal, and found that it had crept to its mother's body, and was fondling it. I took it in my arms, and retreated to where I had left my duck frock, and throwing everything else out, I put the animal in, and tied up the end, so that it could not escape. I then sat down to recover myself from the excitement occasioned by this first engagement I had ever been in, quite delighted with my newly-acquired treasure.

I then thought what I should do. It was now within an hour of dark, and was too late to return to the other side of the island, or I would have done so, as I was anxious to get my seal home. At last I decided that I would go farther from the beach, and take up my quarters for the night. I collected my provision, and with my seal under my arm, I walked away about one hundred yards from the water's edge, and took up a position under a large rock; here I ate my supper, and then untied the line which closed up the frock, and had a parting look at my little friend before I went to sleep. He had struggled a good deal at first, but was now quiet, although he occasionally made attempts to bite me. I coaxed him and fondled him a good deal, and then put him into his bag again, and made him secure, which appeared to annoy him very much, as he was not half as quiet in a bag as he was when I held him in my lap. I then took my book to read over again the history of the seal, and I found that their skins were valuable, and also that they gave a great deal of oil, but I had no use for oil, though I thought that their skins might be very comfortable in my bed-place. I shut my book and lay down to sleep, but I could not obtain any till near daylight, I had been so excited, and was so anxious about my treasure. The sun shining in my eyes woke me up; I found my seal was lying very quiet; I touched him to see that he was not dead, and the cry that he gave assured me to the contrary. I then walked back to where I had left the bodies of the parents. I found on examination that they were both dead, and also that their furs were very beautiful, and I resolved that I would have their skins. But here was a difficulty. If I took off the skins, I could not carry them with me, and I was anxious to get the young one home, lest it should die of hunger, so I decided that I would first take home the young one, give it food and warm it, and then return and skin the old ones.

I therefore made my breakfast, and leaving the remainder of my provision in a cleft in the rock, that I might not have the trouble of bringing it again, I set off on my return, and used such diligence that I was back at the cabin by noon. I found my birds all well, and apparently quite satisfied with the provision that I had left them, for they were most of them asleep, and those that were awake did not notice my arrival.

"Ah," thought I, "you only like me for what I give you; next time I go away I will leave you hungry, and then when you see me come back, you will all flutter your wings with gladness."

I was puzzled where to put my seal so as to keep him safe: at last I decided upon opening the seaman's chest and putting him in that. I did so, and gave him a piece of fish which the birds had not eaten. The little creature devoured it eagerly, and I took my lines and went down to catch some fish for a further supply. In half an hour I returned with two large fish, and I then took the seal out of the chest and fed him again. He ate very heartily; and I was glad to perceive that he appeared much tamer already. I threw some of the insides of the fish to the birds, who were now become of very inferior interest to me. Having fed my animals, I then thought of myself, and, as I took my meal, I arranged that the next morning I would go over to the other side of the island, skin the two seals, and spread out the skins on the rocks to dry, and would leave them there till I had a better opportunity of bringing them to the cabin; at present I could not be away from my new acquaintance, which I wished to make tame and fond of me. Having fed him again in the morning, I put down the lid of the chest, and then started for the lee side of the island.

CHAPTER XVII

I arrived early, skinned both the seals, and dragged the skins up from the water-side, though with difficulty, especially that of the large one, to the rock where I had taken up my quarters the night before. Here I spread them out to dry, putting large pieces of rock upon the edges, that they might not be blown away. It was nearly dusk when I had finished, but I set off, and an hour after dark arrived at the cabin; for now that I knew my way so well, I got over the ground twice as fast as I did before. I crawled into my bed-place in the dark, and slept soundly after my fatigue. I awoke the next morning with the plaintive cry of my seal in the chest, and I hastened to get some fish to feed him with. I took him out and fed him; and was astonished how tame the little animal had become already. He remained very quietly with me after he had been fed, nestling close to my side, as if I had been his mother, and even making a half attempt to follow me when I left him.

My birds appeared very dull and stupid, and I observed also that they were very dirty, and always rushed to the kid when it was full of water, trying to get into it. This made me think that they required bathing in salt water, and I took one down to the bathing-pool, with a long line to its leg, and put it in. The manner in which the poor creature floundered, and dipped and washed itself, for several minutes, proved my supposition correct; so, after allowing it half an hour for its recreation, I took it back, and went down with the others until they had all indulged in the luxury of a bath; and from that time, as I took them down almost every day, it was astonishing how much brighter and sleeker their plumage became.

I remained a week in the cabin, taming my seal, which now was quite fond of me; and one night, as I was going to bed, he crawled into my bed-place, and from that time he was my bed-fellow. At the end of a week I went over to the other side of the island, and contrived to carry up the two skins to the summit. It was a hard day's work. The day afterwards I conveyed them to the cabin, and, as they were quite dry, I put them into my bed-place to lie down upon, as I did not like the smell of the birds' feathers, although I had so long been accustomed to them.

And now, what with my seal, my birds, and my garden, and the occupation they gave me, the time passed quickly away, until, by my reckoning, it was nearly the period for the birds to come again. I observed, as the time drew near, that my birds were uneasy. They had paired, as I mentioned before, and when their plumage was complete, it was evident that they had paired male and female, as I had supposed. They had not been tethered for a long while, and appeared to me now very much inclined to fly, especially the male birds. At first I thought that I would cut all their wings, as I was fearful that they would join the other birds on their arrival, but observing that they were so fond of their mates, I resolved to cut the wing of the females only, as I did not think that the male birds would leave them. I did so, and took my chance; for since I had the seal for a companion, I did not care so much for the birds as before. At last the birds came, and took possession of the guano-ground as usual, and I went for fresh eggs; at the same time I found that my females were scratching, as if they would make their nests, and a few days afterwards they began to lay. I then thought that as soon as they had young ones they would wish to go away, so I took the eggs that were laid, to prevent them, but I found that as fast as I took away the eggs they laid more, and this they did for nearly two months, supplying me with fresh eggs long after the wild birds had hatched, and left the island. The male birds, at the time that the females first laid their eggs, tried their wings in short flights in circles, and then flew away out to sea. I thought that they were gone, but I was deceived, for they returned in about a quarter of an hour, each with a fish in its beak, which they laid down before their mates. I was much pleased at this, and I resolved that in future they should supply their own food, which they did; and not their own food only, but enough for the seal and me also when the weather was fine, but when it was rough, they could not obtain any, and then I was obliged to feed them. The way I obtained from them the extra supply of fish was, that when they first went out, I seized, on their return, the fish which they brought, and as often as I did this they would go for more, until the females were fed.

But I had one difficulty to contend with, which was, that at the time the birds could not obtain fish, which was when the weather was rough, I could not either, as they would not take the bait. After some cogitation, I decided that I would divide a portion of the bathing-pool farthest from the shore, by a wall of loose rock which the water could flow through, but which the fish could not get out of, and that I would catch fish in the fine weather to feed the seal and the birds when the weather was rough and bad. As soon as I had finished curing my stock of provisions and got it safely housed in the cabin, I set to work to make this wall, which did not take me a very long while, as the water was not more than two feet deep, and the pool about ten yards across. As soon as it was finished, I went out every day, when it was fine, and caught as many fish as I thought I might require, and put them into this portion of the bathing-pool. I found the plan answer well, as the fish lived, but I had great difficulty in getting them out when I wanted them, for they would not take the bait.

As my birds were no longer a trouble to me, but rather, on the contrary, a profit, I devoted my whole time to my seal. I required a name for him, and reading in the book of Natural History that a certain lion was called Nero, I thought it a very good name for a seal, and bestowed it on him accordingly, although what Nero meant I had no idea of. The animal was now so tame that he would cry if ever I left him, and would follow me as far as he could down the rocks, but there was one part of the path leading to the bathing-pool which was too difficult for him, and there he would remain crying till I came back. I had more than once taken him down to the bathing-pool to wash him, and he was much pleased when I did. I now resolved that I would clear the path of the rocks, that he might be able to follow me down the whole way, for he had grown so much that I found him too heavy to carry. It occupied me a week before I could roll away and remove the smaller rocks, and knock off others with the axe, but I finished it at last, and was pleased to find that the animal followed me right down and plunged into the water. He had not been down since I had made the wall of rock to keep the fish in, and as soon as he was in, he dived and came out with one of the fish, which he brought to land. "So now," thought

I, "I shall know how to get the fish when I want them—I shall bring you down, Nero." I may as well here observe that Nero very soon obeyed orders as faithfully as a dog. I had a little switch, and when he did wrong, I would give him a slight tap on the nose. He would shake his head, show his teeth, and growl, and then come fondly to me. As he used to follow me every day down to the pool, I had to break him off going after the fish when I did not want them taken, and this I accomplished. No one who had not witnessed it, could imagine the affection and docility of this animal, and the love I had for him. He was my companion and playmate during the day, and my bedfellow at night. We were inseparable.

It was at the latter portion of the second year of my solitude that a circumstance occurred, that I must now relate. Nero had gone down to the pool with me, and I was standing fishing off the rocks, when he came out of the pool and plunged into the sea, playing all sorts of gambols, and whistling with delight. I did not think anything about it. He plunged and disappeared for a few minutes, and then would come up again close to where my line was, but he disturbed the fish and I could not catch any. To drive him farther off, I pelted him with pieces of rock, one of which hit him very hard, and he dived down. After a time I pulled up my line, and whistling to him to return, although I did not see him, I went away to the cabin, fully expecting that he would soon follow me, for now he could walk (after his fashion) from the cabin to the pool as he pleased. This was early in the morning, and I busied myself with my garden, which was now in great luxuriance, for I had dressed it with guano; but observing about noon that he had not returned, I became uneasy, and went down to the pool to look for him. He was not there, and I looked on the sea, but could not perceive him anywhere. I called and whistled, but it was of no use, and I grew very much alarmed at the idea that my treasure had deserted me. "It could not be because I threw the pieces of rock at him," thought I; "he would not leave me for that." I remained for two or three hours, watching for him, but it was all in vain; there was no seal—no Nero,—my heart sank at the idea of the animal having deserted me, and for the first time in my life, as far as I can recollect, I burst into a flood of tears. For the first time in my life, I may say, I felt truly miserable—my whole heart and affections were set upon this animal, the companion and friend of my solitude, and I felt as if existence were a burden without him. After a while, I retraced my steps to the cabin, but I was miserable, more so than I can express. I could not rest quiet. Two hours before sunset, I went down again to the rocks, and called till I was hoarse. It was all in vain; night closed in, and again I returned to the cabin, and threw myself down in my bed-place in utter despair.

"I thought he loved me," said I to myself, "loved me as I loved him; I would not have left him in that way." And my tears burst out anew at the idea that I never should see my poor Nero again.

The reader may think that my grief was inordinate and unwarrantable, but let him put himself in my position—a lad of sixteen, alone on a desolate island, with only one companion—true, he was an animal, and could not speak, but he was affectionate; he replied to all my caresses; he was my only companion and friend, the only object that I loved or cared about. He was intelligent, and I thought loved me as much as I loved him, and now he had deserted me, and I had nothing else that I cared about or that cared for me. My tears flowed for more than an hour, till at last I was wearied and fell asleep.

CHAPTER XVIII

It was early in the morning, and yet dark, when I felt something touch me. I started up—a low cry of pleasure told me at once that it was Nero, who was by my side. Yes, it was Nero, who had come back, having climbed up again the steep path to the cabin, to return to his master. Need I say that I was overjoyed, that I hugged him as if he had been a human being, that I wept over him, and that in a few minutes afterwards we were asleep together in the same bed-place. Such was the fact, and never was there in my after life, so great a transition from grief to joy.

"Oh! now, if you had left me,"—said I to him, the next morning, when I got up; "you naughty seal, to frighten me and make me so unhappy as you did!" Nero appeared quite as happy as I was at our reunion, and was more affectionate than ever.

I must now pass over many months in very few words, just stating to the reader what my position was at the end of three years, during which I was alone upon the island. I had now arrived at the age of near seventeen, and was tall and strong for my years. I had left off wearing my dress of the skins of birds, having substituted one of the seaman's shirts, which I had found in the chest. This, however, was the whole of my costume, and although, had it been longer it would have been more correct, still, as I had no other companion but Nero, it was not necessary to be so very particular, as if I had been in society. During these three years, I think I had read the Bible and Prayer-book, and my Natural History book, at least five or six times quite through, and possessing a retentive memory, could almost repeat them by heart; but still I read the Bible as a sealed book, for I did not understand it, having had no one to instruct me, nor any grace bestowed upon me. I read for amusement, and nothing more.

My garden was now in a most flourishing condition, the climbing plants had overrun the cabin, so as to completely cover the whole of the roof and every portion of it, and they hung in festoons on each side of the door-way. Many of the plants which I had taken up small, when I moved them, had proved to be trees, and were now waving to the breeze, high above the cabin roof; and everything that I had planted, from continual watering and guano, had grown most luxuriantly. In fact, my cabin was so covered and sheltered, that its original form had totally disappeared, it now looked like an arbour in a clump of trees, and from the rocks by the bathing-pool it had a very picturesque appearance.

I had, of course, several times gone up the ravine, and now that my axe had become useful, I had gradually accumulated a large stock of wood down by the bathing-pool, more than I could use for a long while, as I seldom lighted a fire, but the cutting it was employment, and employment was to me a great source of happiness. I had been several times to the other side of the island, and had had more encounters with the seals, of which I killed many, for I found their skins very comfortable and useful in the cabin. I had collected about three dozen of the finest skins, which were more than I required, but I had taken them for the same reason that I had collected the firewood, for the sake of employment, and in this instance, I may add, for the sake of the excitement which the combats with the seals afforded me.

I have not narrated any of these conflicts, as I thought that they might weary the reader, I must, however, state what occurred on one occasion, as although ludicrous, it nearly cost me my life. I had attacked a large male seal, with a splendid fur, for I always looked out for the best skinned animals. He was lying on a rock close to the water, and I had gone into the water to cut him off and prevent his escape by plunging in, as he would otherwise have done; but as I aimed the usual blow at his nose, my foot slipped on the wet rock, and I missed the animal, and at the same time fell down on the rock with the axe in my hand. The animal, which was a male of the largest size, seized hold of my shirt (which I then wore) with his teeth, and, plunging with me into the sea, dived down into the deep water. It was fortunate that he had seized my shirt instead of my body, and also that I could swim well. He carried me along with him—the shirt, for a few seconds, drawn over my head, when, disembarrassing myself of the garment, by slipping my head and arms out, I left it in his possession, and regained the surface of the water, almost suffocated. It was fortunate that I did not wear sleeve-buttons; had I had them, I could not have disengaged myself, and must have perished. I climbed the rock again, and turning round, I perceived the seal on the surface, shaking the shirt in great wrath. This was a sad discomfiture, as I lost not only my shirt but my axe, which I dropped when I was dragged into the water; nothing was saved except my knife, which I carried by a lanyard round my neck. Why I mention this circumstance particularly, is, that having felt great inconvenience for want of sleeve-buttons to hold the wristbands of my shirt together, I had thought of making use of those of the mate, which the reader may recollect had been given with his watch into Jackson's care, to take home to his wife; but on second consideration I thought it very possible I might lose them, and decided that the property was in trust, and that I had no right to risk it. This correct feeling on my part, therefore, was probably the saving of my life.

I have only now to mention my birds, and of them I can merely say that they went on as before; they bathed constantly, at the right season they laid eggs, the male birds caught fish and brought them to the cabin, and they were just as stupid and uninteresting as they were at first; however, they never left me, nor indeed shewed any intention to leave me, after the first season of the birds returning to the island. They were useful but not very ornamental, and not at all interesting to one who had such an intelligent companion as Nero.

Having now brought up my history, in a few words, until the time referred to, I come to the narrative of what occurred to produce a change in my condition. I have said that in the chest there was a spy-glass, but it had been wetted with salt-water, and was useless. Jackson had tried to shew me how to use it, and had shewn me correctly, but the glasses were dimmed by the wet and subsequent evaporation from heat. I had taken out all the glasses and cleaned them, except the field-glass as it is called, but that being composed of two glasses, the water had penetrated between them, and it still remained so dull that nothing could be distinguished through it, at the time that Jackson was shewing me how to use the instrument; it was therefore put on one side as useless. A year afterwards, I took it out, from curiosity, and then I discovered that the moisture between the two glasses had been quite dried up, and that I could see very clearly through it, and after a little practice I could use it as well as anybody else. Still I seldom did use it, as my eyesight was particularly keen, and I did not require it, and as for any vessel coming off the island, I had gradually given up all thoughts of it. It was one evening when the weather was very rough and the sea much agitated, that I thought I saw something unusual on the water, about four miles distant. I supposed at first it might be a spermaceti whale, for numbers used to play round the island at certain seasons, and I used to watch their blowing and their gambols, if I may use the term, and Jackson often told me long stories about the whale fisheries; but a ray of the setting sun made the object appear white, and I ran for the glass, and made out that it was a boat or a very small vessel, with a sail out, and running before the gale right down to the island. I watched it till it was dark with much interest, and with thoughts of various kinds chasing each other; and then I began to consider what was best to do. I knew that in an hour the moon would rise, and as the sky was not cloudy, although the wind and sea were high, I should probably be able to see it again. "But they never can get on shore on this side of the island," thought I, "with so much sea. Yes they might, if they ran for the bathing-pool." After thinking a while, I decided that I would go down to the bathing-pool, and place lighted faggots on the rocks on each side of the entrance, as this would shew them where to run for, and how to get in. I waited a little longer, and then taking my spy-glass and some tinder with me, I went down to the pool, carried two faggots to the rocks on each side, and having set them on fire and taken up others to replace them as soon as they were burnt out, I sat down with my spy-glass to see if I could make out where the boat might be.

As the moon rose, I descried her now within a mile of the island, and her head directed towards the beacon lights made by the burning faggots. I threw another faggot on each and went down for a further supply. The gale had increased, and the spray now dashed over the rocks to where the faggots were burning, and threatened to extinguish them, but I put on more wood and kept up a fierce blaze. In a quarter of an hour I could distinguish the boat; it was now close to the island, perhaps three hundred yards distant, steering not directly for the lights, but more along shore.

The fact was that they had hauled up, not knowing how they could land until they had observed the two lights clear of each other, and then they understood why they had been made; and a moment afterwards they bore up right for the entrance to the bathing-pool, and came rushing on before the rolling seas. I still trembled for them, as I knew that if the sea receded at the time that they came to the ledge of rocks at the entrance, the boat would be dashed to pieces, although their lives might be saved, but fortunately for them, it was not so—on the contrary, they came in borne up on a huge wave which carried them clear over the ledge, right up to the wall of rock which I had made across the pool, and then the boat grounded.

"Hurrah! well done, that," said a voice from the boat. "Lower away the sail, my lads; all's right."

The sail was lowered down, and then, by the light of the fire, I discovered that there were several people in the boat. I had been too much excited to say anything; indeed, I did not know what to say. I only felt that I was no more alone, and the reader may imagine my joy and delight.

CHAPTER XIX

As soon as the sail was lowered, the men leaped over the sides of the boat into the water, and waded to the rocks.

"Who are you?" said one of the men, addressing me, "and how many of you are there here?"

"There is no one on the island but myself," replied I; "but I'm so glad that you have come."

"Are you? Then perhaps you'll tell us how to get something to eat, my hearty?" replied he.

"Oh yes, wait a little, and I'll bring you plenty," replied I.

"Well, then, look smart, that's a beauty, for we are hungry enough to eat you, if you can find us nothing better."

I was about to go up to the cabin for some birds, when another man called out—

"I say—can you get us any water?"

"Oh yes, plenty," replied I.

"Well then, I say, Jim, hand us the pail out of the boat."

The one addressed did so, and the man put it into my hands, saying, "Bring us that pail, boy, will you?" I hastened up to the cabin, filled the pail full of water, and then went for a quantity of dried birds, with which I hastened down again to the bathing-pool; I found the men had not been idle, they had taken some faggots off the stack and made a large fire under the rocks, and were then busy making a sort of tent with the boat's sails.

"Here's the water, and here's some birds," said I, as I came up to them.

"Birds! what birds?" said the man who had first spoken to me, and appeared to have control over the rest. He took one up and examined it by the light of the fire, exclaiming, "Queer eating, I expect."

"Why, you didn't expect a regular hotel when you landed, did you, mate?" said one of the men.

"No, if I had, I would have called for a glass of grog," replied he. "I suspect I might call a long while before I get anyone to bring me one here."

As I knew that Jackson called the rum by the name of grog, I said, "There's plenty of grog, if you want any."

"Is there, my hearty,—where?"

"Why, in that cask that's in the water on the other side of your little ship," replied I. "I can draw you some directly."

"What! in that cask? Grog floating about in salt water, that's too bad. Come here all of you—You're in earnest, boy—no joking I hope, or you may repent it."

"I'm not joking," said I—"there it is."

The man, followed by all the rest, excepting one of the party, waded into the water, and went to the cask of rum.

"Take care," said I, "the spiles are in."

"So I see—never fear, my hearty—come now all of us." So saying, the whole of them laid hold of the cask by the chains, and lifting it up, they carried it clean out of the water, and placed it on the rocks by the side of the pool.

"Hand us the little kid out of the boat, Jim," said the man; "we'll soon see if it's the right stuff."

He took out the spiles, drew off some of the liquor, and tasting it, swore it was excellent. It was then handed round, and all the men took some.

"We're in luck to-night; we're fallen upon our legs," said the first man. "I say, Jim, put them dried chickens into the pitch-kettle along with some taters out of the bag—they'll make a good mess; and then with this cask of grog to go to, we shan't do badly."

"I say, old fellow," said he, turning to me, "you're a regular trump. Who left you on shore to get all ready for us?"

"I was born here," replied I.

"Born here! well, we'll hear all about that to-morrow—just now, we'll make up for lost time, for we've had nothing to eat or drink since Wednesday morning. Look alive, my lads! get up the hurricane-house. Jim, put the pail of water into the kettle, and send the islander here for another pailful, for grog."

The pail was handed to me, and I soon returned with it full, and, as I did not see that they had a pannikin, I brought one down and gave it to them.

"You're a fine boy," said the mate; (as I afterwards found out that he was). "And now, I say, where do you hold out? Have you a hut or a cave to live in?"

"Yes," replied I; "I have a cabin, but it is not large enough for all of you."

"No, no! we don't want to go there—we are very well where we are, alongside of the cask of rum, but you see, my lad, we have a woman here."

"A woman!" said I; "I never saw a woman. Where is she?"

"There she is, sitting by the fire."

I looked round, and perceived that there was one of the party wrapped up in a blanket, and with a wide straw hat on the head, which completely concealed the form from me. The fact is, that the woman looked like a bundle, and remained by the fire quite as inanimate. At my saying that I never saw a woman, the man burst into a loud laugh.

"Why, did you not say that you were born on the island, boy?" said the mate at last. "Were you born without a mother?"

"I cannot recollect my mother—she died when I was very young; and therefore I said, that I had never seen a woman."

"Well, that's explained; but you see, my lad—this is not only a woman, but a very particular sort of a woman; and it will not do for her to remain here after we have had our supper—for after supper, the men may take a drop too much, and not behave themselves; so I asked you about your cabin, that you might take her there to sleep. Can you do that?"

"Yes," replied I; "I will take her there, if she wishes to go."

"That's all right then, she'll be better there than here, at all events. I say, boy, where did you leave your trousers?"

"I never wear any."

"Well then, if you have any, I advise you to put them on, for you are quite old enough to be breeched."

I remained with them while the supper was cooking, asking all manner of questions, which caused great mirth. The pitch kettle, which was a large iron pot on three short legs, surprised me a good deal, I had never seen such a thing before, or anything put on the fire. I asked what it was, and what it was made of. The potatoes also astonished me, as I had never yet seen an edible root.

"Why, where have you been all your life?" said one of the men.

"On this island," replied I, very naively.

I waded into the water to examine the boat as well as I could by the light of the fire, but I could see little, and was obliged to defer my examination till the next day. Before the supper was cooked and eaten, I did, however, gain the following information.

That they were a portion of the crew of a whaler, which had struck on a reef of rocks about seventy miles off, and that they had been obliged to leave her immediately, as she fell on her broadside a few minutes afterwards; that they had left in two boats, but did not know what had become of the other boat, which parted company during the night. The captain and six men were in the other boat, and the mate with six men in the one which had just landed— besides the lady.

"What's a lady?" said I.

"I mean the woman who sits there; her husband was killed by some of the people of the Sandwich Isles, and she was going home to England. We have a consort, another whaler, who was to have taken our cargo of oil on board, and to have gone to England with that and her own cargo, and the missionary's wife was to have been sent home in her."

"What's a missionary?" inquired I.

"Well, I don't exactly know; but he is a preacher who goes out to teach the savages."

By this time the supper was cooked, and the odour from the pitch kettle was more savoury than anything that I had ever yet smelt. The kettle was lifted off the fire, the contents of it poured into a kid, and after they had given a portion in the small kid to the woman, who still remained huddled up in the blanket by the fire, they all sat round the large kid, and commenced their supper.

"Come, boy, and join us," said the mate, "you can't have had your supper; and as you've found one for us, it's hard but you should share it with us."

I was not sorry to do as he told me, and I must say that I never enjoyed a repast so much in my life.

"I say, boy, have you a good stock of them dried chickens of yours?" said the mate.

"Yes, I have a great many, but not enough to last long for so many people."

"Well, but we can get more, can't we?"

"No!" replied I, "not until the birds come again, and that will not be for these next five moons."

"Five moons! what do you mean?"

"I mean, five full moons must come, one after another."

"Oh, I understand; why then we must not remain on the island."

"No," replied I, "we must all go, or we shall starve; I am so glad that you are come, and the sooner you go the better. Will you take Nero with you?"

"Who is Nero?"

"Nero—my seal—he's very tame."

"Well, we'll see about it; at all events," said he, turning to the other men, "we must decide upon something, and that quickly, for we shall starve if we remain here any time."

It appeared that they had left the whaler in such a hurry, that they had only had time to throw into the boat two breakers of water, four empty breakers to fill with saltwater for ballast to the boat, and the iron pitch kettle, with a large sack of potatoes.

As soon as supper was finished, they went to the cask for the rum, and then the mate said to me—

"Now I'll go and speak to the woman, and you shall take her to sleep in your cabin."

During the whole of this time the woman, as the mate called her, had never spoken a word. She had taken her supper, and eaten it in silence, still remaining by the fire, huddled up in the blanket. On the mate speaking to her, she rose up, and I then perceived that she was much taller than I thought she could have been; but her Panama hat still concealed her face altogether.

"Now then, my lad," said the mate, "shew the lady where she is to sleep, and then you can join us again if you like."

"Will you come with me?" said I, walking away.

The woman followed me up the path. When we arrived at the platform opposite the cabin, I recollected Nero, whom I had ordered to stay there till my return.

"You won't be afraid of the seal," said I, "will you? he is very good-natured. Nero, come here."

It was rather dark as Nero came shuffling up, and I went forward to coax him, for he snarled a little at seeing a stranger.

"Have you no light at hand?" said my companion, speaking for the first time in a very soft, yet clear voice.

"No, I have not, but I will get some tinder, and make a fire with one of the faggots, and then you will be able to see."

"Do so, then, my good lad," replied she.

I thought her voice very pleasing.

I soon lighted the faggot and enabled her to see Nero (who was now quite quiet) and also the interior of the cabin.

She examined the cabin and the bed-places, and then said,

"Where do you sleep?"

I replied by shewing her my bed-place. "And this," said I, pointing to the one opposite, "was Jackson's, and you can sleep in that. Nero sleeps with me. Here are plenty of seal skins to keep you warm if you are cold. Are your clothes wet?"

"No, they are quite dry now," replied she; "if you will get me some seal skins, I will lie down on them, for I am very tired."

I spread five or six skins one on the other, in Jackson's bed-place, and then I went out and threw another faggot on the fire, that we might have more light.

"Do you want anything else?" said I.

"Nothing, I thank you. Are you going to bed now?"

"I was meaning to go down again to the men, but now I think of it, I do not like to leave you alone with Nero, as he might bite you. Are you afraid of him?"

"No, I'm not much afraid, but still I have no wish to be bitten, and I am not used to sleep with such animals, as you are."

"Well then, I'll tell you how we'll manage it. I will take some skins outside, and sleep there. Nero will not leave me, and then you won't be afraid. The weather is clearing up fast, and there's very little wind to what there was—besides, it will be daylight in three or four hours."

"As you please," was the reply.

Accordingly I took some seal skins out on the platform, and spreading them, I lay down upon them, wishing her good-night, and Nero soon joined me, and we were both fast asleep in a few minutes.

CHAPTER XX

Nero, who was an early riser, woke me up at day-break, or I should have slept much longer; for I had been tired out with the fatigue and excitement of the night before. As soon as I was up, I looked into the cabin, and found the woman was fast asleep; her straw hat was off, but she had lain down in her clothes. Her black hair was hanging about her shoulders. Having only seen Jackson with his bushy beard, I had been somewhat surprised when I first saw the men on their landing so comparatively clear of hair on their face; my astonishment at the clear white skin of a woman—and in this instance, it was peculiarly white and pallid—was very great. I also perceived how much more delicate her features were than those of the men; her teeth, too, were very white, and Jackson's were discoloured and bad; I longed to see her eyes, but they were closed. Any other difference I could not perceive, as she had drawn the blanket close up to her chin.

"This is then a woman," said I to myself: "yes, and it's very like what I used to see in my dreams." I looked a little longer, and then, hearing Nero coming into the cabin behind me, and afraid that she would awake, I made a hasty retreat.

I remained at this part of the cabin considering what I should do. I thought I would light a fire, and go down for a fish to broil on the embers for her breakfast, so I called Nero to come down with me. On arriving at the pool, I found all the seamen fast asleep under the tent they had made with the boat's sails; and they appeared to be much the same as Jackson used to be after he had got drunk the night before; I presumed therefore, that such was their state, and was not far wrong. Nero went into the pool and brought out a fish, as I ordered him, and I then walked to the boat to examine it. This took me half an hour, and I was sorry that none of the men were awake, that so I might ask any questions I wished. I examined the pitch-kettle, and the boat's sails, and the breakers. Breakers are small casks, holding about six to seven gallons of water, and are very handy for boats. I remained about an hour, and then went back to the cabin, carrying a faggot on my shoulder, Nero following with the fish in his mouth. We were met by the woman, who came out of the cabin; she no longer had the blanket round her, for it was a beautiful bright morning, and very warm.

"Nero is bringing you your breakfast," said I, "so you ought to like him."

"I dare say I shall, if we are to be companions in future," replied she.

"Do you want anything?" said I.

"Yes, a little water, if you can get me some."

I filled the kid from the spring, put it down by her, and then took out the inside of the fish, and fed the birds, who were crowding round me.

The woman washed her face and hands, braided up her hair, and then sat down on the rock. In the meantime, I had lighted my faggot, cleaned the fish, and waited till the wood was burnt to ashes before I put the fish on the fire. Having then nothing to do, I thought that reading would amuse the woman, and I went in for the Bible.

"Shall I read to you?" said I.

"Yes," replied she, with some astonishment in her looks.

I read to her the history of Joseph and his brethren, which was my favourite story in the Bible.

"Who taught you to read?" said she, as I shut the book, and put the fish on the embers.

"Jackson," said I.

"He was a good man, was he not?" replied she.

I shook my head. "No, not very good," said I, at last. "If you knew all about him, you would say the same; but he taught me to read."

"How long have you been on this island?" said she.

"I was born on it, but my father and mother are both dead, and Jackson died three years ago—since that I have been quite alone, only Nero with me."

She then asked me a great many more questions, and I gave her a short narration of what had passed, and what Jackson had told me; I also informed her how it was I procured food, and how we must soon leave the island, now that we were so many, or the food would not last out till the birds came again.

By this time the fish was cooked, and I took it off the fire and put it into the kid, and we sat down to breakfast; in an hour or so, we had become very sociable.

I must however now stop a little to describe her. What the men had told me was quite true. She had lost her husband, and was intending to proceed to England. Her name was Reichardt, for her husband was a German, or of German family. She was, as I have since ascertained, about thirty-seven years old, and very tall and elegant; she must have been very handsome when she was younger, but she had suffered much hardship in following her husband as she had done, through all the vicissitudes of his travels.

Her face was oval; eyes black and large; and her hair black as the raven's wing; her features were small and regular; her teeth white and good; but her complexion was very pallid, and not a vestige of colour on her cheeks. As I have since thought, it was more like a marble statue than anything I can compare her to. There was a degree of severity in her countenance when she did not smile, and it was seldom that she did. I certainly looked upon her with more awe than regard, for some time after I became acquainted with her; and yet her voice was soft and pleasant, and her manners very amiable; but it must be remembered I had never before seen a woman. After breakfast was over, I proposed going down to where the seamen lay, to see if they were awake, but I told her I thought that they would not be.

"I will go with you, as I left a basket with some things of mine in the boat, and it will be as well to bring them up at once."

We therefore set off together, I having ordered Nero to stay in the cabin. On our arrival at the pool we found the men still fast asleep; and by her directions I went into the water to the boat, and brought out a basket and a small bundle which she pointed out.

"Shall I wake them?" said I.

"No, no," replied she; "so long as they sleep, they will be doing no harm. But," said she, "we may as well take some potatoes up with us; fill both these handkerchiefs," continued she, taking two out of the bundle. I did so, and she took one and I the other, and we returned to the cabin.

"Are these all the birds that you have for food?" said she, looking at the pile in the cabin.

"Yes," replied I. "But what are we to do with the potatoes?"

"We can roast them by the fire if we like," said she; "but at present we had better take them into the cabin. Did you plant all these flowers and creepers which grow over the cabin?"

"Yes," replied I. "I was alone and had nothing to do, so I thought I would make a garden."

"They are very pretty. Now that I am back, you can go down to the men if you please, and tell them, when they wake up, that I wish to have the smallest of the boat's sails, to make a screen of. Tell the mate, he is the most civil."

"I will," said I. "Is there anything else?"

"Yes, bring up a few more potatoes; they will let you take them if you say that I told you."

"Shall I take Nero with me?"

"Yes, I do not want his company, for I am a little afraid of him."

I called Nero, who came after me, and went down to the pool, when I found that the men had all woke up, and were very busy, some lighting a fire, some washing potatoes, and some trying to catch the fish in the pool.

"Oh, here he is. Come, boy, what have you got for our breakfast? We've been trying to catch some of these fish, but they're as quick as eels."

"Nero will soon catch you what you want," replied I. "Here, Nero, in."

Nero plunged in, and soon brought out a fish, and I then sent him in for another.

"Thanks, lad," said the mate; "that will be enough for our breakfast. That seal of yours is a handy fellow, and well trained."

While the other men were getting breakfast, one of them went up to Nero, I believe with the intention of making friends with him, but Nero rejected his advances, and showed his sharp teeth, snapping at him several times. The man became angry, and caught up a piece of rock to throw at the seal. He aimed at the animal's nose, and narrowly missed hitting it. Had he done so, he would probably have killed it. This made me very angry, and I told the man not to do so again; upon this, he caught up another, and was about to throw it, when I seized him by the collar with my left hand, and with my right drawing my American knife, I threatened to stab him with it, if he attacked the beast. The man started back, and in so doing, fell over a piece of rock, on his back. This quarrel brought the mate to us, along with two or three of the men. My knife was still lifted up, when the mate said—

"Come, my hearty, no knives, we don't allow them. That's not English. Put it up, no one shall hurt the beast, I promise you. Bob, you fool, why couldn't you leave the animal alone? You forget you are among savages, here."

At this, the other men burst out into a laugh.

"Yes," observed one; "I can swear, when I get back, that the natives of this island are savages, who eat raw flesh, have seals for playmates, and don't wear clothes enough for common decency."

This made them laugh more, and the man who had attacked Nero, and who had got upon his legs again, joined with the others; so all was again good-humour. The men sat down to their breakfast, while I examined the boat again, and afterwards asked many questions, with which they were much amused, every now and then observing, "Well, he is a savage!"

After they had breakfasted, I made Nero catch another fish and sent him up to the cabin with it, as I was afraid that the man might do him an injury, and then told the mate that the woman had desired me to bring up some potatoes.

"Take them," said he; "but you have nothing to carry them up with. Here, fill the pail, and I will go to the cabin with you."

"She told me that I was to ask you for a small boat's sail, to hang up as a screen."

"Well, she shall have the boat's mizen. We don't want it. I'll carry it up."

The mate threw the sail and yard over his shoulder, and followed me up to the cabin. On our arrival, we found the missionary's wife sitting on the platform, Nero lying not far from her, with the fish beside him. The mate took off his hat, and saluted my new companion, saying, "That he hoped she was comfortable last night."

"Yes," replied she, "as much so as I could expect; but I turned this good lad out of his cabin, which I do not wish to do again, and therefore I requested the sail for a screen. Now, John Gough, what do you intend to do?" continued she.

The mate replied, "I came up here to see what quantity of provisions the lad might have. By his account, it will not last more than a month, and it will take some time before we can reach where we are likely to fall in with any vessel. Stay here we cannot, for we shall only eat the provision and lose time, therefore, the sooner we are off the better."

"If you take all the provision, of course you will take the lad with you?" replied she.

"Of course we will."

"And my chest, and my seal?" inquired I.

"Yes, your chest, certainly, but as for your seal, I do not know what to say to that—he will be starved in the boat, and if you give him his liberty, he will do well enough."

"What you say is very true," replied the woman. "I am afraid, boy, that you will have to part with your friend. It will be better for both of you."

I made no reply, for it cut me to the heart to think of parting with Nero; but still I had sense enough to perceive that what they said was right.

The mate then went into the cabin, and examined the heap of dried birds which I had collected, and having made his calculation, said that there were sufficient for three weeks, but not more.

"And when do you think of leaving this island?" inquired the woman.

"The day after to-morrow, if I can persuade the men, madam," replied he; "but you know they are not very easy to manage, and very thoughtless, especially now that they have so unexpectedly fallen in with liquor."

"That I admit," replied she; "but as they will probably take the liquor in the boat, that will not make so great a difference."

"I shall go down and speak to them now they're all sober," replied the mate, "and will let you know in the evening, or to-morrow morning, perhaps, will be better." The mate then saluted her by touching his hat, and left us.

CHAPTER XXI

There was one thing which had made a great impression on me in the conversation with the men in the morning. They called me a Savage, and said that I had not sufficient clothes on; and as I observed that they were all dressed in jackets and trousers, which covered them from head to foot, I took it for granted that my shirt, which was all that I wore, was not a sufficient clothing. This had never occurred to me before, nor can the reader be surprised at it. I had been like our first parents in Eden—naked but not ashamed— but now that I had suddenly come in contact with my fellow-men, I felt as if something were amiss. The consequence was, that I went to the chest and got out a pair of white trousers, and put them on. I thought them very uncomfortable and very unnecessary articles, but others wore them, and I felt that I must do so also. They were rather long for me, but I rolled up the bottoms of the legs, as I observed that the seamen did, and then came out on the platform, where the missionary's wife was still seated, looking out upon the waves as they lashed the rocks. She immediately observed the addition that I had made to my dress, and said,

"That is a great improvement. Now you look like other people. What is your name? you have not told me."

When I had answered the question, I said to her—

"I have brought up more of the potatoes, as you call them; what am I to do with them?"

"First tell me, have you any spot that you know about the island where there is mould—that is, earth, like you have in your garden—where we can plant them?"

"Yes," replied I, "there is some up there," and I pointed to one-third up the ravine. "I brought all this earth from there, and there is plenty of it; but what is the good of planting them?"

"Because," said she, "one of the potatoes planted will, in a very short time, grow, and then it will produce perhaps thirty or forty potatoes at its roots as large as these; they are excellent things for food, and where there is nothing else to be had, may be the means of preserving life."

"Well, that may be," replied I, "and if we were going to remain on the island, it would be well to plant them, but as we are going away the day after to-morrow, what's the use of it? I know that they are very nice, for I had some for supper last night."

"But are we only to think of ourselves in this world, and not of others?" replied she. "Suppose, two or three years hence, another boat were to be cast away on this island, and not find, as we have, you here, with provisions ready for them, they would starve miserably; whereas, if we plant these potatoes, they may find plenty of food and be saved. Only think how glad your father and mother would have been to have found potatoes on the island when they were thrown on it. We must not live only for ourselves, but we must think and try to do good to others—that is the duty of a Christian."

"I think you are very right," replied I, "and a very kind person too. If you wish it I will go and plant the potatoes this day. How am I to plant them?"

"They have a shovel in the boat," said she, "for I saw them throwing the water out with it. Go down and get it, and then I will go with you and show you."

I went down and the mate gave me the shovel, which I carried up to her. I found her cutting the potatoes into pieces, and she showed me how she cut them, leaving an eye in each piece, and explained the reason for it. I was soon very busy cutting away alongside of her, and before long the pail of potatoes was all ready to be planted.

We then walked to the ravine, and she showed me how to use the shovel, and I made the holes. Before noon we had planted all that we had cut, but we had still the two handkerchiefs full that we had at first brought up with us. We returned to the cabin, and I prepared the fish for dinner. After it was on the embers, she wished to have the screen put up beside her bed-place.

"Go down to the mate," said she, "and ask him for the hammer and three or four nails. I know they have them in the boat."

"I may as well take them down some birds for their dinner," replied I, "for they will want them."

"Yes, do so; and then come back to me as soon as you can."

The mate gave me the hammer, an article I had never seen before, and five or six nails, with which I returned to the cabin, and nailed up the sail as a screen.

"Now you will be able to sleep in your own bed-place to-night," said she.

I made no reply, but I could not imagine why I could not have done so the night before, for I had only gone out of the cabin that she might not be frightened by Nero being so close to her.

After we had eaten our dinner, she said to me—

"How could you contrive to live on this island, if you had no dried birds?"

"How?" replied I; "why, very badly. I might catch fish; but there are times in the year when you can catch no fish, they won't take bait, neither will they when the weather is rough. Besides, I have only two lines, and I might lose them both—then what would become of me? I should starve."

"Well, then, you see under all circumstances, it was just as well to plant the potatoes, for other people may come here and be in your position."

"Yes, that is true, but we shall not be here long now, and you don't know how glad I am to go. I want to see all the things that I have read about in my books. I want to go to England and look for somebody; but you don't know all that I know; some day I will tell you all—everything. I am so tired of living here by myself—nothing to say—no one to talk to—no one to care for, except Nero, and he can't speak. I can't bear the idea of parting with him though."

"Would you rather stay on the island with Nero, than go away without him?"

"No," replied I; "go I must, but still I do not like to part with him. He is the only friend that I ever had, that I can remember."

"When you have lived longer, and mixed more with the world, my poor boy, you will then find how many sacrifices you will be obliged to make, much more serious than parting with an animal that you are attached to. I suppose you expect to be very happy if ever you get back to England?"

"Of course I do; why should I not be?" replied I; "I shall be always happy."

The Missionary's wife shook her head. "I fear not. Indeed, I think if you live long enough, you will acknowledge that the happiest of your days were passed on this barren rock."

"Jackson said otherwise," replied I. "He was always grieving at being on the island, and not able to get back to England, and he told me so many stories about England, and what is done there, and what a beautiful place it is, that I'm sure I shall like it better than being here, even if I had somebody with me."

"Well, you are in the hands of God, and you must put your trust in him. He will do with you as he thinks best for you—that you know, as you read your Bible."

"No, I didn't know that," replied I. "God lives beyond the stars, a long way off."

"Is that all you have gained by reading your Bible?" inquired she, looking me in the face.

"No, not all," replied I; "but I do not understand a great deal that I read, I want some one to tell me. I am so glad you came with the men in the boat, for I never saw a woman before. I used to see somebody in my dreams, and now I know it was a woman. It was my mother, but I have not seen her for a long while now, and I have nobody but Nero."

"My poor boy, you have a father in heaven."

"Yes," replied I; "I know he is in heaven, and so is my mother, for Jackson said that they were both very good."

"I mean your Heavenly Father, God. Do you not say in the Lord's Prayer, 'Our Father which art in heaven.' You must love him."

I was about to reply, when John Gough, the mate, came up, and told my companion that he had been speaking to the men, and they had agreed that the day after the next they would, if the weather permitted, leave the island; that they had examined the boat, and found it required very little repair, and that all would be ready the next day.

"I hope that they will not overload the boat," said she.

"I fear that they will, but I must do all I can to prevent it. The cask of rum was rather an unfortunate discovery, and we had been better without it. Leave it they will not, so we must put out of the boat all that we can possibly do without, for we shall be nine of us, and that will be plenty of weight with the addition of the cask."

"You promised to take my chest, you remember," said I.

"Yes, I will do so if I possibly can; but recollect, I may not be able to keep my promise—for now that they have the liquor, the men do not obey me as they did before, ma'am," said the mate. "Perhaps he had better take the best of his clothes in a bundle, in case they should refuse to take in the chest; and I must say that, loaded as the boat will be, they will be much to blame if they do not refuse, for the boat is but small for stowage, and there's all the provisions to put in her, which will take up a deal of room."

"That is very true," replied the woman. "It will be better to leave the chest here, for I do not think that the boat will hold it. You must not mind your chest, my good boy; it is of no great value."

"They take my rum and all my birds, and they ought to take both me and my chest."

"Not if it takes up too much room," replied the woman. "You cannot expect it. The wishes of one person must give way to the wishes of many."

"Why they would have starved if it had not been for me," replied I, angrily.

"That's very true, boy," replied the mate; "but you have to learn yet, that might is right; and recollect that what you did this morning has not made you any great favourite with them."

"What was that?" inquired my companion.

"Only that he nearly drove his knife through one of the men, that's all," replied the mate; "English sailors ar'n't fond of knives."

He then touched his hat, and went down again to the pool, desiring me to follow him with a kid for our share of the supper. I did so, and on my return she asked me why I had drawn my knife upon the seaman, and I narrated how it occurred. She pointed out to me the impropriety of what I had done, asking me whether the Bible did not tell us we were to forgive injuries.

"Yes," replied I; "but is it not injuries to ourselves? I did forgive Jackson; but this was to prevent his hurting another."

"Another! why you talk of Nero as if the animal was a rational being, and his life of as much consequence as that of a fellow-creature. I do not mean to say but that the man was very wrong, and that you must have felt angry if an animal you were so fond of

130

had been killed; but there is a great difference between the life of an animal and that of a fellow-creature. The animal dies, and there is an end of it; but a man has an immortal soul, which never perishes, and nothing can excuse your taking the life of a man, except in self-defence. Does not the commandment say, 'Thou shalt not kill?'"

She then talked to me a long while upon the subject, and fully made me understand that I had been very wrong, and I confessed that I had been so.

CHAPTER XXII

I now resolved to speak to her relative to the belt which contained the diamonds; and I was first obliged to narrate to her in a few words what Jackson had told me. She heard me with great interest, now and then asking a question. When I had told her all, I said—

"Now, as they talk of not taking my chest, what shall I do? Shall I wear the belt myself, or shall I put it in the bundle? or will you wear it for me, as my mother would have done, if she had been alive?"

She did not reply for some time, at last she said, as if talking to herself, and not to me—

"How unsearchable are thy ways, O God!"

Indeed, although I did not feel it at the time, I have afterwards thought, and she told me herself, how great her surprise was at finding in the unshorn little Savage, thus living alone upon a desolate rock, a lad of good birth, and although he did not know it, with a fortune in his charge, which would, in all probability, be ultimately his own. This is certain, that the interest she felt towards me increased every hour, as by degrees I disclosed my history.

"Well," replied she, "if you will trust me, I will take charge of your belt. To-morrow we will select out of the chest what will be best to take with you, and then we will arrange as you wish."

After about an hour's more conversation, she went into the cabin, and retired behind the screen which had been fixed up, telling me that she did not mind Nero, and that I might go to bed when I pleased. As I was not much inclined to go down to the seamen, I followed her advice and went to bed; but I could not sleep for a long time from the noise which the men made, who were carousing at the bathing-pool. The idea of parting with Nero also lay heavy upon my heart, though the woman had almost satisfied me that as soon as I was gone, the animal would resume its natural habits, and care nothing for me.

I was up the next morning early, and went down with Nero to obtain the fish which we required. I left some on the rocks for the seamen's breakfast (for they were all sound asleep), and then returned to the cabin, and prepared for our own. Mrs Reichardt, as I shall now call her, soon came out to me, and when breakfast was over, proposed that we should plant the remainder of the potatoes before we packed up the things in the chest. As soon as they were all cut, we set off to the ravine, and had finished our task before noon, at which time there were but few of the seamen stirring, they had remained up so long the night before, drinking. The mate was one of those who were on their legs, and he asked me if I thought we should have smooth water to launch the boat on the following day. I replied in the affirmative, and went with Mrs Reichardt to the cabin, and putting down the shovel, I hauled my chest out on the platform to select what articles I should take.

While we were thus employed, and talking at times, the men came up for the dried birds to take down ready for putting them in the boat on the following day, and in two trips they had cleared out the whole of them.

"Have you used all the potatoes you brought up?" said one of the men; "for we shall be short of provisions."

Mrs Reichardt replied that we had none left.

"Well then," said the man, "the mate says you had better bring down that brute of yours to catch the rest of the fish in the pond, that we may cook them before we start, as they will make two days' meals at least."

"Very well," replied I; "I will come down directly." I did so, and Nero, in a quarter of an hour, had landed all the fish, and I then returned with him to the cabin. Mrs R. had selected the best of the clothes, and made them up in a tight bundle, which she sewed up with strong thread. My books she had left out, as well as the spy-glass, and the tools I had, as they might be useful. I asked her whether I should carry them down to the bathing-pool, but she replied that on the morning when we embarked would be quite time enough. I then went to the hole under Jackson's bed-place, and brought out the belt and the few articles that were with it. Mrs R., after having examined them, said that she would take care of them all; the watch and other trinkets she put in her basket, the belt she took to the bed-place, and secreted it.

She appeared very silent and thoughtful, and on my asking her whether I should not take down the shovel, and the pail, and hammer, she replied, "No, leave all till we are ready to go to the boat. It will be time enough."

Shortly afterwards, the mate brought us up some of the fish which they had cooked for supper, and when we had eaten it we went to bed.

"This is the last night we shall sleep together, Nero," said I, kissing my favourite, and the thought brought tears into my eyes. "But it can't be helped." I was however soon fast asleep with my arm round the animal.

When I went out the next morning, I found that the weather was beautifully fine, the water smooth, and only rippled by a light breeze. As Mrs R. had not yet made her appearance, I went down to the bathing-pool, where I found all the men up and in full activity. The boat had been emptied out, the oars, masts, and sails, were on the rocks and the men were turning the bows to the seaward in readiness for launching her over the ledge of rocks. The dried birds lay in a heap by the side of the cask of rum, and the fish which had been baked were in a large kid. The six breakers were also piled up together, and the mate and some of the men were disputing as to how many of them should be filled with water. The mate wanted them all filled; the men said that three would be sufficient, as the boat would be so loaded. At last the mate gained his point, and the men each took a breaker, and went up to the cabin for the water. I went with them to fill the breakers, and also to see that they did no mischief, for they appeared very unruly and out of temper; and I was afraid that they would hurt Nero, who was at the cabin, if I was not there to prevent them; but with the exception of examining the cabin, and forcing themselves in upon Mrs Reichardt, they did nothing. When the breakers were full, which took at least half an hour, they did indeed try to catch the birds, and would have wrung their necks, but the males flew away, and the females I put into the bed-place that was screened off in the cabin, and near which Mrs Reichardt was sitting. They all appeared to have a great awe and respect for this woman, and a look from her was more effectual than were any words of the mate.

"We don't want you," said one of the men, as they went down to the bathing-pool with the breakers on their shoulders. "Why don't you keep up with the lady? You're quite a lady's man, now you've white trousers on."

The others who followed him laughed at this latter remark.

"I'm of no use up there, at present," said I; "and I may be down below."

The men set down the breakers on the rocks by the pool, and then, under the directions of the mate, prepared to launch the boat over the ledge. The masts of the boat were placed athwartships, under her keel, for her to run upon, and being now quite empty, she was very light. She was what they call a whale-boat, fitted for the whale fishery, pointed at both ends, and steered by an oar; she was not very large, but held seven people comfortably, and she was remarkably well fitted with sails and masts, having two lugs and a mizen. As soon as they were all ready, the men went to the side of the boat, and in a minute she was launched into the sea without injury. The mate said to me, as they brought her broadside to the ledge—

"Now, my lad, we don't want you any more; you may go up to the cabin till we are ready, and then we will send for you and the lady."

"Oh! but I can be of use here," replied I; "and I am of none up there."

The mate did not reply, and the men then went to the rum cask, and rolled it towards the boat; and when they had it on the ledge, they parbuckled it, as they term it, into the boat with a whale-line that they happened to have, and which was of great length. After the cask of rum was got in amidships, (and it took up a great deal of space, reaching from one gunnel to the other, and standing high above the thwarts) they went for the breakers of water, which they put in, three before and three behind the cask, upon the floor of the boat.

"She will be too heavy," said one of the men, "with so much water."

"We can easily get rid of it," replied the mate. "If you had said she would be too heavy with so much liquor on board, you had better explained the matter; however, you must have your own ways, I suppose."

The next articles that they brought to stow away were the provisions. The kid of fish was put amidships on the breakers, and the dried birds, which they carried down in their arms, were packed up neatly in the stern-sheets. They were soon up to the gunnel, and the mate said,

"You had better stow away forward now—there will be little room for the lady as it is."

"No, no, stow them all aft," replied one of the men, in a surly tone; "the lady must sit where she can. She's no better than we."

"Shall this go in?" said I, pointing to the coil of whale-line, and addressing the mate.

"No, no; we must leave that," replied one of the men in the boat; "we shall be wedged enough as it is; and I say, Jim, throw that old saw and the bag of nails out of the boat—we can have no use for them."

The masts were then stepped, and the rigging set up to the gunnel of the boat, the yards and sails handed in, and hooked on the halyards ready for hoisting. In fact the boat was now all ready for starting; they had only the iron kettle and two or three other articles to put in.

"Shall we have the mizen?" inquired one of the men, pointing to the mast, which lay on the rocks.

"No, she steers quite as well without it," replied the mate. "We'll leave it. And now, lads, hand the oars in."

They were brought to the boat, but owing to the puncheon of rum in the centre, they could not lie flat, and after a good deal of arguing and disputing, four oars and a boat-hook were lashed to the gunnel outside, and the rest were left on the rocks.

At this time there was some consultation between the mate and some of the men—the mate being evidently opposed by the others. I could not hear what it was about, but the mate appeared very angry and very much annoyed. At last he dashed his hat down on the rocks in a great passion, saying,

"No good will come of it. Mark my words. No good ever did or ever will. Be it so, you are too many for me; but I tell you again, no good will come of it."

The mate then sat down on the rocks by himself, and put his head down on his knees, covering it with his hands.

The man with whom he had been disputing went to the others in the boat, and spoke to them in a low tone, looking round at me, to ascertain if I was within hearing.

After a minute or two they all separated, and then one of them said to me—

"Now, my lad, we're all ready. Go up to the cabin and bring down your bundle and her basket, and tell the lady we are waiting for her."

"There's the shovel," said I, "and the boat's sail—must I bring them down?"

"Oh yes, bring them down, and also two or three sealskins for the lady to sit upon."

Off I went on my errand, for I was delighted with the idea of leaving the island, and my patience had been almost exhausted at the time they had taken in the stowage of the boat. As I hastened up the path, I heard loud contention, and the mate's voice speaking very angrily, and I stopped for a short time to listen, but the noise ceased, and I went on again. I found Nero on the platform, and I stopped a minute to caress him. "Good bye, my poor Nero, we shall never see one another again," said I. "You must go back to the sea, and catch fish for yourself;" and the tears started in my eyes as I gave the animal a farewell kiss.

I then went into the cabin, where I found Mrs Reichardt sitting very quietly.

"They are all ready," said I, "and have sent me up for you but I am to bring down the boat's sail and some seal skins for you to sit upon. I can carry both if you can carry my bundle. Have you put the belt on?"

"Yes," replied she, "I am quite ready. I will carry the bundle, and the books and spy-glass, as well as my basket; but we must pack them close," added she, "and roll the sail up round the yard, or you will not be able to carry it."

We took the sail down, and got it ready for carrying, and I rolled up the two best seal skins, and tied them with a piece of fishing line, and then we were all ready. I shouldered my burden, and Mrs Reichardt took the other articles, as proposed, and we left the cabin to go down the path to the bathing-pool.

"Good bye, Nero—good bye, birds—good bye, cabin—and good bye, garden," said I, as I went along the platform; and having so done, and ordered Nero back with a tremulous voice, I turned my head in the direction of the bathing-pool. I stared and then screamed, dropping my burden, as I lifted up my hands in amazement—

"Look!" cried I to my companion. "Look!" repeated I, breathless.

She did look, and saw as I did—the boat under all sail, half a mile from the pool, staggering under a fresh breeze, which carried her away at the rate of seven or eight miles an hour.

They had left us—they had deserted us. I cried out, like a madman, "Stop! stop! stop!" and then, seeing how useless it was, I dashed myself on the rock, and for a minute or two was insensible.

"Oh!" groaned I, at last, as I came to my senses.

"Frank Henniker," said a sweet firm voice.

I opened my eyes, and saw Mrs Reichardt standing by me.

"It is the will of Heaven, and you must submit to it patiently," continued she.

"But so cruel, so treacherous!" replied I, looking at the fast-receding boat.

"I grant, most cruel, and most treacherous, but we must leave them to the judgment of God. What can they expect from him in the way of mercy when they have shewn none? I tell you candidly, that I think we are better in our present forlorn state upon this rock, than if in that boat. They have taken with them the seeds of discord, of recklessness, and intemperance, in an attempt which requires the greatest prudence, calmness, and unanimity, and I fear there is little chance of their even being rescued from their dangerous position. It is my opinion, and I thought so when I first knew they had found the cask, that liquor would prove their ruin, and I say again, that boat will never arrive at its destination, and they will all perish miserably. It has pleased God that they should leave us here, and depend upon it, it has been so decided for the best."

"But," replied I, looking again at the boat, "I was tired of being here—I was so anxious to get off—and now to be left! And they have taken all our provisions, everything, even the fish in the pool. We shall starve."

"I hope not," replied she, "and I think not; but we must exert ourselves, and trust to Heaven."

But I could not heed her—my heart was bursting. I sobbed, as I sat with my hands covering up my face.

"All gone!" cried I. "No one left but you and I."

"Yes," replied she, "one more."

"Who?" cried I, looking up.

"God!—who is with us always."

CHAPTER XXIII

I heard what she said, but my head was too confused to weigh the words. I remained silent, where I was. A few seconds elapsed, and she spoke again:

"Frank Henniker, rise, and listen to me."

"We shall starve," muttered I.

As I said this, one of the male birds returned from the sea with a large fish, of which Mrs Reichardt took possession, as she had seen me do, and the gannet flew away again to obtain more. Immediately afterwards, the other two birds returned with fish, which were in a like way secured by my companion.

"See how unjust and ungrateful you are," observed she. "Here are the birds feeding us, as the ravens did Elijah in the wilderness, at the very time that you are doubting the goodness and mercy of God. There is a meal for us provided already."

"My head! my head!" exclaimed I, "it is bursting, and there is a heavy weight rolling in it—I cannot see anything."

And such was the fact: the excitement had brought on a determination of blood to the head, and my senses were rapidly departing. Mrs Reichardt knelt by my side, and perceiving that what I had said was the case, went into the cabin and brought out a cloth, which she wetted with water from the spring, and laid across my forehead and temples. I remained motionless and nearly senseless for half an hour, during which she continued to apply fresh cold water to the cloth, and by degrees I recovered from my stupor. In the meantime, the weather being so fine and the water smooth, the gannets continued to return with the fish they caught, almost all of which were taken from them by my companion, until she had collected more than a dozen fish, from half a pound to a pound weight, which she put away, so that the birds and seal might not devour them.

I was still in a half dozing state, when the breathing and cold nose of Nero touched my cheek, and the murmurings of my favourite roused me up, and I opened my eyes.

"I am better now," said I to Mrs Reichardt. "How kind you have been!"

"Yes, you are better, but still, you must remain quiet. Do you think that you could walk to your bed-place?"

"I'll try," replied I, and with her assistance I rose up; but, when I afterwards gained my feet, I should have fallen if she had not supported me; but, assisted by her, I gained my bed and sank down again.

She raised my head higher, and then applied the linen cloth and cold water as before.

"Try now," said she, "if you cannot go to sleep. When you awake again, I will have some dinner ready for you."

I thanked her and shut my eyes. Nero crawled to my bed-place, and with my hand upon his head, I fell asleep, and remained so till near sunset, when I awoke with very little pain in my head, and much refreshed. I found Mrs Reichardt by my side.

"You are better now," said she. "Can you eat any dinner? I must make friends with Nero, for he has been disputing my right to come near your bedside, and his teeth are rather formidable. However, I gave him the inside of the fish when I cleaned them, and we are better friends already. There is your dinner."

Mrs Reichardt placed before me some of the fish, broiled on the embers, and I ate very heartily.

"It is very kind of you," said I, "to be working for me, when I ought to be working for you—but you must not do it again."

"Only my share of the work when you are well," replied she; "but my share I always shall do. I cannot be idle, and I am strong enough to do a great deal; but we will talk about that to-morrow morning. You will be quite well by that time, I hope."

"Oh! I feel well now," replied I, "only I am very weak."

"You must put your trust in God, my poor boy. Do you ever pray to him?"

"Yes, I try a little sometimes—but I don't know how. Jackson never taught me that."

"Then I will. Shall I pray now for both of us?"

"Will God hear you? What was it that you said just before I forgot everything this morning?"

"I told you that there was another here besides ourselves, a good and gracious God, who is always with us and always ready to come to our assistance if we call upon him."

"You told me God lived beyond the stars."

"My poor boy, as if he were a God who was afar off and did not attend to our prayers! Such is not the case. He is with us always in spirit, listening to all our prayers, and reading every secret thought of our hearts."

I was silent for some time, thinking upon what she had told me; at last I said—

"Then pray to him."

Mrs Reichardt knelt down and prayed in a clear and fervent voice, without hesitation or stop. She prayed for protection and support in our desolate condition, that we might be supplied with all things needful for our sustenance, and have a happy deliverance from our present position. She prayed that we might be contented and resigned until it should please him to rescue us—that we might put our whole trust and confidence in him, and submit without murmuring to whatever might be his will. She prayed for health and strength, for an increase of faith and gratitude towards him for all his mercies. She thanked him for our having been preserved by being left on the desolate rock, instead of having left it in the boat with the seamen. (This surprised me.) And then she prayed for me, entreating that she might be the humble instrument of leading me to my Heavenly Father, and that he would be pleased to pour down upon me his Holy Spirit, so that I might, by faith in Christ, be accepted, and become a child of God and an inheritor of eternal bliss.

There was something so novel to me and so beautiful in her fervency of prayer, that the tears came into my eyes, and about a minute after she had finished, I said—

"I now recollect, at least, I think I do—for the memory of it is very confused-that my mother used to kneel down by me and pray just as you have done. Oh, how I wish I had a mother!"

"My child," replied she, "promise me that you will be a good and obedient son, and I will be a mother to you."

"Will you? Oh! how kind of you. Yes, I will be all you wish; I will work for you day and night if it is necessary. I will do everything, if you will but be my mother."

"I will do my duty to you as a mother most strictly," replied she; "so that is agreed upon. Now, you had better go to sleep, if you can."

"But I must first ask you a question. Why did you thank God for the seamen having left us here, instead of taking us with them?"

"Because the boat was overloaded as it was; because the men, having liquor, would become careless and desperate, and submit to no control; and therefore I think there is little or no chance of their ever arriving anywhere safe, but that they will perish miserably in some way or another. This, I consider, is the probability, unless the Almighty in his mercy should be pleased to come to their assistance, and allow them to fall in with some vessel soon after their departure."

"Do you think, then, that God prevented our going with them on purpose that we might not share their fate?"

"I do! God regulates everything. Had it been better for us that we should have gone, he would have permitted it; but he willed it otherwise, and we must bow to his will with a full faith, that he orders everything for the best."

"And you say that God will give us all that we ask for in our prayers?"

"Yes, if we pray fervently and in faith, and ask it in the name of Jesus Christ; that is, he will grant all we pray for, that is good for us, but not what is not good for us; or when we ask anything, we do not know that we are asking what is proper or not—but he does. We may ask what would be hurtful to us, and then, in his love for us, he denies it. For instance, suppose you had been accustomed to pray, you must have prayed God that he would permit you to leave this island in the boat, as you are so anxious to go away; but supposing that boat is lost, as I imagine it will be, surely it would have been a kindness in God, who knew that it would be lost, not to grant your prayer. Is it not so?"

"Yes, I see now, thank you; now I will go to sleep—good-night."

CHAPTER XXIV

I awoke the next morning quite recovered from my illness of the day before, and was out of the cabin before Mrs Reichardt, who still remained behind the screen which she had put up after I had gone to sleep. It was a beautiful morning, the water was smooth, and merely rippled with a light breeze, and the sun shone bright. I felt well and happy. I lighted a fire to broil the fish for breakfast, as there was a sufficiency left, and then got my fishing-lines ready to catch some larger fish to reinhabit my pond at the bathing pool. Mrs Reichardt came out of the cabin and found me playing with Nero.

"Good morning, dear mother," said I, for I felt most kindly towards her.

"Good morning, my dear boy," replied she. "Are you quite well?"

"Quite well; and I have got my lines all ready, for I have been thinking that until the birds come, we must live on fish altogether, and we can only take them in fine weather like this; so we must not lose such a day."

"Certainly not. As soon as we have breakfasted, we will go down and fish. I can fish very well, I am used to it. We must both work now; but first go for your Bible, that we may read a little."

I did so, and after she had read a chapter she prayed, and I knelt by her side; then we breakfasted, and as soon as we had breakfasted, we set off to the bathing-pool.

"Do you know if they left anything behind them, Frank?"

"Yes," replied I, "they left some oars, I believe, and a long line and we have the shovel, and the hammer, and the boat's small sail, up at the cabin."

"Well, we shall see very soon," replied she, as we went down the path.

When we arrived at the bathing-pool, the first thing that met my eyes made me leap with joy. "Oh! mother! mother! they've left the iron pot; I did so long for it; and as I lay awake this morning, I thought that if I prayed for anything, it would be for the iron pot. I was tired of dried birds, and they ate so different when they were boiled up in the pot with potatoes."

"I am equally glad, Frank, for I do not like victuals uncooked; but now let us first see what else they have thrown out of the boat."

"Why they have put on shore three of the little casks of water," said I; "they took them all on board."

"They have so, I suppose, because the boat was too heavy, and they would not part with the liquor. Foolish men, they will now not have more than six days' water, and will suffer dreadfully."

We then looked round the rocks and found that they had left the iron kettle, three breakers, five oars, and a harpoon and staffs; a gang-board, a whale line of 200 fathoms, an old saw, a bag of broad-headed nails, and two large pieces of sheet-iron.

"That saw may be very useful to us," said Mrs Reichardt, "especially as you have files in your chest. Indeed, if we want them, we may convert one-half of the saw into knives."

"Into knives! How?"

"I will shew you; and these pieces of sheet-iron I could use again. You see the sheet-iron was put on to repair any hole which might be made in the boat, and they have thrown it out, as well as the hammer and nails. I wonder at John Gough permitting it."

"I heard them quarrelling with him as I came out yesterday to fetch you down; they would not mind what he said."

"No, or we should not have been left here," replied she; "John Gough was too good a man to have allowed it, if he could have prevented it. That sheet-iron will be very useful. Do you know what for? to broil fish on, or anything else. We must turn up the corners with the hammer. But now we must lose no more time, but fish all day long, and not think of eating till supper time."

Accordingly we threw out our lines, and the fish taking the bait freely, we soon hauled in more than a dozen large fish, which I put into the bathing-pool.

"What use can we make of that long line which they have left?"

"A good many; but the best use we can make of it, is to turn it into fishing-lines, when we require new ones."

"But how can we do that, it is so thick and heavy?"

"Yes, but I will show you how to unlay it, and then make it up again. Recollect, Frank, that I have been the wife of a Missionary, and have followed my husband wherever he went; sometimes we have been well off, sometimes as badly off as you and I are now—for a Missionary has to go through great dangers, and great hardships, as you would acknowledge if you ever heard my life, or rather that of my husband."

"Won't you tell it to me?"

"Yes, perhaps I will, some day or another; but what I wish to point out to you now is, that being his wife, and sharing his danger and privation, I have been often obliged to work hard and to obtain my living as I could. In England, women do little except in the house, but a Missionary's wife is obliged to work with the men, and as a man very often, and therefore learns to do many things of which women in general are ignorant. You understand now?"

"Oh yes. I have thought already that you appear to know more than Jackson did."

"I should think not; but Jackson was not fond of work I expect, and I am. And now, Frank, you little thought that when you so tardily went to work the other day to plant potatoes for the benefit of any one that might hereafter come to the island, that you were planting for yourself, and would reap the benefit of your own kind act; for if you had not assisted, of course I could not have done it by myself: so true it is, that even in this world you are very often rewarded for a good action."

"But are not you always?"

"No, my child, you must not expect that; but if not rewarded in this world, you will be rewarded in the next."

"I don't understand that."

"I suppose that you hardly can, but I will explain all that to you, if God spare my life; but it must be at a more seasonable time."

We continued fishing till late in the afternoon, by which time we had taken twenty-eight large fish, about seven to nine pounds' weight; Mrs Reichardt then proposed that we should leave off, as we had already provision for a fortnight.

I hauled out one more fish, which she took with her to cook for our supper, and having coiled up my lines, I then commenced, as she had told me to do, carrying up the articles left by the boat's crew at the bathing-pool. The first thing I seized upon was the coveted iron kettle; I was quite overjoyed at the possession of this article, and I had good reason to be. In my other hand I carried the saw and the bag of nails. As soon as I had deposited them at the cabin, I went down again, and before supper was ready I had brought up everything except the three breakers of water, which I left where they were, as we did not want them for present use, whatever we might hereafter. We were both rather tired, and were glad to go to bed after we had taken our supper.

CHAPTER XXV

When we met the following morning, my mother, as I shall in future call her, said to me, "This will be a busy day, Frank, for we have a great many arrangements to make in the cabin, so that we may be comfortable. In future the cabin must be kept much more clean and tidy than it is—but that is my business more than yours. Let us get our breakfasts, and then we will begin."

"I don't know what you want me to do," replied I; "but I will do it if I can, as soon as you tell me."

"My dear boy, a woman requires a portion of the cabin to herself, as it is not the custom for women to live altogether with men. Now, what I wish is, that the hinder part of the cabin, where you used to stow away your dried birds, should be made over to me. We have oars with which we can make a division, and then nail up seal skins, so that I may have that part of the cabin to myself. Now, do you understand what I want?"

"Yes, but the oars are longer than the cabin is wide," observed I. "How shall we manage it?"

"We have the old saw, and that will do well enough to cut them off, without its being sharpened."

"I never saw one used," replied I, "and I don't understand it."

"I will soon show you. First, we must measure the width of the cabin. I shall not take away more than one third of it."

My mother went into the cabin, and I followed her. With a piece of fishing-line, she took the width of the cabin, and then the height up to the rafters for the door posts. We then went out, and with the saw, which she showed me how to use, and which astonished me very much, when I perceived its effects, the oars were cut up to the proper length. Gimlets I had already from the sea-chest, and nails and hammer we had just obtained from the boat, so that before the forenoon was over, the framework was all ready for nailing on the seal skins. The bag of broad-headed short nails, which had been thrown on the rocks, were excellent for this purpose, and, as I had plenty of skins, the cabin was soon divided off, with a skin between the door-jambs hanging down loose, so that any one might enter. I went inside after it was complete. "But," said I, "you have no light to see what you are about."

"Not yet, but I soon will have," replied my mother. "Bring the saw here, Frank. Observe, you must cut through the side of the cabin here, a square hole of this size; three of the planks cut through will be sufficient. Begin here."

I did as she directed me, and in the course of half an hour, I had cut out of the south side of the cabin a window about two feet square, which admitted plenty of light.

"But won't it make it cold at night?" said I.

"We will prevent that," replied she, and she took out a piece of white linen, and with some broad-headed nails, she nailed it up, so as to prevent the air from coming in, although there was still plenty of light. "There," said she, "that is but a coarse job, which I will mend bye-and-bye, but it will do for the present."

"Well, it is very nice and comfortable now," said I, looking round it. "Now what shall I bring in?"

"Nothing for the bed but seal skins," said she. "I do not like the feathers. The seal skins are stiff at present, but I think we may be able to soften them bye-and-bye. Now, Frank, your chest had better come in here, as it is of no use where it is, and we will make a storeroom of it, to hold all our valuables."

"What, the diamonds?" replied I.

"My dear boy, we have articles to put into the chest, which, in our present position, are more valuable to us than all the diamonds in the world. Tell me now, yourself, what do you prefer and set most value upon, your belt of diamonds, or the iron kettle?"

"The iron kettle, to be sure," replied I.

"Exactly so; and there are many things in our possession as valuable as the iron kettle, as you will hereafter acknowledge. Now do you go and get ready some fire for us, and I will finish here by myself. Nero, keep out, sir—you are never to come into this cabin."

I went with Nero for a fish and when I returned, I determined that I would use the iron kettle. I put it on with water and boiled the fish, and I thought that it ate better than broiled on the embers, which made it too dry.

As we sat at our meal, I said, "Dear mother, what are we to do next?"

"To-morrow morning we will put the cabin into better order, and put away all our things instead of leaving them about the platform in this way. Then I will carefully look over all that we have got, and put them away in the chest. I have not yet seen the contents of the chest."

The next day it was very cloudy and, rough weather, blowing fresh. After breakfast we set to work. We cleared out the floor of the cabin, which was strewed with all manner of things, for Jackson and I had not been very particular. The whale line was coiled up and put into one corner, and every thing else was brought in and a place found for it.

"We must contrive some shelves," said my mother, "that we may put things on them, or else we never can be tidy; and we have not one except that which holds the books. I think we can manage it. We have two oars left besides the boat's yard; we will nail them along the side of the cabin, about a foot or more from it, and then we will cut some of the boat's sail, and nail the canvas from the side of the cabin to the oars, and that will make a sort of shelf which will hold our things."

I brought in the oars, they were measured and cut off and nailed up. The canvas was then stretched from the side of the cabin to the oar, and nailed with the broad-headed nails, and made two capital shelves on each side of the cabin, running from one end to the other.

"There," said my mother, "that is a good job. Now we will examine the chest and put everything away and in its place."

My mother took out all the clothes, and folded them up. When she found the roll of duck which was at the bottom, she said—

"I am glad to find this as I can make a dress for myself much better for this island than this black stuff dress which I now wear, and which I will put by to wear in case we should be taken off the island some of these days, for I must dress like other people when I am again among them. The clothes are sufficient to last you for a long while, but I shall only alter two shirts and two pair of trousers to your present size, as you will grow very fast. How old do you think you are now?"

I replied, "About sixteen years old, or perhaps more."

"I should think that was about your age."

Having examined and folded up every article of clothing in the chest, the tools, spyglass, &c., were put by me on the shelves, and then we examined the box containing the thread, needles, fishhooks, and other articles, such as buttons, &c.

"These are valuable," said she; "I have some of my own to put along with them. Go and fetch my basket, I have not yet had time to look into it since I left the ship."

"What is there in it?"

"Except brushes and combs, I can hardly say. When I travelled about, I always carried my basket, containing those things most requisite for daily use, and in the basket I put everything that I wished to preserve, till I had an opportunity to put it away. When I embarked on board of the whaler, I brought my basket on my arm as usual, but except opening it for my brushes and combs or scissors, I have not examined it for months."

"What are brushes and combs and scissors?"

"That I will shew you," replied she, opening the lid of the basket. "These are the brushes and combs for cleaning the hair, and these are scissors. Now we will take everything out."

The basket did indeed appear to contain a wonderful quantity of things, almost all new to me. There were two brushes, twelve combs, three pair of scissors, a penknife, a little bottle of ink, some pens, a woman's thimble, a piece of wax, a case of needles, thread and silk, a piece of India ink, and a camel's-hair brush, sealing-wax, sticking plaster, a box of pills, some tape and bobbin, paper of pins, a magnifying glass, silver pencil case, some money in a purse, black shoe ribbon, and many other articles which I have forgotten. All I know is that I never was so much interested ever after at any show as I was with the contents of this basket, all of which were explained to me by my mother, as to their uses, and how they were made. There were several little papers at the bottom of the basket which she said were seeds of plants, which she had collected to take to England with her, and that we would plant them here. As she shook the dust out of the basket after it was empty, two or three white things tumbled out, which she asked me to pick up and give to her.

"I don't know how they came here," said she, "but three of them are orange-pips which we will sow to-morrow, and the other is a pea, but of what kind I know not, we will sow that also—but I fear it will not come up, as it appears to me to be one of the peas served out to the sailors on board ship, and will be too old to grow. We can but try. Now we will put into the chest, with the other things that you have, what we do not want for present use, and then I can drive a nail into the side of my bedroom and hang my basket on it."

"But," said I, "this round glass—what is that for?"

"Put it on one side," replied she, "and to-morrow, if it is fine, I will shew you the use of it; but there are some things we have forgotten, which are your belt and the other articles you gave me to take for you when you thought we were to leave the island. They are in the bed-place opposite to yours."

I brought them, and she put away the mate's watch and sleeve buttons, and the other trinkets, &c., saying that she would examine the letters and papers at another time. The belt was examined, counting how many of the squares had stones in them, and then, with her scissors, she cut open one of the squares, and took out a white glittering thing like glass as it appeared to me, and looked at it carefully.

"I am no great judge of these things," said she, "but still I have picked up some little knowledge. This belt, if it contain all stones like this, must be of considerable value; now I must get out my needle and thread and sew it up again." She did, and put the belt away with the other articles in the chest. "And now," said she, "we have done a good day's work, and it is time to have something to eat."

CHAPTER XXVI

I must say that I was much better pleased with the appearance of the cabin, it was so neat and clean to what it had been, and everything was out of the way. The next day was a calm and clear day, and we went down to fish. We were fortunate, and procured almost as many as we had done at the previous fishing—they were all put in the bathing pool as before. When we went up to the cabin, as soon as the fish was put on the fire, under the direction of my mother, I turned up the sides of one of the pieces of sheet iron, so as to make a sort of dish. The other piece I did the same to, only not so high at the sides, as one piece was kept for baking the fish on and the other as a dish to put our dinner upon when cooked. That day we had been too busy with fishing to think of anything else, but on the following I recollected the magnifying glass, and brought it to her. She first showed me the power it had to magnify, with which I was much amused for a time, and she explained as well as she could to me the cause of its having that power, but I could not well understand her; I was more pleased with the effect than cognisant of the cause. Afterwards she sent me to the cabin for some of the dried moss which I used for tinder, and placing the glass so as to concentrate the rays of the sun, to my astonishment I saw the tinder caught fire. It was amazement more than astonishment, and I looked up to see where the fire came from. My mother explained to me, and I, to a certain degree, comprehended, but I was too anxious to have the glass in my own hands and try experiments. I lighted the tinder again-then I burnt my hand—then I singed one of the gannet's heads, and lastly, perceiving that Nero was fast asleep in the sun, I obtained the focus on his cold nose. He started up with a growl, which made me retreat, and I was perfectly satisfied with the result of my experiments. From that time, the fire was, when the sun shone, invariably lighted by the burning-glass, and very useful did I find it. As it was so portable, I always carried it with me, and when I had nothing to do, I magnified, or set fire, according to the humour of the moment.

Although I have not mentioned it, not a morning rose, but before breakfast, I read the Scriptures to my mother.

"There's so much in that book which I cannot understand," said I, one morning.

"I suspect that, living as you have, alone on this island, and having seen nothing of the world," replied my mother, "that there are not many books that you would understand."

"But I understand all that is said in the Beast and Bird Book," replied I.

"Perhaps you may, or think you do; but, Frank, you must not class the Bible with other books. The other books are the works of man, but the Bible is the word of God. There are many portions of that book which the cleverest men, who have devoted their lives to its study, cannot understand, and which never will be understood as long as this world endures. In many parts the Bible is a sealed book."

"But will it never be understood then by anybody?"

"There is quite as much of the Bible as is necessary for men to follow its precepts, and this is so clear that anybody may understand it—it contains all that is necessary for salvation; but there are passages, the true meaning of which we cannot explain, and which God, for his own purposes, will not permit us to. But if we do not know them now, we shall probably hereafter, when we have left this world, and our intellects more nearly approach God's."

"Well, I don't understand why we should not understand it."

"Frank," replied she, "look at that flower just in bloom. Do you understand how it is that that plant keeps alive—grows every year—every year throws out a large blue flower? Why should it do so? why should the flower always be blue? and whence comes that beautiful colour? Can you tell me? You see, you know that it does do so; but can you tell me what makes it do so?"

"No."

"Look at that bird. You know it is hatched from an egg. How is it that the inside of an egg is changed into a bird? How is it that the bird is covered with feathers, and has the power to fly? Can you explain to me yourself? You can walk about just as you please—you have the power of reasoning, and thinking, and of acting; but by what means is it that you possess that power? Can you tell? You know that is so, but you know no more. You can't tell why or how or what causes produce these effects—can you?"

"No."

"Well, then, if you are surrounded by all manner of things, living and dead, and see every day things which you cannot explain, or understand, why should you be surprised that, as God has not let you know by what means these effects are produced, that in his written word he should also keep from you that which for good purposes you are not permitted to know. Everything here is by God's will, and that must be sufficient for us. Now do you understand?"

"Yes, I see now what you mean, but I never thought about these things before. Tell me some more about the Bible."

"Not now. Some day I will give you a history of the Bible, and then you will understand the nature of the book, and why it was written; but not at present. Suppose, as we have nothing particular to do, you tell me all you know about yourself from Jackson, and all that happened while you lived with him. I have heard only part, and I should like to know all."

"Very well," replied I. "I will tell you everything, but it will take a long while."

"We shall have plenty of time to spare, my dear boy, I fear, before we leave this place; so, never mind time—tell me everything."

I commenced my narrative, but I was interrupted.

"Have you never been able to call your own mother to your memory?" said she.

"I think I can now, since I have seen you, but I could not before. I now can recollect a person dressed like you, kneeling down and praying by my side; and I said before, the figure has appeared in my dreams, and much oftener since you have been here."

"And your father?"

"I have not the slightest remembrance of him, or anybody else except my mother."

I then proceeded, and continued my narrative until it was time to go to bed; but as I was very circumstantial, and was often interrupted by questions, I had not told a quarter of what I had to say.

CHAPTER XXVII

Mrs Reichardt had promised to give me a history of the Bible; and one day, when the weather kept us both at home, she thus commenced her narrative:—

"The Bible is a history of God's doings for the salvation of man. It commences with the fall of man by disobedience, and ends with the sacrifice made for his reinstatement. As by one man, Adam, sin came into the world, so by one man, Jesus Christ, was sin and death overcome. If you will refer to the third chapter of Genesis, at the very commencement of the Bible, you will find that at the same time that Adam receives his punishment, a promise is made by the Lord, that the head of the serpent shall hereafter be bruised. The whole of the Bible, from the very commencement, is an announcement of the coming of Christ; so that as soon as the fault had been committed, the Almighty, in his mercy, had provided a remedy. Nothing is unknown or unforeseen by God.

"Recollect, Frank, that the Bible contains the history of God's doings, but it does not often tell us why such things were done. It must be sufficient for us to know that such was the will of God; when he thinks proper, he allows us to understand his ways, but to our limited capacities, most of his doings are inscrutable. But, are we to suppose that, because we, in our foolishness, cannot comprehend his reasons, that therefore they must be cavilled at? Do you understand me, Frank?"

"Yes," replied I; "I do pretty well."

"As I pointed out to you the other day, you see the blade of grass grow, and you see it flower, but how it does so you know not. If then you are surrounded all your life with innumerable things which you see but cannot comprehend—when all nature is a mystery to you—even yourself—how can you expect to understand the dealings of God in other things? When, therefore, you read the Bible, you must read it with faith."

"What is faith? I don't quite understand, mother."

"Frank, I have often told you of many things that are in England, where you one day hope to go. Now, if when you arrive in England, you find that everything that I have told you is quite true, you will be satisfied that I am worthy of belief."

"Yes."

"Well, suppose some one were to tell you something relative to any other country, which you could not understand, and you came to me and asked me if such were the case, would you, having found that I told you truth with regard to England, believe that what you had been told of this other country was true, if I positively asserted that it was so?"

"Of course I should, mother."

"Well, then, Frank, that would be faith; a belief in things not only not seen, but which you cannot understand. But to go on, I mention this because some people are so presumptuous as to ask the why and the wherefore of God's doings, and attempt to argue upon their justice, forgetting that the little reason they have is the gift of God, and that they must be endowed with intellect equal to the Almighty, to enable them to know and perceive that which he decides upon. But if God has not permitted us to understand all his ways, still, wherever we can trace the finger of God, we can always perceive that everything is directed by an all-wise and beneficent hand; and that, although the causes appear simple, the effects produced are extraordinary and wonderful. We shall observe this as we talk over the history of the Jews, in the Bible. But, I repeat, that we must study the whole of the Bible with faith, and not be continually asking ourselves, 'Why was this done?' If you will turn to the ninth chapter of the Epistle to the Romans, you will see what the Apostle Paul says on the subject: 'Nay but, O man, who art thou that repliest against God?' Shall the thing formed say to him that formed it, 'Why hast thou made me thus?' Do you not understand in what spirit the Bible should be read?"

"Yes, I do. We must read it as the Word of God, and believe all that we read in it."

"Exactly;—now we will proceed. After Adam's fall, the earth became so wicked that God destroyed it, leaving but Noah and his family to re-people it; and as soon as this was done, the Almighty prepared for his original intention for the future salvation of men. He selected Abraham, who was a good man, and who had faith, to be the father of a nation chosen for his own people—that was the Jewish nation. He told him that his seed should multiply as the stars in the heavens, and that all the nations of the earth should be blessed in him; that is, that from his descendants should Christ be born, who should be the salvation of men. Abraham's great-grandchildren were brought into Egypt, to live apart in the land of Goshen. You have read the history of Joseph and his brethren?"

"Oh yes; I know that well."

"Well, the Almighty wished the Jews should be a nation apart from others, and for that purpose he brought them into Egypt. But observe, Frank, by what simple and natural causes this was effected. It was by a dream of Joseph's, which, when he told them of it, irritated his brothers against him; they sold him as a slave, and he was sent into Egypt. There, having explained the dream of Pharaoh, he was made a ruler over Egypt, and saved that country from the famine which was in every other land. His brothers come down to buy corn, and he recognises them. He sends for his father and all the family, and establishes them in the land of Goshen, as shepherds, apart from the Egyptians. Here they multiplied fast; but after Joseph's elevation they were cruelly treated by the Egyptians, who became afraid of their rapid increase, and eventually the Kings of Egypt gave orders that all the male children of the Jews should be destroyed. It was at this time, when they were so oppressed and cruelly treated by the Egyptians, that God interfered and sent for Moses. Moses, like all the rest of the Jews, knew nothing of the true God, and was difficult to persuade, and it was only by miracles that he was convinced."

"Why did God keep the Jews apart from the Egyptians, and have them thrown in bondage?"

"Because he wished to prepare them to become his own peculiar people. By their being descended from Abraham, and having never intermarried with other nations, they had become a pure race; by being in bondage and severely treated, they had suffered and become united as a people. They knew no Gods but those worshipped by the Egyptians, and these Gods it was now the intention of the Almighty to confound, and prove to the Jews as worthless. At the same time he worked with his own nation in mystery, for when Moses asked him what God he was to tell his people that he was, the Almighty only replied by these words— *I am*, having no name like all the false Gods worshipped by the Egyptians. He was now about to prove, by his wonderful miracles, the difference between himself and the false Gods."

"What are miracles?"

"A miracle is doing that which man has no power of doing, proving that the party who does it is superior to man: for instance— to restore a dead man to life is a miracle, as none but God, or those empowered by God could do. Miracles were necessary, therefore, to prove to the Jews that the Almighty was the true God, and were resorted to by him in this instance, as well as in the coming of Our Saviour, when it was also necessary to prove that he was the Son of God. When the Almighty sent Moses to Pharaoh to demand that the Israelites should have permission to sacrifice in the desert, he purposely hardened the heart of Pharaoh that he might refuse the request."

"But why did he so?"

"Because he wanted to prove to the Israelites that he was the only true God and had Pharaoh consented to their going away, there would have been no opportunity of performing those miracles by which the Israelites were to be delivered, and by which they were to acknowledge him as their God."

Mrs Reichardt often renewed this conversation, till I became acquainted with Scriptural History.

CHAPTER XXVIII

The following morning, I went with Nero to take a couple of fish out of the pool. As soon as Nero had caught them, he went into the other part of the bathing pool to amuse himself, while I cleaned the fish, which I generally did before I went up to the cabin, giving him the heads and insides for his share, if I did not require any portion for the birds. Nero was full of play that morning, and when I threw the heads to him, as he frolicked in the water, he brought them out to the rocks, but instead of eating them, as usual, he laid them at my feet. I threw them in several times, and he continued to bring them out, and my mother, coming down to me, was watching him.

"I think," said she, "you must teach Nero to fetch and carry like a dog—try. Instead of the heads, throw in this piece of wood;" which she now broke off the boat-hook staff.

I did so, and Nero brought it out, as he had done the heads of the fish. I patted and coaxed the animal, and tried him again several times with success.

"Now," said my mother, "you must accustom him to certain words when you send him for anything. Always say, 'Fetch it, Nero!' and point with your finger."

"Why am I to do that, mother?" I asked.

"Because the object to be gained is, not that the animal should fetch out what you throw in, but what you send it to bring out which you have not thrown in. Do you understand?"

"Yes," replied I. "You mean if there were anything floating near on the sea, I should send him for it."

"Exactly. Then Nero would be of some use."

"I will soon teach him," replied I; "to-morrow I will send him into the sea after the piece of spar. I've no fear that he will go away now."

"I was thinking last night, Frank, whether they had taken the pail with them in the boat."

"The pail," said I; "I know where it is, but I quite forgot it. We left it up the ravine the last day we planted the potatoes."

"We did so, now I recollect. I will go for it while you get the breakfast ready."

We had now been for many weeks on a fish diet, and I must confess that I was tired of it, which was not the case when I lived upon the dried birds during the whole of the year. Why so I cannot tell, but I was soon to learn to relish fish, if I could obtain them.

It was not often that the wind blew direct on the shore, but coming from the northward and eastward, it was in a slanting direction, but occasionally, and chiefly about the time of the Equinoxes, the gales came on very heavy from the eastward, and then the wash of the seas upon the rocky coast was tremendous. Such was the case about this time. A fierce gale of wind from the eastward raised a sea which threw the surf and spray high over the loftiest of the rocks, and the violence of the wind bore the spray far inland. The gale had come on in the evening, and my mother and I, when we rose in the morning, were standing on the platform before the cabin, admiring the grandeur of the scene, but without the least idea that it was to be productive of so much misery to ourselves. My mother pointed out to me some passages in the Psalms and Old Testament bearing strongly upon the scene before us; after a time I called Nero, and went down with him to take fish out of the pool for our day's consumption. At that time we had a large supply in the pool—more than ever, I should say. When I arrived at the pool, I found the waves several feet in height rolling in over the ledges, and the pool one mass of foam, the water in it being at least two or three feet higher than usual; still it never occurred to me that there was any mischief done, until I had sent Nero in for the fish, and found that, after floundering and diving for some time, he did not bring out one. My mind misgave me, and I ordered him in again. He remained some time and then returned without a fish, and I was then satisfied that from the rolling in of the waves, and the unusual quantity of the water in the pool, the whole of the fish had escaped, and that we were now without any provisions or means of subsistence, until the weather should settle, and enable us to catch some more.

Aghast at the discovery, I ran up to the cabin, and called to my mother, who was in her bedroom.

"Oh, mother, all the fish have got out of the pool, and we have nothing to eat. I told you we should be starved."

"Take time, Frank, and take breath," replied she, "and then tell me what has happened, to cause this alarm and dismay, that you appear to be in."

I explained to her what had happened, and that Nero could not find one fish.

"I fear that what you say must be correct," replied she; "but we must put our trust in God. It is his will, and whatever he wills must be right."

I cannot say I was Christian enough at the time to acknowledge the truth of her reply, and I answered, "If God is as good and as gracious as you say, will he allow us to starve? Does he know that we are starving?" continued I.

"Does he know, Frank?" replied my mother; "what does the Bible say—that not a sparrow falls to the ground without his knowledge; and of how much more worth are you than many sparrows? Shame upon you, Frank!"

I was abashed but not satisfied, I therefore replied quietly, "We have nothing to eat, mother."

"Granted that we have lost all our fish, Frank, still we are not yet starving; the weather may moderate tomorrow, and we may catch some more, or even if it should not till the day afterwards, we can bear to be two days without food. Let us hope for the best and put our trust in God—let us pray to him and ask him for his assistance. He can rebuke these stormy waters—he can always find means of helping those who put confidence in him, and will send us aid when all hope appears gone. Pray, Frank, as I will do, fervently, and believing that your prayer is heard—pray with faith, and your prayer will be answered."

"It is not always so," replied I; "you have told me of many people who have died of starvation."

"I grant it, and for all wise purposes they were permitted so to do, but the Almighty had reasons for permitting it, unknown to us, but which you may depend upon it, were good. We cannot fathom his decrees. He may even now decide that such is to be our fate; but if so, depend upon it, Frank, all is right, and what appears to you now as cruel and neglectful of you, would, if the future could be looked into by us, prove to have been an act of mercy."

"Do you think, then, that we shall starve?"

"I do not—I have too much faith in God's mercy, and I do not think that he would have preserved our lives by preventing the men from taking us into the boat, if we were now to starve. God is not inconsistent; and I feel assured that, forlorn as our present position appears to be, and tried as our faith in him may be, we shall still be preserved, and live to be monuments of his gracious love and kindness."

These words of my mother and the implicit confidence which she appeared to have, much revived me. "Well," said I, "I hope you are right, my dear mother, and now I think of it," continued I, brightening up at the idea, "if the worst come to the worst, we can eat the birds; I don't care much for them now, and if I did, you should not starve, mother."

"I believe you would not hesitate to sacrifice the birds, Frank, but a greater sacrifice may be demanded of you."

"What?" inquired I; and then after a little thought, I said, "You don't mean Nero, mother?"

"To tell the truth, I did mean Nero, Frank, for the birds will not be a support for more than a day or two."

"I never could kill Nero, mother," replied I gloomily, and walking away into the cabin, I sat down very melancholy at the idea of my favourite being sacrificed; to me it appeared quite horrible, and my mother having referred to it, made her fall very much in my good opinion. Alas! I was indeed young and foolish, and little thought what a change would take place in my feelings. As for the birds, as I really did not care for them, I resolved to kill two of them for our day's meal, and returning to the platform I had laid hold of the two that were there and had seized both by the neck, when my mother asked me what I was going to do.

"Kill them, and put them in the pot for our dinner," replied I.

"Nay, Frank! you are too hasty. Let us make some little sacrifice, even for the poor birds. We surely can fast one day without very great suffering. To-morrow will be time enough."

I dropped the birds from my hand, tacitly consenting to her proposal. It was not, however, for the sake of the birds that I did so, but because one day's respite for the birds would be a day's respite for Nero.

"Come," said my mother, "let us go into the cabin and get some work. I will alter some of the clothes for you. What will you do?"

"I don't know," replied I, "but I will do whatever you tell me."

"Well, then, I perceive that the two fishing-lines are much worn, and they may break very soon, and then we shall be without the means of taking fish, even if the weather is fine, so now we will cut off some of the whale line, and when it is unravelled, I will show you how to lay it up again into fishing line; and, perhaps, instead of altering the clothes, I had better help you, as fishing-lines are now of more consequence to us than anything else."

This was an arrangement which I gladly consented to. In a short time the whale line was unravelled, and my mother showed me how to lay it up in three yarns, so as to make a stout fishing line. She assisted, and the time passed away more rapidly than I had expected it would.

"You are very clever, mother," said I.

"No, my child, I am not, but I certainly do know many things which women in general are not acquainted with; but the reason of this is, I have lived a life of wandering, and occasional hardships. Often left to our own resources, when my husband and I were among strangers, we found the necessity of learning to do many things for ourselves, which those who have money usually employ others to do for them; but I have been in situations where even money was of no use, and had to trust entirely to myself. I have therefore always made it a rule to learn everything that I could; and as I have passed much of my life in sailing over the deep waters, I obtained much useful knowledge from the seamen, and this of laying up fishing lines is one of the arts which they communicated to me. Now, you see, I reap the advantage of it."

"Yes," replied I; "and so do I. How lucky it was that you came to this island!"

"Lucky for me, do you mean, Frank?"

"No, mother! I mean how lucky for me."

"I trust that I have been sent here to be useful, Frank, and with that feeling I cheerfully submit to the will of God. He has sent me that I may be useful to you, I do not doubt; and if by my means you are drawn towards him, and, eventually, become one of his children, I shall have fulfilled my mission."

"I do not understand you quite, mother."

"No, you cannot as yet, but everything in season," replied she, slowly musing; "'First the blade, then the ear, and then the full corn in the ear,'"

"Mother," said I, "I should like to hear the whole story of your life. You know I have told you all that I know about myself. Now suppose you tell me your history, and that of your husband. You did say that perhaps, one day you would. Do you recollect?"

"Yes, I do recollect that I did make a sort of promise, Frank, and I promise you now that some day I will fulfil it; but I am not sure that you will understand or profit by the history now, so much as you may bye-and-bye."

"Well, but mother, you can tell me the story twice, and I shall be glad to hear it again, so tell it to me now, to amuse me, and bye-and-bye that I may profit by it."

My mother smiled, which she very seldom did, and said—

"Well, Frank, as I know you would at any time give up your dinner to listen to a story, and as you will have no dinner to-day, I think it is but fair that I should consent to your wish. Who shall I begin with—with my husband or with myself?"

"Pray begin with your own history," replied I.

CHAPTER XXIX

"I am the daughter of a parish clerk in a small market town near the southern coast of England, within a few miles of a large seaport."

"What is a parish clerk?" I asked, interrupting my mother at the commencement of her promised narrative.

"A parish clerk," she replied, "is a man who is employed in the parish or place to which he belongs, to fulfil certain humble duties in connection with the church or place of worship where the people meet together to worship God."

"What does he do there?" I inquired.

"He gives out the psalms that are to be sung, leads the congregation in making their responses to the minister appointed to perform the services of the church; has the custody of the registry of births, deaths, and burials of the inhabitants, and the care of the church monuments, and of other property belonging to the building. In some places he also fulfils the duties of bell-ringer and grave-digger; that is to say, by ringing a large bell at the top of the church, he summons the people to their devotions, during their lives, and digs a hole in consecrated ground, surrounding the sacred building, to receive their bodies when dead."

I mused on this strange combination of offices, and entertained a notion of the importance of such a functionary, which I afterwards found was completely at variance with the real state of the case.

"My father," she resumed, "not only fulfilled all these duties, but contrived to perform the functions of schoolmaster to the parish children."

"What are parish children?" I asked eagerly. "I know what children are, as Jackson represented to me that I was the child of my father and mother, but what makes children, parish children?"

"They are the children of the poor," Mrs Reichardt replied, "who, not being able to afford them instruction, willingly allow them to be taught at the expense of the people of the parish generally."

I thought this a praiseworthy arrangement. I knew nothing of poors-rates, and the system of giving relief to the poor of the parish, so long used in England, afterwards explained to me, but the kindness and wisdom of this plan of instruction became evident to my understanding. I was proceeding to ask other questions, when my mother stopped them by saying, that if I expected her to get through her story, I must let her proceed without further interruption; for many things would be mentioned by her which demanded explanation, for one so completely unaware of their existence as myself, and that it would be impossible to make me thoroughly acquainted with such things within any reasonable time; the proper explanations, she promised, should follow. She then proceeded.

"My father, it may be thought, had enough on his hands, but in an obscure country town, it is not unusual for one man to unite the occupations of several, and this was particularly the case with my father, who, in addition to the offices I have enumerated, was the best cattle-doctor and bone-setter within ten miles; and often earned his bread at different kinds of farmer's work, such as thatching, hedging, ditching and the like. Nevertheless, he found time to read his Bible, and bring up his only daughter religiously. This daughter was myself."

"What had become of your mother?" I asked, as I thought it strange Mrs Reichardt should only mention one parent.

"She had died very soon after my birth," she answered, "and I was left at first to the care of a poor woman, who nursed me; as soon, however, as I could run about, and had exhibited some signs of intelligence, my father began to get so partial to me, that he very reluctantly allowed me to go out of his sight. He took great pains in teaching me what he knew, and though the extent of his acquirements was by no means great, it was sufficient to lay a good foundation, and establish a desire for more comprehensive information, which I sought every available means to obtain.

"I remember that at a very early age I exhibited an extraordinary curiosity for a child; constantly asking questions, not only of my father, but of all his friends and visitors, and, as they seemed to consider me a quick and lively child, they took pleasure in satisfying my inquisitive spirit. In this way I gained a great deal of knowledge, and, by observation of what passed around me, a great deal more.

"It soon became a source of pride and gratification with my father, to ask me to read the Bible to him. This naturally led to a good many inquiries on my part, and numerous explanations on his. In course of time, I became familiar with all the sacred writings, and knew their spirit and meaning much better than many persons who were more than double my age.

"My fondness for such studies, and consequent reputation, attracted the attention of Dr Brightwell, the clergyman of our parish, who had the kindness to let me share the instructions of his children, and still further advanced my education, and still more increased my natural predilection for religious information. By the time I was thirteen, I became quite a prodigy in Christian learning, and was often sent for to the parsonage, to astonish the great people of the neighbourhood, by the facility with which I answered the most puzzling questions that were put to me, respecting the great mysteries of Christianity."

CHAPTER XXX

It was about this time that I first became acquainted with an orphan boy, an inmate of the workhouse, who had been left to the care of the parish by the sudden death of his parents, a German clock-maker and his wife, from a malignant fever which had visited the neighbourhood, and taken off a considerable portion of the labouring population. I had been sent on errands from my father, to the master of the workhouse, a severe, sullen man, of whom I had a great dread, and I noticed this child, in consequence of his pale and melancholy countenance, and apparently miserable condition. I observed that no one took any notice of him; and that he was allowed to wander about the great straggling workhouse, among the insane, the idiotic, and the imbecile, without the slightest attention being paid to his going and coming; in short, he lived the wretched life of a workhouse boy.

"I see that you are eager to ask what is a workhouse boy," said my mother, "so I will anticipate your question. There is, in the various parishes of the country to which we both belong, a building expressly set apart for the accommodation and support of the destitute and disabled poor. It usually contains inmates of all ages, from the infant just born, to the very aged, whose infirmities shew them to be on the verge of the grave. They are all known to be in a state of helpless poverty, and quite unable to earn a subsistence for themselves. In this building they are clothed and fed; the younger provided with instruction necessary to put them in the way of earning a livelihood; the elders of the community enjoying the consolations of religion, accorded to them by the regular visits of the chaplain."

"I suppose," I here observed, "that the people who lived there, were deeply impressed with their good fortune in finding such an asylum?"

"As far as I could ever ascertain," Mrs Reichardt replied, "it was exactly the reverse. It was always thought so degrading to enter a workhouse, that the industrious labourer would endure any and every privation rather than live there. An honest hard-working man must be sorely driven indeed, to seek such a shelter in his distress."

"That seems strange," I observed. "Why should he object to receive what he so much stands in need of?"

"When he thus comes upon the funds of the parish," answered my mother, "he becomes what is called a pauper, and among the English peasantry of the better sort, there is the greatest possible aversion to be ranked with this degraded class. Consequently, the inmates of the workhouses are either those whose infirmities prevent their earning a subsistence, or the idle and the dissolute, who feel none of the honest prejudices of self-dependence, and care only to live from day to day on the coarse and meagre fare afforded them by the charity of their wealthier and more industrious fellow-creatures.

"The case of this poor boy I thought very pitiable. I found out that his name was Heinrich Reichardt. He could speak no language but his own, and therefore his wants remained unknown, and his feelings unregarded. He had been brought up with a certain sense of comfort and decency, which was cruelly outraged by the position in which he found himself placed by the sudden death of his parents. I observed that he was often in tears, and his fair features and light hair contrasted remarkably with the squalid faces and matted locks of his companions. His wretchedness never failed to make a deep impression on me.

"I brought him little presents, and strove to express my sympathy for his sufferings. He seemed, at first, more surprised than grateful, but I shortly discovered that my attentions gave him unusual pleasure, and he looked upon my visits as his only solace and gratification.

"Even at this period I exercised considerable influence over my father, and I managed to interest him in the case of the poor foreign boy to such an extent, that he was induced to take him out of the workhouse, and find him a home under his own roof. He was at first reluctant to burden himself with the bringing up of a child, who, from his foreign language and habits, could be of little use to him in his avocations; but I promised to teach him English, and all other learning of which he stood most in need, and assured my father that in a prodigious short time I would make him a much abler assistant than he was likely to find among the boys of the town.

"My father's desire to please me, rather than any faith he reposed in my assertions, led him to allow me to do as I pleased in this affair. I lost no time, therefore, in beginning my course of instruction, and in a few weeks ascertained that I had an apt pupil, who was determined to proceed with his education as fast as circumstances would admit. We were soon able to express our ideas to each other, and in a few months read together the book out of which I had received so many invaluable lessons.

"In a short time, I became not less proud of, than partial to, my pupil. I took him through the same studies which I had pursued under the auspices of our clergyman, and was secretly pleased to find, not only that he was singularly quick in imbibing my instructions, but displayed a strong natural taste for those investigations towards which I had shown so marked a bias.

"Day after day have we sat together discoursing of the great events recorded in Holy Writ: going over every chapter of its marvellous records, page by page, till the whole was so firmly fixed upon our minds, that we had no necessity during our conversations for referring to the Sacred Book. We found examples we held up to ourselves for imitation; we found incidents we regarded as promises of Divine protection; we found consolation and comfort, as well as exhortation and advice; and, moreover, we found a sort of instruction that led us to select for ourselves duties that apparently tended to bring us nearer to the Great Being whose goodness we had so diligently studied.

"My father seemed as much pleased with my successful teaching, as he had been with my successful learning; and when young Reichardt turned out a remarkably handy and intelligent lad, to whose assistance in some of his avocations he could have recourse with perfect confidence in his cleverness and discretion, he grew extremely partial to him. Dr Brightwell also proved his friend, and in a few years, the condition of the friendless workhouse boy was so changed, he could not have been taken for the same person.

"He was a boy of a very grateful spirit, and always regarded me with the devotion of a most thankful heart. Often would he contrast the wretchedness of his previous condition, with the happiness he now enjoyed, and express in the warmest terms his obligations to me for the important service I had rendered him in rescuing him from the abject misery of the workhouse. Under these circumstances, it is not extraordinary, that we should learn to regard each other with the liveliest feelings of affection, and while we were still children, endured all the transports and torments which make up the existence of more experienced lovers."

"I do not like interrupting you," I here observed, "but I certainly should like to know what is meant by the word lovers?"

"I can scarcely explain it to you satisfactorily at present," said Mrs Reichardt, with a smile; "but I have no doubt, before many years have passed over your head—always provided that you escape from this island—you will understand it without requiring any explanation. But I must now leave my story, as many things of much consequence to our future welfare now demand my careful attention."

I could not then ascertain from her what was meant by the word whose meaning I had asked. It had very much excited my curiosity, but she left me to attend to her domestic duties, of which she was extremely regardful, and I had no opportunity at that time of eliciting from her the explanation I desired.

CHAPTER XXXI

It is impossible for me to overrate the value of Mrs Reichardt's assistance. Indeed had it not been for her, circumstanced as I was at this particular period, I should in all probability have perished. Her exhortations saved me from despair, when our position seemed to have grown quite desperate. But example did more, even, than precept. Her ingenuity in devising expedients, her activity in putting them in force, her unfailing cheerfulness under disappointment, and Christian resignation under privation, produced the best results. I was enabled to bear up against the ill effects of our crippled resources, consequent upon the ill conduct of the sailors of the whaler, and the failure of our fish-pond.

She manufactured strong lines for deep sea fishing, and having discovered a shelf of rock, little more than two feet above the sea, to which with a good deal of difficulty I could descend, I took my stand one day on the rock with my lines baited with a piece of one of my feathered favourites, whom dire necessity had at last forced me to destroy. I waited with all the patience of a veteran angler. I knew the water to be very deep, and it lay in a sheltered nook or corner of the rocks about ten feet across; I allowed the line to drop some three or four yards, and not having any float, could only tell I had a bite by feeling a pull at the line, which was wound round my arm.

After some time having been passed in this way, my attention was withdrawn from the line, and given to the narrative I had so lately heard—that is to say, though my eyes were still fixed upon the line, I had completely given up my thoughts to the story of the poor German boy, who had been snatched from poverty by the interference of the parish clerk's daughter, and I contrived to speculate on what I should have done under such circumstances, imagining all sorts of extravagances in which I should have indulged, to testify my gratitude to so amiable and benevolent a friend.

A singular course of ideal scenes followed each other in quick succession in my mind—as I fancied myself the hero of a similar adventure. I regarded my imaginary benefactress with feelings of such intensity as I had never before experienced; and it seemed that I was to her the exciting object of sentiments of a like nature, the knowledge of which awoke in our hearts the most agreeable sensations.

I was rudely disturbed out of this day-dream by finding myself suddenly plunged into the deep water beneath me. The shock was so startling, that some seconds elapsed before I could comprehend my situation; and then it became clear that I must have hooked a fish, that had not only succeeded in pulling me off my balance, but the line by which he was held being round my arm, cutting painfully into the flesh, threatened drowning by keeping me under water. With great difficulty I managed to rise to the surface, and loosened the windings of the line from my limb; then, anxious to retain possession of what from its force must have been a fish well worth some trouble in catching, I held on with both hands, and pulled with all my strength.

At first, by main force I was drawn through the water; then when I found the strain slacken, I drew in the line. This manoeuvre was repeated several times, till I succeeded in obtaining a view of what I had caught; or, more properly speaking, of what had caught me. It was merely a glimpse; for the fish, which was a very large one, getting a sight of me within a few yards of him, made some desperate plunges, and again darted off, dragging me along with him, sometimes under the water, and sometimes on the surface.

His body was nearly round, and about seven or eight feet long— rather a formidable antagonist for close quarters; nevertheless, I was most eager to get at him, the more so, when I ascertained that his resistance was evidently decreasing. I continued to approach, and at last got near enough to plunge my knife up to the haft in his head, which at once put an end to the struggle.

But now another difficulty presented itself. In the ardour of the chase I had been drawn nearly a mile from the island, and I found it impossible to carry back the produce of my sport, exhausted as I was by the efforts I had made in capturing him. I knew I could not swim with such a burthen for the most inconsiderable portion of the distance. My fish therefore must be abandoned. Here was a bountiful supply of food, as soon as placed within reach, rendered totally unavailable.

I thought of Mrs Reichardt. I thought how gratified she would have been, could I have brought to her such an excellent addition to our scanty stock of food. Then I thought of her steadfast reliance upon Providence, and what valuable lessons of piety and wisdom she would read me, if she found me depressed by my disappointment.

CHAPTER XXXII

As soon as I could disconnect my tackle from the dead fish, I turned my face homewards, and struck out manfully for the shore; luckily I did not observe any sharks. I landed safely without further adventure, and immediately sought my kind friend and companion, whom I found, as usual, industriously employed in endeavouring to secure me additional comforts. If she was not engaged in ordinary women's work, making, mending, cleaning, or improving, in our habitation, she was sure to be found doing something in the immediate neighbourhood, which, though less feminine, shewed no less forethought, prudence, and sagacity.

Our garden had prospered wonderfully under her hands. The ground seemed now stocked with various kinds of vegetation, of which I neither knew the value, nor the proper mode of cultivation; and we seemed about to be surrounded with shrubs and plants— many of very pleasing appearance—that must in a short time entirely change the aspect of the place.

She heard my adventure with a good deal of interest, only remonstrating with me upon my want of caution, and dwelling upon the fatal consequences that must have ensued to herself, had I been drowned or disabled by falling from the rock, or devoured by the sharks.

"You may consider yourself, my dear son," she observed, with serious earnestness, "to have been under the Divine care. Nothing can be clearer than that a wise and kind Providence is continually watching over his creatures when placed in unusual or perilous circumstances. He occasionally affords them manifestations of his favour, to encourage them when engaged in good works. This shews the comprehensive eye of the master of many workmen, who overlooks the labours of his more industrious servants, and indicates to them his regard for their welfare and appreciation of their labours."

"But surely," I interposed, "if I had been under the superintendence of the Providence of which you speak, I should not have been obliged to abandon so capital a fish, when I had endured such trouble to capture it, and when its possession was so necessary to our comfort, nay, even to our existence."

"The very abandonment of so unwieldy a creature," she replied, "is unanswerable evidence of a Divine interposition in your favour; for had you persisted in your intention of carrying it to the shore, there is but little doubt that its weight would have overpowered you, and that you would have been drowned; and then what would have become of me? A woman left in this desolate spot to her own resources, must soon be forced to give up the struggle for existence, from want of physical strength. Nevertheless, there are numerous instances on record, of women having surmounted hardships which few men could endure. Supported by our Heavenly Father, who is so powerful a protector of the weak, and friend of the helpless, the weakest of our weak sex may triumph over the most intolerable sufferings. I, however, am not over confident of being so supported, and therefore, I think it would be but shewing a proper consideration for your fellow exile, to act in every emergency with as much circumspection and prudence as possible."

I promised that for the future I would run no such risks, and added many professions of regard for her safety. They had the desired effect; I pretended to think no more of my disappointment, nevertheless, I found myself constantly dwelling on the size of my lost fish, and lamenting my being obliged to abandon him to his more voracious brethren of the deep. These thoughts so filled my mind that at night I continued to dream over again the whole incident, beginning with my patient angling from the rock, and concluding with my disconsolate swim to shore—and pursued my scaly antagonist quite as determinedly in my sleep as I had done in the deep waters.

I rose early after having passed so disturbed a night, and soon made my way to the usual haunt of Nero, whom I discovered in the sea near the rocks making all sorts of strange tumblings and divings, apparently after some dark object that was floating in the water. I called him away, to examine what it was that had so attracted his attention, and my surprise may be imagined when I made out the huge form of my enemy of the preceding day. My shouts and exclamations of joy soon brought Mrs Reichardt to the scene, and when she discovered the shape of this prodigious fish, her surprise seemed scarcely less than my own.

How to land him was our first consideration; and after some debate on the ways and means, I got a rope and leaped into the water with it, fastened a noose round his gills, and then swimming back and climbing the rock; we jointly tried to pull him up on to the shore. We hauled and tugged with all our force for a considerable time, but to very little effect; he was too heavy to pull up perpendicularly. At last we managed to drag him to a low piece of rock, and there I divided him into several pieces, which Mrs Reichardt carried away to dry and preserve in some way that she said would make the fish capital eating all the year round.

It was very palatable when dressed by her, and as she changed the manner of cooking several times, I never got tired of it. By its flavour, as far as I could judge from subsequent knowledge, the creature was something of the sturgeon kind of fish, but its proper name I never could learn; nor was I ever able to catch another, therefore, I must presume that it was a stranger in those seas. Nevertheless, he proved most acceptable to us both, for we should have fared but ill for some time, had it not been for his providential capture.

It was one afternoon, when we had been enjoying a capital meal at the expense of our great friend, that I led the subject to Mrs Reichardt's adventures, subsequently to where she broke off in the story of herself and the poor German boy; and though not without considerable reluctance, I induced her to proceed with her narrative.

CHAPTER XXXIII

"Our good minister Dr Brightwell," she commenced, "was a man of considerable scholastic attainments, and he delighted in making a display of them. At one time, he had been master of an extensive grammar school, and now he employed a good deal of his leisure in teaching those boys and girls of the town, who indicated the possession of anything like talent. The overseers used to talk jestingly to my father of the Doctor teaching plough-boys Greek and Latin; and wenches, whose chief employment was stone-picking in the fields, geography and the use of the globes. Even the churchwardens shook their heads, and privately thought the Rector a little out of his seven senses for wasting his learning upon such unprofitable scholars. Nevertheless, he continued his self-imposed task, without meeting any reward beyond the satisfaction of his own conscience. It was not till he added to his pupils myself and young Reichardt, that he felt he was doing his duty with some prospect of advantage.

"The spirit of emulation roused both of us to make extraordinary efforts to second our worthy master's endeavours: and this did not, as is usually the case, proceed from rivalry—it arose entirely from a desire of the one to stand well in the estimation of the other. In this way we learned the French and Latin languages, geography, and the usual branches of a superior education: but our bias was more particularly for religious knowledge, and our preceptor encouraged this, till we were almost as good theologians as himself.

"While this information was being carefully arranged and digested, there sprung up in our hearts so deep a devotion for each other, that we were miserable when absent and enjoyed no gratification so much as being in each other's society. We knew not then the full power and meaning of this preference, but, as we changed from boy and girl-hood to adult life, our feelings developed themselves into that attachment between the sexes, which from time immemorial has received the name of love."

"I think I know what that means, now," said I, as my day-dream, which was so rudely disturbed by my fall into the sea occurred to me.

"It would be strange if you did," she replied, "considering that it is quite impossible you should have become acquainted with it."

"Yes, I am certain I understand it very well," I rejoined, more confidently, and then added, not without some embarrassment, "If I were placed in the position of Heinrich Reichardt, I am quite sure I should feel towards any young female, who was so kind to me, the deepest regard and affection. I should like to be constantly near her, and should always desire that she should like me better than anyone else."

"That is quite as good an explanation of the matter, as I could expect from you," she observed, smiling. "But to return to my story. Our mutual attachment attracted general attention, and was the subject of much observation. But we had no enemies: and when we were met strolling together in the shady lanes, gathering wild flowers, or wandering through the woods in search of wild strawberries, no one thought it necessary to make any remark if we had our arms round each other's waist. My father, if he heard anything about it, did not interfere. Young Reichardt had made himself so useful to him, and shewed himself so remarkably clever in everything he undertook, that the old man loved him as his own son.

"It was a settled thing between us, that we were to become man and wife, as soon as we should be permitted. And many were our plans and schemes for the future. Heinrich considered himself to be in the position of Jacob, who served such a long and patient apprenticeship for Rachel; and though he confessed he should not like to wait so long for his wife as the patriarch had been made to do, he acknowledged he would rather serve my father to the full period, than give up all hope of possessing me.

"This happy state of things was, however, suddenly put an end to, by Dr Brightwell one day sending for my father. It was a long time before he came back, and when he did, he looked unusually grave and reserved. In an hour or so he communicated to me the result of his long interview with the Rector. The Doctor had resolved to send young Reichardt to a distant place, where many learned men lived together in colleges, for the purpose of further advancing his education, and fitting him for a religious teacher, to which vocation he had long expressed a desire to devote himself. The idea of separation seemed very terrible, but I at last got reconciled to it, in the belief that it would be greatly for Heinrich's advantage, and we parted at last with many tears, many protestations, some fears, but a great many more hopes.

"For some days after he had left me, everything seemed so strange, every one seemed so dull, every place seemed so desolate, that I felt as if I had been transported into some dismal scene, where I knew no one, and where there was no one likely to care about me in the slightest degree. My father went about his avocations in a different spirit to what he had so long been used to exhibit; it was evident he missed Heinrich as much as I did, and the villagers stared whenever I passed them—as though my ever going about without Heinrich, was something which they had never anticipated.

"In course of time, however, to all appearance, everything and every one went on in their daily course, as though no Heinrich had ever been heard of. My father would sometimes, when overpressed by business, refer to the able assistant he had lost, and now and then I heard a conjecture hazarded by some one or other of his most confidential friends, as to what young Reichardt was doing with himself. My conjectures, and my references to him, were far from being so occasional; there was scarce an hour of the day I did not think of him; but, believing that I should please him most by endeavouring to improve as much as possible during his absence, I did not give myself up to idle reflections respecting the past, or anticipations, equally idle, respecting the future.

"My great delight was in hearing from him. At first, his letters expressed only his feelings for me; then he dwelt more largely on his own exertions for preparing himself for the profession he desired to adopt; and after a time, his correspondence was almost entirely composed of expositions of his views of a religious life, and dissertations on various points of doctrine. He evidently was growing more enthusiastic in religion, and less regardful of our attachment.

"Yet I entertained no apprehensions or misgivings. I did not think it necessary to consider myself slighted because the thoughts of my future husband were evidently raised more and more above me; the knowledge of this only made me more anxious to raise myself more and more towards the elevation to which his thoughts were so intently directed.

"Things went on in this way for two or three years. I never saw him all this time; I heard from him but seldom. He excused his limited correspondence on the plea that his studies left him no time for writing. I never blamed him for this apparent neglect—indeed I rather encouraged it, for my exhortations were always that he should address his time and energies towards the attainment of the object I knew him to have so much at heart—his becoming a minister of our Lord's Gospel.

"One day my father came home from the rectory with a troubled countenance. Dr Brightwell was very indignant because Heinrich had joined a religious community that dissented from the Articles of the Church of England. The Doctor had offered to get him employment in the Church, if he would give up his new connections: but the more earnest character of his new faith exerted so much influence over his enthusiastic nature, that he willingly abandoned his bright prospects to become a more humble labourer in a less productive vineyard.

"My father, as the clerk of the parish, seemed to think himself bound to share in the indignation of his pastor for this desertion, and Heinrich was severely condemned by him for displaying such ingratitude to his benefactor: I was commanded to think no more of him.

"This, however, was not so easy a matter, although our correspondence appeared to have entirely ceased. I knew not where to address a letter to him and was quite unaware of what his future career was now to be."

CHAPTER XXXIV

"Time passed on. With all, except myself, Heinrich Reichardt appeared to be forgotten; in the opinion of all, except myself, he had forgotten our house, and all the friends he had once made there. Our good Rector had been removed by death from the post he had so ably filled; and my father being incapacitated by age and infirmity from attending his duties in the church, had his place filled by another. He had saved sufficient to live upon, and had built himself a small cottage at the end of the village, where we lived together in perfect peace, if not in perfect happiness.

"I had long grown up to womanhood, and having some abilities, had been employed as one of the teachers of the girls' school, of which I had raised myself to be mistress. I conducted myself so as to win the respect of the chief parochial officers, from more than one of whom I received proposals of marriage: but I never could reconcile myself to the idea of becoming the wife of any man but the long-absent Heinrich, and the new clerk and the overseer were fain to be content with my grateful rejection of their proposals.

"I determined to wait patiently till I could learn from Heinrich's own lips that he had abandoned his early friend. I could never get myself to believe in the possibility of his unfaithfulness; and the remembrances of our mutual studies in the Book of Truth seemed always to suggest the impossibility of his acting so completely at variance with the impressions he had thence received.

"I was aware that if I had mentioned my hopes of his one day coming to claim me, I should be laughed at by everyone who knew anything of our story—so I said nothing; but continued the more devotedly in my heart to cherish that faith which had so long afforded me support against the overwhelming evidence of prolonged silence and neglect.

"There was a congregation of Dissenters in the town, and I had been once or twice prevailed on to join their devotions. One day I heard that proceedings of extraordinary interest would take place at the meeting-house. A minister of great reputation had accepted the situation of Missionary to preach the Gospel to the heathen, and he was visiting the different congregations that lay in his route to the seaport whence he was to embark to the Sandwich Islands. He was expected to address a discourse to the Dissenters of our parish, and I was induced to go and hear him.

"The meeting-house was very much crowded, but I contrived to get a seat within a short distance of the speakers, and waited with much interest to behold the man, who, like some of the first preachers, had chosen the perilous task of endeavouring to convert a nation of savage idolaters to the faith of the true Christ.

"After a short delay he appeared on a raised platform, and was introduced to this congregation by their minister. I heard nothing of this introduction, though it seemed a long one; I saw nothing of the speaker, though his was a figure which always attracted an attentive audience. I saw only the stranger. In those pale, grave, and serious features then presented to me, I recognised Heinrich Reichardt."

"He had come back to you at last," I exclaimed; "I thought he would. After all you had done for the poor German boy, it was impossible that he should grow up to manhood and forget you."

"You shall hear," she replied. "For some time my heart beat wildly, and I thought I should be obliged to leave the place, my sensations became so overpowering; but the fear of disturbing the congregation, and of attracting attention towards myself, had such influence over me, that I managed to retain sufficient control over my feelings to remain quiet. Nevertheless, my eyes were upon Heinrich, and my whole heart and soul were exclusively engrossed by him while he continued before me.

"Presently he began to speak. As I have just said, I paid no attention to the preliminary proceedings. I know nothing of the manner in which he was introduced to his audience; but when he became the speaker, every word fell upon my ear with a distinctness that seemed quite marvellous to me.

"And how could it be otherwise? His tall figure, his melancholy yet expressive features, his earnest manner, and clear and sonorous voice, invested him with all the power and dignity of an Apostle, and when with these attributes were joined those associations of the past with which he was so intimately connected, it is impossible to exaggerate the influence he exercised over me.

"He began with a fervent blessing on all who had sought the sanctity of that roof, and his hearers, impressed with the thrilling earnestness of his delivery, became at once hushed into a kind of awe-struck attention. They knelt down, and bowed their heads in prayer.

"I appeared to have no power to follow the general example, but remained the only sitter in the entire congregation with my eyes, nay, all my senses, fixed, rivetted upon the preacher. This, of course, attracted his attention. I saw him look towards me with surprise, then he started, his voice hesitated for a moment, but he almost immediately continued his benediction, and, as it seemed to me, with a voice tremulous with emotion.

"Then followed a discourse on the object of the preacher in presenting himself there. He described the wonderful goodness of the Creator in continually raising up the most humble instruments of his will to perform the most important offices; in illustration of which he referred to the numerous instances in the Old and New Testaments, where God's preference in this way is so clearly manifested.

"He then stated that 'a case had arisen for Divine interposition, equal in necessity to any which had occurred since the first commencement of Christianity.' He explained that 'there were nations still existing in a distant portion of the globe in a state of the wildest barbarism. Ignorant savages were they, with many cruel and idolatrous customs, who were cannibals and murderers, and given up to the worst vices of the heathen. Their abject and pitiable state, he told us, the Lord God had witnessed with Divine commiseration, and had determined that the light of Christian love should shine upon their darkness, and that Almighty wisdom should dissipate their besotted ignorance.

"'But who' he asked, 'was to be the ambassador from so stupendous a Power to these barbarous states? Who would venture to be a messenger of peace and comfort to a cruel and savage nation? Was there no man,' he again asked, 'great enough and bold enough to undertake a mission of such vast importance, attended by such terrible risks?

"'The Almighty Ruler seeks not for his ministers among the great and bold,' he added, 'as it is written, He hath put down the mighty from their seats, and hath exalted the humble and meek. And it will be peculiarly so on this occasion, for the exaltation is from the humblest origin; so humble it is scarcely possible to imagine so miserable a beginning, in the end attaining distinction so honorable.

"'Imagine, if you can, my brethren,' he said, 'in the building set apart in your town for the reception of your destitute poor, a child parentless, friendless, and moneyless, condemned, as it seemed, to perpetual raggedness and intolerable suffering. A ministering angel, under the direction of the Supreme Goodness, took that child by the hand and led it out of the pauper walls that enclosed it, and under its auspices the child grew and flourished, and learned all that was excellent in faith and admirable in practice.

"'It was ordained that he should lose sight of his angelic teacher. A dire necessity compelled him to withdraw from that pure and gracious influence. He had to learn in a different school, and prepare himself for heavier tasks. Manhood, with all its severe responsibilities, came upon him. He sought first to render himself competent for some holy undertaking, before he could consider himself worthy again to claim that notice which had made him what he was. Earnestly he strove for the Divine assistance and encouragement; and as his qualifications increased, his estimate of the worthiness necessary for the object he had in view, became more and more exalted.

"'At last,' he continued, 'it became known to him that a Missionary was required to explain to the savage people to whom I have already alluded, the principles of Christianity. He was appointed to this sacred trust: and he then determined, before he left this country for the distant one of his ministry, to present himself before that beneficent being who had poured out before him so abundant a measure of Christian virtue; that they might be joined together in the same great vocation, and support each other in the same important trust.'

"I heard enough," continued Mrs Reichardt. "All was explained, and I was fully satisfied. The discourse proceeded to identify the speaker with the poor boy who had been preserved for such onerous duties. Then came an appeal to the congregation for their prayers, and such assistance as they could afford, to advance so holy a work as the conversion of the heathen.

"I was in such a tumult of pleasant feelings that I retained but a confused recollection of the subsequent events. I only remember that as I was walking home from the meeting, I heard footsteps quickly following; in a few minutes more the voice that had so lately filled my heart to overflowing with happiness, again addressed me. I was too much excited to remain unconcerned on suddenly discovering that Heinrich was so near, and I fell fainting into his arms.

"I was carried into a neighbouring cottage, but in a short time was enabled to proceed home. In a week afterwards we were married: a few days more sufficed for the preparations that were required for my destination, and then we proceeded to the port, and embarked on board the ship that was to take us over many thousand miles of sea, to the wild, unknown country that was to be the scene of our mission."

CHAPTER XXXV

Mrs Reichardt was obliged to break off her narrative, where it concluded at the end of the last chapter. As I have said, her household duties, being very numerous, and requiring a great deal of attention, took up nearly the whole of her time.

The garden now presented a most agreeable appearance, possessing several different kinds of vegetables, and various plants that had been raised from seed. We had succeeded in raising several young orange trees from the pips she had brought in her basket; and they promised to supply us with plenty of their luscious fruit. Even the peas we thought so dry and useless had germinated, and provided us with a welcome addition to our table. I shall never forget the first day she added to our scanty meal of dried fish a dish of smoking potatoes fresh out of the moist earth. After enjoying sufficiently my wonder at their appearance, and delight at their agreeable taste, she informed me of their first introduction into Europe, and their gradual diffusion over the more civilised portions of the globe.

I speak of Europe now, because I had learned from my companion, not only a good deal of geography, but had obtained some insight into several other branches of knowledge. In particular, she had told me much interesting information about England, much more than I had learned from Jackson; dwelling upon its leading features, and the most remarkable portions of its history; and I must acknowledge that I felt a secret pride in belonging to so great a country.

I considered that I belonged to it, for my father and mother were English, and though I might be called The Little Savage, and be fixed to an obscure island in the great ocean, I felt that my real home was in this great country my mother talked about so glowingly, and that my chief object ought to be to return into the hands of my grandfather the belt that had in so singular a manner come into my possession.

I often thought of this great England whose glory had been so widely spread and so durably established, and longed for some means of leaving our present abode, and going in search of its time-honoured shores. But I asked myself how was this desirable object to be effected? We had no means of transporting ourselves from the prison into which we had been accidentally cast. We had nothing resembling a boat on the island, and we had no tools for making one; and even had we been put in possession of such a treasure, we had no means of launching it. The rocky character of the coast made the placing of a boat on the water almost impossible.

The expectation of a vessel appearing off the island appeared quite as unreasonable. We had seen no ships for a long time, and those we had observed were a great deal too far off to heed our signals.

We had no help for it, but to trust to Providence and bear our present evil patiently. Nevertheless, I took my glass and swept the sea far and wide in search of a ship, but failed to discover anything but a spermaceti whale blowing in the distance, or a shoal of porpoises tumbling over each other nearer the shore, or a colony of seals basking in the sun on the rocks nearest the sea. My disappointment was shared by Nero, who seemed to regard my vexation with a sympathising glance, and even the gannets turned their dull stupid gaze upon me, with an expression as if they deeply commiserated my distress.

I had for a long time employed myself in making a shelving descent to the sea, on the most secure part of the rock, intending that it should be a landing place for a boat, in case any ship should come near enough to send one to our rescue. It was a work of great labour, and hatchet and spade equally suffered in my endeavours to effect my object; but at last I contrived to take advantage of a natural fracture in the rock, and a subsequent fall of the cliff, to make a rude kind of inclined plane, rather too steep, and too rough for bad climbers, but extremely convenient for my mother and me, whenever we should be prepared to embark for our distant home.

My thoughts were now often directed to the possibility of making on the island some kind of boat that would hold ourselves and sufficient provisions for a voyage to the nearest of the larger islands. I spoke to Mrs Reichardt on the subject, but she dwelt upon the impossibility without either proper tools, or the slightest knowledge of boat-building, of producing a vessel to which we could trust ourselves with any confidence, neither of us knowing anything about its management in the open sea; and then she spoke of the dangers a small boat would meet with, if the water should be rough, or if we should not be able to make the island in any reasonable time.

Yet I was not daunted by difficulties, nor dissuaded by discouraging representations. I thought at first of fastening all the loose timber together that had drifted against the rocks, as much in the shape of a boat as I could get it, but on looking over my stock of nails, I found they fell very far short of the proper quantity; consequently that mode of effecting my purpose was abandoned.

I then thought of felling a tree and hollowing it out by charring the timber. As yet I had discovered nothing on the island but shrubs. I was quite certain that no tree grew near enough to the sea to be available, and if I should succeed in cutting down a large one and fashioning it as I desired, I had no means of transport.

I might possibly make a boat capable of carrying all I wanted to put into it, but as I could neither move the water up to the boat, nor the boat down to the water, for all the service I wanted of it, even if the island contained a tree large enough, I might just as well leave it untouched.

Still I would not altogether abandon my favourite project. I thought of the willows that grew on the island, and fancied I could make a framework by twisting them strongly together, and stretching seal skins over them. I laboured at this for several weeks,—exercising all my ingenuity and no slight stock of patience, to create an object with which I was but imperfectly acquainted.

I did succeed at last in putting together something in a remote degree resembling the boat that brought part of the whaler's crew to the island and had taken them away, but it was not a quarter the size, and was so light that I could carry it without much difficulty to the landing I had constructed on the cliff. When I came to try its capabilities, I found it terribly lop-sided—it soon began to leak, and in fact it exhibited so many faults, that I was forced to drag it again on shore, and take it to pieces.

I called in Mrs Reichardt to my assistance, and though at first she seemed averse to the experiment, she gave me a great deal of information respecting the structure of small boats, and the method of waterproofing leather and other fabrics. I attended carefully to all she said, and commenced re-building with more pretensions to art.

I now made a strong frame-work, tolerably sharp at each end, and as nearly as possible resembling a keel at the bottom. I covered this on both sides with pieces of strong cloth saturated with grease from the carcases of birds, and then covered the whole with well-dried seal skins, which I had made impervious to wet. The inside of the boat nearest the water I neatly covered with pieces of dry bark, over which I fixed some boards, which had floated to the island from wrecked ships. Finally I put in some benches to sit on, and then fancied I had done everything that was necessary.

I soon got her into the fishing-pool, and was delighted to find that she floated capitally—but I still had a great deal to do. I had made neither oars to propel her through the water, nor sail to carry her through the waves, when rowing was impossible. I remembered the whaler's spare oars and mizen, but they were too large; nevertheless, they served me as models to work upon, and in time I made a rough pair of paddles or oars, which, though rudely fashioned, I hoped would answer the purpose pretty well.

The next difficulty was how to use the oars, and I made many awkward attempts before I ascertained the proper method of proceeding. Again my companion, on whom nothing which had once passed before her eyes had passed in vain, shewed me how the boat should be managed.

In a short time I could row about the pool with sufficient dexterity to turn the boat in any direction I required, and I then took Nero as a passenger, and he seemed to enjoy the new gratification with a praiseworthy decorum; till, when I was trying to turn the boat round, the movement caused him to attempt to shift his quarters, which he did with so little attention to the build of our vessel, that in one moment she was capsized, and in the next we were swimming about in the pool with our vessel bottom upwards.

As she was so light, I soon righted her, and found that she had received no injury, and appeared to be perfectly water-tight.

CHAPTER XXXVI

I could not prevail upon Mrs Reichardt to embark in my craft, the fate of my first passenger which she had witnessed from the shore, had deterred her from attempting a voyage under such unpromising circumstances.

As soon as I had dried my clothes, I was for making another experiment, and one too of a more hazardous nature. I would not be parted from Nero, but I made him lie at the bottom of the boat, where I could have him under strict control. With him I also took my little flock of gannets, who perched themselves round me, gazing about them with an air of such singular stupidity as they were being propelled through the water, that I could not help bursting out laughing.

"Indeed," said Mrs Reichardt, "such a boat's crew and such a boat has never been seen in those seas before. A young savage as captain, a tame seal as boatswain, and a flock of gannets as sailors, certainly made up as curious a set of adventurers as ever floated upon the wide ocean."

I was not the least remarkable of the strange group, for I had nothing on but a pair of duck trousers, patched in several places; and my hair, which had grown very long, hung in black wavy masses to my shoulders. My skin was tanned by the sun to a light brown, very different from the complexion of Mrs Reichardt, which had ever been remarkable for its paleness. Indeed she told me I should find some difficulty in establishing my claim to the title of European, but none at all to that of Little Savage, which she often playfully called me.

Nevertheless, in this trim, and with these companions, I passed out of the fishing-pool into the sea, with the intention of rowing round the island. Mrs Reichardt waved her hand as I departed on my voyage, having exhorted me to be very careful, as long as I was in hearing; she then turned away, as I thought, to return to the hut.

The day was remarkably fine. There was not so much as a cloud on the horizon, and scarcely a ripple on the water: therefore, everything seemed to favour my project, for if there had been anything of a breeze, the beating of the waves against the rock would have been a great obstacle to my pursuing my voyage with either comfort or safety. The water too was so clear, that although it was of great depth, I could distinguish the shells that lay on the sand, and observe various kinds of fish, some of most curious shape, that rushed rapidly beneath the boat as it was urged along.

I was delighted with the motion, and with the agreeable appearance of the different novelties that met my gaze. The light boat glided almost imperceptibly through the water at every stroke of the oar. Nero lay as still as if his former lesson had taught him the necessity of remaining motionless; and the gannets now and then expressed their satisfaction by a shrill cry or a rapid fluttering of their wings.

In this way, we passed on without any adventure, till I found it necessary for me to row some distance out to sea, to round a projecting rock that stood like a mighty wall before me. I pulled accordingly, and then had a better opportunity of seeing the island than I had ever obtained. I recognised all the favourite places, the ravine, the wood, the hut covered with beautiful creepers, and the garden, full of flowers, looked very agreeable to the eye: but every part seemed to look pleasant, except the great savage rocks which enclosed the island on every side: but even these I thought had an air of grandeur that gave additional effect to the scene.

Much to my surprise, I recognised Mrs Reichardt walking rapidly towards a part of the shore, near which I should be obliged to pass. From this I saw that she was intent on watching me from point to point, to know the worst, if any accident should befall me, and be at hand should there be a necessity for rendering assistance. I shouted to her, and she waved her hand in reply.

On rounding the headland, my astonishment was extreme on finding my little bark in the midst of a shoal of enormous sharks. If I came in contact with one of them I was lost, for the frail boat would certainly be upset and as Jackson had assured me, if ever I allowed these monsters to come near enough, one snap of their jaws, and there would be an end of the Little Savage. I thought of the warning of Mrs Reichardt, and was inclined to think I had better have taken her advice, and remained in the fishing-pool; nevertheless, I went on as quietly and deliberately as possible, exercising all my skill to keep clear of my unexpected enemies.

It was not till I had got into the middle of the shoal that the sharks seemed to be aware there was anything unusual in their neighbourhood, but as soon as they were fully aware of the presence of an intruder, they exhibited the most extraordinary excitement, rushing together in groups, with such rapid motion, that the water became so agitated, I was obliged to exercise all my skill to keep the boat steady on her course.

They dived, and rushed to and fro, and jostled each other, as I thought, in anything but an amicable spirit; still, however, keeping at a respectful distance from the boat, for which I was extremely thankful. I urged her on with all my strength, for the purpose of getting away from such unpleasant neighbours; but they were not to be so easily disposed of. They came swimming after the boat, then when within a few yards dived, and in a moment they were before it, as if to bar any further progress.

I however pushed on, and they disappeared, but immediately afterwards rose on all sides of me. They were evidently getting more confidence; a fact I ascertained with no slight apprehension, for they began to approach nearer, and their gambols threatened every minute to overwhelm my poor craft, that, light as a cork, bounced up and down the agitated waves, as if quite as much alarmed for our safety as ourselves.

The captain was not the only one who began to fear evil; the gannets were very restless, and it was only by strong admonitions I could prevail on Nero to retain his recumbent attitude at my feet; their instinct warned them of approaching danger, and I felt the comfortable assurance that my own rashness had brought me into my present critical position, and that if the menaced destruction did arrive, there was no sort of assistance at hand on which I could rely.

Every moment the sharks became more violent in their demonstrations, and more bold in their approaches, and I could scarcely keep the boat going, or prevent the water rushing over her sides. The gannets, having shewn themselves for some minutes uneasy, had at last flown away to the neighbouring rock, and Nero began to growl and snap, as though meditating a forcible release from his prostrate position, to see what mischief was brewing.

As I was coaxing him to be quiet, I felt a tremendous blow given to the boat, evidently from beneath, and she rose into the air several yards, scattering Nero and myself, and the oars, in different directions.

The noise we made in falling appeared for the instant to have scattered the creatures, for I had struck out for the rock and nearly reached it before a shark made its appearance.

Just then I saw a large monster rushing towards me. I thought all was over. He turned to open his great jaws, and in another instant I should have been devoured.

At that critical period I saw a second object dart in between me and the shark, and attack the latter fiercely. It was Nero, and it was the last I ever saw of my faithful friend. His timely interposition enabled me to reach a ledge in the cliff, where I was in perfect safety, hanging by some strong seaweed, although my feet nearly touched the water, and I could retain my position only with the greatest difficulty.

The whole shoal were presently around me. They a first paid their attentions to the boat and the oars, which they buffeted about till they were driven close to the rock, at a little distance from the place where I had found temporary safety. They left these things unharmed as soon as they caught sight of me, and then their eagerness and violence returned with tenfold fury. They darted towards me in a body, and I was obliged to lift my legs, or I should have had them snapped off by one or other of the twenty gaping jaws that were thrust over each other, in their eagerness to make a mouthful of my limbs.

This game was carried on for some minutes of horrible anxiety to me. I fancied that my struggles had loosened the seaweed, and that in a few minutes it must give way, and I should then be fought for and torn to pieces by the ravenous crew beneath. I shouted with all the strength of my lungs to scare them away; but as if they were as well aware that I could not escape them as I was myself, they merely left off their violent efforts to reach my projecting legs, and forming a semi-circle round me, watched with upturned eyes, that seemed to possess a fiendish expression that fascinated and bewildered me, the snapping of the frail hold that supported me upon the rock.

In my despair I prayed heartily, but it was rather to commend my soul to my Maker, than with any prospect of being rescued from so imminent and horrible a peril. The eyes of the ravenous monsters below seemed to mock my devotion. I felt the roots of the seaweed giving way: the slightest struggle on my part would I knew only hasten my dissolution, and I resigned myself to my fate.

In this awful moment I heard a voice calling out my name. It was Mrs Reichardt on the cliff high above me. I answered with all the eagerness of despair. Then there came a heavy splash into the water, and I heard her implore me to endeavour to make for a small shrub that grew in a hollow of the rock, at a very short distance from the tuft of seaweed that had become so serviceable.

I looked down. The sharks had all disappeared; I knew, however, that they would shortly return, and lost not a moment in making an effort to better my position in the manner I had been directed. Mrs Reichardt had thrown a heavy stone into the water among the sharks, the loud splash of which had driven them away. Before they again made their appearance, I had caught a firm hold of the twig, and flung myself up into a position of perfect safety.

"Thank God he's safe!" I heard Mrs Reichardt exclaim.

The sharks did return, but when they found their anticipated prey had escaped, they swam lazily out to sea.

"Are you much hurt, Frank Henniker?" she presently cried out to me.

"I have not a scratch," I replied.

"Then thank God for your deliverance," she added.

I did thank God, and Mrs Reichardt joined with me in prayer, and a more fervent thanksgiving than was ours, it is scarcely possible to imagine.

CHAPTER XXXVII

I had several times pressed Mrs Reichardt for the conclusion of her story, but she had always seemed reluctant to resume the subject. It was evidently full of painful incidents, and she shrunk from dwelling upon them. At last, one evening we were sitting together, she working with her needle and I employed upon a net she had taught me how to manufacture, and I again led the conversation to the narrative my companion had left unfinished. She sighed heavily and looked distressed.

"It is but natural you should expect this of me, my son," she said; "but you little know the suffering caused by my recalling the melancholy events that I have to detail. However, I have led you to expect the entire relation, and, therefore, I will endeavour to realise your anticipations."

I assured her I was ready to wait, whenever it might be agreeable for her to narrate the termination of her interesting history.

"It will never be agreeable to me," she replied mournfully; "indeed I would forget it, if I could; but that is impossible. The struggle may as well be made now, as at any time. I will therefore commence by informing you, that during our long voyage to the Sandwich Islands, I found ample opportunity for studying the disposition of my husband. He was much changed since he first left me, but his was still the same grateful nature, full of truth and purity, that had won me towards him when a child. A holy enthusiasm seemed now to exalt him above ordinary humanity. I could scarcely ever get him to talk upon any but religious subjects, and those he treated in so earnest and exalted a manner, that it was impossible to avoid being carried away with his eloquence.

"He seemed to feel the greatness of his destination, as though it had raised him to an equality with the adventurous Saints, who established the banner of Christ among the Pagan nations of Europe. He was fond of dilating upon the importance of his mission, and of dwelling on the favour that had been vouchsafed him, in causing him to be selected for so high and responsible a duty.

"It was evident that he would rather have been sent to associate with the barbarous people whom he expected to make his converts, than have been raised to the richest Bishopric in England. And yet, with this exultation, there was a spirit of deep melancholy pervading his countenance, as well as his discourses, that seemed to imply a sense of danger. The nimbus of the saint in his eyes was associated with the crown of martyrdom. He seemed to look forward to a fatal termination of his ministry, as the most and proper conclusion of his labours.

"His conversation often filled me with dread. His intimations of danger seemed at first very shocking, but, at last, I got more familiar with these terrible suggestions, and regarded them as the distempered fancies of an overworked mind.

"In this way our long voyage passed, and we arrived at last at our place of destination. When we had disembarked, the scene that presented itself to me was so strange, that I could almost believe I had passed into a new world. The most luxurious vegetation, of a character I had never seen before—the curious buildings—the singular forms of the natives, and their peculiar costume—excited my wonder to an intense degree.

"My husband applied himself diligently to learn the language of the people, whilst I as intently studied their habits and customs. We both made rapid progress.

"As soon as I could make myself understood, I endeavoured to make friends with the women, particularly with the wives of the great men, and although I was at first the object of more curiosity than regard, I persisted in my endeavours, and succeeded in establishing with many a good understanding.

"I found them ignorant of everything that in civilised countries is considered knowledge—their minds being enveloped in the most deplorable darkness—the only semblance of religion in use amongst them, being a brutal and absurd idolatry.

"I often tried to lead them to the consideration of more humanising truths, for the purpose of preparing the way for the inculcation of the great mysteries of our holy religion: but the greater portion of my hearers were incompetent to understand what I seemed so desirous of teaching, and my making them comprehend the principles of Christianity appeared to be a hopeless task.

"Yet I continued my pious labours, without allowing my exertions to flag—making myself useful to them and their families in every way I could—attending them when sick—giving them presents when well—and showing them every kindness likely to make a favourable impression on their savage natures. In this way I proceeded doing good, till I found an opportunity of being of service to a young girl, about twelve years of age, who was a younger sister of one of the wives of a great chief. She had sprained her ankle and was in great pain, when I applied the proper remedies and gave her speedy relief. Hooloo, for that was her name, from that moment became warmly attached to me, and finding her of an affectionate and ingenuous disposition, I became extremely desirous of improving upon the good impression I had made.

"At the same time my husband sought, by his knowledge of the mechanical arts, and some acquaintance with medicine, to recommend himself to the men. He also met with much difficulty at first, in making his information properly appreciated. He sought to increase their comforts—to introduce agricultural implements of a more useful description, and to lead them generally towards the conveniences and decencies of civilisation. He built himself a house, and planted a garden, and cultivated some land, in which he shewed the superior advantages of what he knew, to what they practised. They seemed to marvel much, but continued to go on in their own way.

"He also went amongst them as a physician, and having acquired considerable knowledge of medicine and simple surgery, he was enabled to work some cures in fevers and spear wounds, that in course of time made for him so great a reputation, that many of the leading chiefs sent for him when anything ailed them or their families, and they were so well satisfied with what he did for them, that he began to be looked upon as one who was to be treated with particular respect and honour, by all classes of the natives, from the highest to the lowest.

"On one occasion the king required his services. He was suffering from a sort of cholic, for which the native doctors could give him no relief. My husband administered some medicines, and stayed with his Majesty until they had the desired effect, and the result being a complete recovery, seemed so astonishing to all the members of his Sandwich Majesty's court, that the doctor was required to administer the same medicine to every one, from the queen to the humblest of her attendants, though all were apparently in good health. He managed to satisfy them with a small portion only of the mixture, which he was quite certain could do them no harm: and they professed to be wonderfully the better for it."

CHAPTER XXXVIII

"His reputation had now grown so great, that whatever he required was readily granted. He first desired to have some children sent him; to learn those things which had enabled him to do so much good, and this having been readily sanctioned, we opened a school for girls and boys, in which we taught the first elements of a civilised education.

"Finding we made fair progress in this way, we commenced developing our real object, the inculcation of Christian sentiments. This meeting with no opposition, and Reichardt having established a powerful influence over the entire community, he next proceeded with the parents, and earnestly strove to induce them to embrace the profession of Christianity.

"His labours were not entirely unproductive. There began to prevail amongst the islanders, a disposition to hear the wondrous discourses of this stranger, and he was employed, day after day, in explaining to large and attentive audiences, the history of the Christian world, and the observances and doctrine of that faith which had been cemented by the blood of the Redeemer. The new and startling subjects of his discourse, as well as the impressive character of his eloquence, frequently deeply moved his hearers; and at his revelations they would often burst forth into piercing shouts and loud expressions of amazement.

"In truth it was a moving scene. The noble figure of the Missionary, with his fine features lighted up with the fire of holy enthusiasm, surrounded by a crowd of dusky savages, armed with spears and war clubs, and partly clothed with feathers, in their features shewing traces of unusual excitement, and every now and then joining in a wild chorus, expressive of their wonder, could not have been witnessed by any Christian, without emotion.

"But when the ceremony of Baptism was first performed before them, their amazement was increased a thousandfold. The first member of our flock was Hooloo, whom I had instructed so far, in the principles of our faith, and I had acquired such an influence over her mind, that she readily consented to abandon her idolatrous customs and become a Christian.

"After a suitable address to the natives, who had assembled in some thousands to witness the spectacle, in which he explained to them the motive and object of baptism, my husband assisted the girl down a sloping green bank which led to a beautiful stream, and walked with her into the water till he was up to his waist; then, after offering up a long and fervent prayer that this first victory over the false worship of the Devil, might be the forerunner of the entire extirpation of idolatry from the land, he, plunging her into the water, baptised her in the name of the Father, the Son, and the Holy Ghost.

"All the people were awed to silence while the ceremony proceeded, but when it was over they burst forth into a loud cry, and came down to meet the new Christian and my husband as they came out of the water, and waved over them boughs of trees, and danced and shouted as though in an ecstasy.

"We however had not proceeded to this extent, without exciting considerable opposition; our disrespect towards their idols had given great offence to those who were identified with the superstitions of the people, and flourished according as these were supported. Complaints were made too of our teaching a new religion, in opposition to the gods they and their fathers had worshipped, and a powerful party was got together for the purpose of pursuing us to destruction.

"My husband was summoned before a council of the great chiefs, to hear the accusations that had been brought against him: and the old idolaters got up and abused him, and threatened him with the punishment of their monstrous gods, for telling lies to the people, and deceiving them with forged tales and strange customs.

"They sought all they could, to move the judges against him, by painting the terrible fate that would befall them if they failed to kill the white stranger, who had insulted their gods; and they predicted hosts of calamities that were to happen, in consequence of their having allowed the teller of lies to work so much mischief against them.

"My husband then being called upon for his defence, first declared to the judges the attributes of the Deity he worshipped: that he created the vast heavens, the stars, the mountains, the rivers, and the sea; his voice spoke in the thunder, and his eye flashed in the lightning. He then dwelt on his goodness to man, especially to the Sandwich Islanders, whom he had created for the purpose of enjoying the fine country around them and of beholding the beauty of the heavens where he dwelt. Then he referred to the gods they had worshipped, and asked how they were made, and what such senseless things could do for them; commenting on their inability to serve them, in any way, or do them any harm; and went on to speak of the benefits he had been able to confer upon them, through the influence of the all powerful God he worshipped; and asked them if he had ever done them anything but good. Lastly, he promised them innumerable benefits, if they would leave their useless gods, and turn to the only God who had the power to serve them.

"It is impossible for me to do justice to the animated manner in which he delivered this discourse. It produced great effect upon the majority of his hearers; but there was a powerful minority it still more strongly influenced against him; and they continued to interrupt him with terrible outcries.

"Most of the leading chiefs were against his suffering any harm. They bore in mind the advantages he had conferred, by his skill in medicine, and superior wisdom in various other things, which the people would lose were he put to death. They also remembered the hope he held out of future benefits, which of course they could not expect, if they offered him any violence.

"The result was, that my husband was suffered to go harmless from the meeting, to the great disappointment of his enemies, who could scarcely be kept from laying violent hands upon him. The danger he had escaped, unfortunately, did not render him more prudent. Far from it. He believed that he was a chosen instrument of the Most High, to win these savages from the depths of idolatry and Paganism; and continued, on every occasion that presented itself, to endeavour to win souls to God.

"The school increased, several of the parents suffered themselves to be baptised, and there was a regular observance of the Lord's Day amongst those who belonged to our little flock. Even many of the islanders, although they did not become Christians, attended our religious services, and spoke well of us.

"We brought up the young people to be able to teach their brethren and sisters; and hoped to be able to establish missions in other parts of the island, to which we sometimes made excursions; preaching the inestimable blessings of the gospel to the islanders, and exhorting them to abandon their dark customs and heathen follies. I was not far behind my husband in this good work, and acquired as much influence among the women as he exercised over the men: indeed we were generally looked upon as holy people, who deserved to be treated with veneration and respect."

CHAPTER XXXIX

"Things went on in this flourishing way for several years; my husband, deeply impressed with the responsibility of his position, as a chosen servant of God, devoted himself so entirely to the great work he had undertaken, that he often seemed to overlook the claims upon his attention of her he had chosen as his partner, in his struggle against the Powers of Darkness. Sometimes I did not see him for several days; and often when we were together, he was so abstracted, he did not seem aware I was present. Whenever I could get him to speak of himself, he would dilate on the unspeakable felicity that he felt in drawing nearer to the end of his work. I affected not to know to what he alluded; but I always felt that he was referring to the impression he entertained of his own speedy dissolution, which he had taken up when he first embraced this mission.

"I tried to get rid of my misgivings by recalling the dangers and difficulties we had triumphantly passed, and referring to the encouraging state of things that existed at the present time; nevertheless, I could not prevent a sinking of the heart, whenever I heard him venture upon the subject; and when he was absent from me, I often experienced an agony of anxiety till his return. I saw, however, no real cause of apprehension, and endeavoured to persuade myself none existed; and very probably I should have succeeded, had not my husband so frequently indulged in references to our separation.

"Alas," she exclaimed, mournfully, "he was better informed than I was of the proximity of that Celestial Home, for which he had been so long and zealously preparing himself. He, doubtless, had his intimation from on high, that his translation to the realms of bliss, was no remote consequence of his undertaking the mission he had accepted; and he had familiarised his mind to it as a daily duty, and by his constant references had sought to prepare me for the catastrophe he knew to be inevitable."

Here Mrs Reichardt became so sensibly affected, that it was some time before she could proceed with her narrative. She, however, did so at last, yet I could see by the tears that traced each other down her wan cheeks, how much her soul was moved by the terrible details into which she was obliged to enter.

"In the midst of our success," she presently resumed, "when we had established a congregation, had baptised hundreds of men, women, and children, had completed a regular place of worship, and an extensive school-house, both of which were fully and regularly attended, some European vessel paid us a short visit, soon after which, that dreadful scourge the small-pox, broke out amongst the people. Both children and adults were seized, and as soon as one died a dozen were attacked.

"Soon the greatest alarm pervaded the natives; my husband was implored to stop the pestilence, which power they felt convinced he had in his hands. He did all that was possible for him to do, but that unfortunately was very little. His recommendation of remedial measures was rarely attended with the desired results. Death was very busy. The people died in scores, and the survivors, excited by the vindictive men who had formerly sought his death for disparaging their gods, began not only to fall off rapidly in their regard and reverence for my husband, but murmurs first, and execrations afterwards, and violent menaces subsequently, attended him whenever he appeared.

"He preached to them resignation to the Divine Will; but resignation was not a savage virtue. He was indefatigable in his attentions to the sick; but those of whom he was most careful seemed the speediest to die. The popular feeling against him increased every hour; he appeared, however, to defy his fate—walking unconcernedly amongst crowds of infuriated savages brandishing heavy clubs, and threatening him with the points of their sharp spears; but his eye never blinked, and his cheek never blanched, and he walked on his way inwardly praising God, careless of the evil passions that raged around him.

"It was on a Sabbath morn—our service had far advanced; we could boast of but a limited congregation, for many had died, some had fled from the pestilence into the interior; others had avoided the place in consequence of the threats of their countrymen. A few children, and two or three women, were all their teacher had to address.

"We were engaged in singing a Psalm, when a furious crowd, mad with rage, as it seemed, screaming and yelling in the most frightful manner, and brandishing their weapons as though about to attack an enemy, burst into our little chapel, and seized my husband in the midst of his devotions.

"I rushed forward to protect him from the numerous weapons that were aimed at his life, but was dragged back by the hair of my head; and with infuriate cries and gestures, that made them look like demons broke loose from hell, they fell upon him with their clubs and spears.

"Reichardt made no resistance, he merely clasped his hands the more firmly, and looked up to Heaven the more devoutly, as he continued the Psalm he had commenced before they entered. This did not delay his fate.

"They beat out his brains so close to me, that I was covered with his blood, and I believe I should have shared the same fate, had I not fainted with terror at the horrible scene of which I was a forced spectator.

"I learned afterwards that some powerful chief interfered, and I was carried away more dead than alive, in which state I long remained. As soon as I became sufficiently strong to be moved, I took advantage of a whaler calling at the island, homeward bound, to beg a passage. The captain heard my lamentable story, took me on board as soon as he could, and shewed a seaman's sympathy for my sufferings.

"I was to have returned to England with him, but off this place we encountered a terrible storm, in which we were obliged to take to the boats, as the only chance of saving our lives. What became of him I know not, as the two boats parted company soon after leaving the wreck. I trust he managed to reach the land in safety, and is now in his own country, enjoying all the comforts that can make life covetable.

"What became of that part of the crew that brought me here in the other boat, led by the fires you had lighted, I am in doubt. But I think on quitting the island, crowded as their boat was, and in the state of its crew, it was scarcely possible for them to have made the distant island for which they steered."

CHAPTER XL

Mrs Reichardt's story made a sensible impression on me. I no longer wondered at the pallor of her countenance, or the air of melancholy that at first seemed so remarkable; she had suffered most severely, and her sufferings were too recent not to have left their effects upon her frame.

I thought a good deal about her narrative, and wondered much that men could be got to leave their comfortable homes, and travel thousands and thousands of miles across the fathomless seas, with the hope of converting a nation of treacherous savages, by whom they were sure to be slaughtered at the first outbreak of ill-feeling.

I could not but admire the character of Reichardt—in all his actions he had exhibited a marked nobility of nature. He would not present himself before the woman who had the strongest claims upon his gratitude, till he had obtained a position and a reputation that should, in his opinion, make him worthy of her; and though he had a presentiment of the fate that would overtake him, he fulfilled his duties as a missionary with a holy enthusiasm that made him regard his approaching martyrdom as the greatest of all earthly distinctions. I felt regret that I had not known such a man. I knew how much I had lost in having missed such an example.

My having heard this story led me into much private communing with myself respecting religion. I could consider myself little better than a savage, like the brutal Sandwich Islanders; my conduct to Jackson had been only in a degree less inhuman than that these idolaters had shewn to their teacher when he was in their power. I fancied at the time that I served him right, for his villainous conduct to my father, and brutal conduct to me: but God having punished him for his misdeeds, I felt satisfied I had no business to put him to greater torment as satisfaction for my own private injuries. I fancied God might have been angry with me, and had kept me on the island as a punishment for my offences; and I had some conversation with Mrs Reichardt on this point.

"Nothing," she observed, "can excuse your ill-feeling towards Jackson; he was a bad man, without a doubt, and he deserved condign punishment for his usage of your parents; but the Divine founder of our religion has urged us to return good for evil."

"Yes," I answered readily, "but I should have suffered as bad as my father and mother, had I not prevented his doing me mischief."

"You do not know that you were to suffer," she replied. "Jackson, without such terrible punishment as he brought upon himself, might eventually have become contrite, and have restored you to your friends as well as enabled you to obtain your grandfather's property. God frequently performs marvellous things with such humble instruments, for he hath said, 'There is more joy in heaven over one sinner that repenteth, than over ninety-nine just men.'"

"Surely, this is raising the wicked man over the good," I cried.

"Not at all," she replied. "The repentant is one gained from the ranks of the great enemy—it is as one that was lost and is found again—it is a soul added to the blessed. Therefore the joy in heaven is abundant at such a conversion. The just are the natural heirs of heaven—their rights are acknowledged without dispute—their claim is at once recognised and allowed, and they receive their portion of eternal joy as a matter of course, without there being any necessity for exciting those demonstrations of satisfaction which hail the advent of a sinner saved."

"I don't think such a villain as Jackson would ever go to heaven," I observed.

"'Judge not, lest ye be judged,'" she answered; "that is a text that cannot be too often impressed upon persons anxious to condemn to eternal torment all those they believe to be worse than themselves. It is great presumption in us poor creatures of clay, to anticipate the proceedings of the Infinite Wisdom. Let us leave the high prerogative of judgment to the Almighty Power, by whom only it is exercised, and in our opinions of even the worst of our fellow-creatures, let us exercise a comprehensive charity, mingled with a prayer that even at the eleventh hour, they may have turned from the evil of their ways, and embraced the prospect of salvation, which the mercy of their Creator has held out to them."

In this and similar conversations, Mrs Reichardt would endeavour to plant in my mind the soundest views of religion; and she spoke so well, and so convincingly, that I had little trouble in understanding her meaning, or in retaining it after it had been uttered.

It was not, as I have before stated, to religion only that she led my thoughts, although that certainly was the most frequent subject of our conversation. She sought to instruct me in the various branches of knowledge into which she had acquired some insight, and in this way I picked up as much information respecting grammar, geography, astronomy, writing, arithmetic, history, and morals, as I should have gained had I been at a school, instead of being forced to remain on a desolate island.

I need not say that I still desired to leave it. I had long been tired of the place, notwithstanding that from our united exertions, we enjoyed many comforts which we could not have hoped for. Our hut we had metamorphosed into something Mrs Reichardt styled a rustic cottage, which, covered as it was with flowers and creepers, really looked very pretty; and the garden added greatly to its pleasant appearance: for near the house we had transplanted everything that bore a flower that could be found in the island, and had planted some shrubs, that, having been carefully nurtured made rapid growth, and screened the hut from the wind.

I had built a sort of out-house for storing potatoes and firewood, and a fowl-house for the gannets, which were now a numerous flock; and had planted a fence round the garden, so that as Mrs Reichardt said, we looked as if we had selected a dwelling in our own beloved England, in the heart of a rural district, instead of our being circumscribed in a little island thousands of miles across the wide seas, from the home of which we were so fond of talking.

Although my companion always spoke warmly of the land of her birth, and evidently would have been glad to return to it, she never grieved over her hard fate in being, as it were, a prisoner on a rock, out of reach of friends and kindred; indeed, she used to chide me for being impatient of my detention, and insensible of the blessings I enjoyed.

"What temptations are we not free from here?" she would say. "We see nothing of the world; we cannot be contaminated with its vices, or suffer from its follies. The hideous wars—the terrible revolutions—the dreadful visitations of famine and pestilence—are completely unknown to us. Robbery, and murder, and fraud, and the thousand other phases of human wickedness, we altogether escape. There was a time, when men, for the purpose of leading holy lives, abandoned the fair cities in which they had lived in the enjoyment of every luxury, and sought a cave in some distant desert, where, in the lair of some wild beast, with a stone for a pillow, a handful of herbs for a meal, and a cup of water for beveridge, they lived out the remnant of their days in a constant succession of mortifications, prayers, and penitence.

"How different," she added, "is our own state. We are as far removed from the sinfulness of the world as any hermit of the desert, whilst we have the enjoyment of comforts to which they were strangers."

"But probably," I observed, "these men were penitents, and went into the desert as much to punish their bodies for the transgressions of the flesh, as to acquire by solitary communion, a better knowledge of the spirit than they were likely to obtain in their old haunts."

"Some were penitents, no doubt," she answered, "but they, having obtained by their sanctity an extraordinary reputation, induced others, whose lives had been blameless, to follow their example, and in time the desert became colonised with recluses, who rivalled each other in the intensity of their devotions and the extent of their privations."

"Would it not have been more commendable," I asked, "if these men had remained in the community to which they belonged, withstanding temptation, and been employed in labour that was creditable to themselves and useful to their country?"

"No doubt it would," she replied; "but religion has, unfortunately, too often been the result of impulse rather than conviction; and at the period to which we are referring, it was thought that sinful human nature could only gain the attributes of saintship by neglecting its social duties, and punishing its humanity in the severest manner. Even in more recent times, and at the present day, in Catholic countries, it is customary for individuals of both sexes, to abandon the world of which they might render themselves ornaments, and shut themselves up in buildings constructed expressly to receive them, where they continue to go through a course of devotions and privations till death puts an end to their voluntary imprisonment.

"In this modified instance of seclusion," she added, "there are features very different from our own case. We are not forced to impoverish our blood with insufficient diet, or mortify our flesh with various forms of punishment. We do not neglect the worship of God. We offer up daily thanks for his loving care of us, and sing his praises in continual hymns: and instead of wasting the hours of the day in unmeaning penances, we fill up our time in employments that add to our health, comfort, and happiness: and that enable us the better to appreciate the goodness of that Power who is so mindful of our welfare."

"Have you no wish then, to leave this island?" I inquired.

"I should gladly avail myself of the first opportunity that presented itself for getting safely to England," she replied. "But I would wait patiently the proper time. It is not only useless repining at our prolonged stay here, but it looks like an ungrateful doubting of the power of God to remove us. Be assured that he has not preserved us so long, and through so many dangers, to abandon us when we most require his interposition in our favour."

I endeavoured to gather consolation from such representations: but perhaps young people are not so easily reconciled to what they do not like, as are their elders, for I cannot say I succeeded in becoming satisfied with my position.

CHAPTER XLI

The perils of my first voyage had deterred me from making a similar experiment; but I recovered my boat, and having further strengthened it, fitted it with what could either be turned into a well or locker: I used to row out a little distance when the sea was free from sharks and fish.

But my grand effort in this direction was the completion of a net, which, assisted by Mrs Reichardt, I managed to manufacture. By this time she had gained sufficient confidence to accompany me in my fishing excursions; she would even take the oars whilst I threw out the net, and assisted me in dragging it into the boat.

The first time we got such a haul, that I was afraid of the safety of our little craft. The locker was full, and numbers of great fish, as I flung them out of the net, were flapping and leaping about the bottom of the boat. It began to sink lower in the water than was agreeable to either of us, and I found it absolutely necessary to throw back into the sea the greater portion of our catch. We then rowed carefully to land, rejoicing that we had at our command, the means of obtaining an abundant supply of food whenever we desired it.

Mrs Reichardt was with me also in our land excursions. Together we had explored every part of the island; our chief object was plants for enriching our garden, and often as we had been in search of novelties, we invariably brought home additions to our collection; and my companion having acquired some knowledge of botany, would explain to me the names, characters, and qualities of the different species, which made our journeys peculiarly interesting.

Our appearance often caused considerable amusement to each other; for our respective costumes must have been extremely curious in the eyes of a stranger. Neither wore shoes or stockings—

these things we did not possess, and could not procure; we wore leggings and sandals of seal skin to protect us from the thorns and plants of the cacti tribe, among which we were obliged to force our way. My companion wore a conical cap of seal skin, and protected her complexion from the sun, by a rude attempt at an umbrella I had made for her.

She had on, on these occasions, a pair of coarse cloth trousers, as her own dress would have been torn to pieces before she had got half a mile through the bush; these were surmounted by a tight spencer she had herself manufactured out of a man's waistcoat, and a dimity petticoat, which buttoned up to her throat, and was fastened in the same way at the wrists.

My head was covered with a broad-brimmed hat, made of dry grass, which I had myself platted. I wore a sailor's jacket, much the worse for wear, patched with seal skin, over a pair of duck trousers, similarly repaired.

Although our expeditions were perfectly harmless, we did not go without weapons. At the instigation of my companion, I had made myself a good stout bow and plenty of arrows, and had exercised myself so frequently at aiming at a mark, as to have acquired very considerable skill in the use of them. I had now several arrows of hard wood tipped with sharp fish-bones, and some with iron nails, in a kind of pouch behind me; in its sheath before me was my American knife, which I used for taking the plants from the ground. I had a basket made of the long grass of the island, slung around me, which served to contain our treasures; and I carried my bow in my hand.

My companion, in addition to her umbrella, bore only a long staff, and a small basket tied round her waist that usually contained a little refreshment; for she would say there was no knowing what might occur to delay our return, and therefore it was better to take our meal with us. And not the least agreeable portion of the day's labour was our repast; for we would seat ourselves in some quiet corner, surrounded by flowers, and shaded by the brushwood from the sun, and there eat our dried fish or pick our birds, and roast our potatoes by means of a fire of dried sticks, and wash down our simple dinner with a flask of pure water—the most refreshing portion of our banquet.

I had, as I have just stated, attained a singular degree of skill in the use of the bow and arrow, which, as we had no fire-arms, was often of important service in procuring food on land.

I had made another use of my skill—an application of it which afforded me a vast deal of satisfaction. My old enemies the sharks used still to frequent a certain portion of the coast in great numbers, and as soon as I became master of my weapon, I would stand as near to the edge of the rock as was safe, and singling out my victim, aim at his upper fin, which I often found had the effect of ridding the place of that fellow.

I bore such an intense hatred to these creatures, for the fright they had put me into during my memorable voyage of discovery, and for the slaughter of my beloved Nero, that I determined to wage incessant war against them, as long as I could manufacture an arrow, or a single shark remained on the coast.

As we had so often traversed the island without accident, we dreamt not of danger. We had never met with any kind of animals, except our old friends the seals, who kept near the sea. Of birds, the gannets were generally the sole frequenters of the island; but we had seen, at rare intervals, birds of a totally different character, some of which I had shot.

Indeed, during our excursions, I was always on the look out for any stranger of the feathered race, that I might exercise my skill upon him. If he proved eatable, he was sure to be very welcome; and even if he could not be cooked, he afforded me some entertainment, in hearing from Mrs Reichardt his name and habits.

We had discovered a natural hollow which lay so low that it was quite hid till we came close to it, when we had to descend a steep declivity covered with shrubs. At the bottom was a soil evidently very productive, for we found trees growing there to a considerable height, that were in marked contrast to the shrubby plants that grew in other parts of the island. We called this spot the Happy Valley, and it became a favourite resting-place.

I remember on one of these occasions, we had made our dinner after having been several hours employed in seeking for plants, of which we had procured a good supply, and the remains of our meal lay under a great tree, beneath the spreading branches of which we had been resting ourselves.

It was quite on the other side of the island, within about a quarter of a mile from the sea. Abundance of curious plants grew about the place, and Mrs Reichardt had wandered to a little distance to examine all within view.

I was peering into the trees and shrubs around to discover a new comer. I had wandered in an opposite direction to that taken by my companion, and was creeping round a clump of shrubs about twenty yards off, in which I detected a chirping noise, when I heard a loud scream.

I turned sharply round and beheld Mrs Reichardt, evidently in an agony of terror, running towards me with prodigious swiftness. She had dropped her umbrella and her staff, her cap had fallen from her head, and her long hair, disarranged by her sudden flight, streamed behind her shoulders.

At first I did not see anything which could have caused this terrible alarm, but in a few seconds I heard a crushing among a thicket of shrubs from which she was running, as if some heavy weight was being forced through them; and presently there issued a most extraordinary monster. It came forward at a quick pace, its head erect above ten feet, its jaws wide open, from the midst of which there issued a forked tongue which darted in and out with inconceivable rapidity. Its body was very long, and thick as an ordinary tree; it was covered over with bright shining scales that seemed to have different colours, and was propelled along the ground in folds of various sizes, with a length of tail of several yards behind. Its eyes were very bright and fierce. Its appearance certainly accounted for my companion's alarm.

"Fly!" she cried in accents of intense terror, as she rushed towards me, "fly, or you are lost!"

She then gave a hurried glance behind her, and seeing the formidable monster in full chase, she just had power to reach the spot to which I had advanced, and sunk overpowered with terror, fainting at my feet.

My first movement was to step across her body for the purpose of disputing the passage of the monster, and in an erect posture, with my bow drawn tight as I could pull it, I waited a few seconds till I could secure a good aim, for I knew everything depended on my steadiness and resolution.

On came my prodigious antagonist, making a terrible hissing as he approached, his eyes flashing, his jaws expanded as if he intended to swallow me at a mouthful, and the enormous folds of his huge body passing like wheels over the ground, crushing the thick plants that came in their way like grass.

I must acknowledge that in my heart I felt a strange sinking sensation, but I remembered that our only chance of escape lay in giving the monster a mortal wound, and the imminence of the danger seemed to afford me the resolution I required.

He was close behind, and in a direct line with the tree under which we had dined, and I was about twenty yards from it. Directly his head darted round and in front of the tree, making a good mark, I let fly the arrow direct, as I thought, for his eye, hoping, by penetrating his brain, to settle him at once. But as he moved his head at that moment, the arrow went into his open jaws, one of which it penetrated, and going deep into the tree behind, pinned his head close to the bark.

As soon as the huge creature found himself hurt, he wound his enormous body round the trunk, and with his desperate exertions swayed the great tree backwards and forwards, as I would have done one of its smallest branches. Fearful that he would liberate himself before I could save my senseless companion, as quick as possible I discharged all my arrows into his body, which took effect in various places. His exertions then became so terrible that I hastily snatched up Mrs Reichardt in my arms, and with a fright that seemed to give me supernatural strength, I ran as fast as I could the shortest way to our hut. Fortunately, before I had gone half a mile, my companion came to her senses, and was able to continue her flight.

We got home at last, half dead with fatigue and fright; nevertheless the first thing we did was to barricade all the entrances. We left loop-holes to reconnoitre; and there we sat for hours after our arrival, waiting the monster's approach in fear and trembling.

We did not go to sleep that night. We did not, either of us, go out the next day. The next night one watched while the other slept. The second day my courage had so far returned, I wanted to go and look after the constant subject of our conversation. But Mrs Reichardt dissuaded me.

She told me it was an enormous python, or serpent of the boa species, that are common on the northern coast of America.

Probably it had been brought to the island on a drifted tree, and being so prodigious a reptile, the wounds it had received were not likely to do it much harm, and it would be no doubt lurking about, ready to pounce upon either of us directly we appeared.

On the third day, nothing having occurred to increase our alarm, I determined to know the worst; so I got by stealth out of the house, and armed with a fresh bow, a good supply of arrows, a hatchet slung at my side, and my American knife—with my mind made up for another conflict if necessary—I crept stealthily along, with my eyes awake to the slightest motion, and my ears open to the slightest sound, till I approached the scene of my late unequal struggle.

I must own I began to draw my breath rather rapidly, and my heart beat more quickly, as I came near the place where I had left my terrible enemy. To my extreme surprise the python had disappeared. There was a tree still standing, though its foliage and branches strewed the ground, and a great portion of its bark was ground to powder. At the base of the trunk was a pool of blood mingled with fragments of bark, broken arrows, leaves, and mould. The reptile had escaped. But where was he? Not altogether without anxiety I began to look for traces of his retreat; and they were easily found. With my arrow ready for immediate flight, I followed a stream of blood that was still visible on the grass, and led from the tree, accompanied by unmistakable marks of the great serpent's progress, in a direct line to the sea. There it disappeared.

When I discovered this, I breathed again. There was no doubt if the monster survived the conflict, he was hundreds of miles away, and was not likely to return to a place where he had received so rough a welcome. It may readily be believed I lost no time in taking the agreeable news to my companion.

CHAPTER XLII

I had become tired of looking out for a ship. Though day after day, and week after week, I made the most careful scrutiny with my glass, as I have said, it brought no result. I sometimes fancied I saw a vessel appearing in the line of the horizon, and I would pile up faggots and light them, and throw on water to make them smoke, as Jackson had done; but all without avail. Either my vision had deceived me, or my signals had not been observed, or the ship's course did not lie in the direction of the island.

We had had storms too on several occasions, but no wreck had been left on our coast. I began to think we were doomed to live out our lives on this rock, and frequently found myself striving very manfully to be resigned to my fate, and for a few days I would cheerfully endeavour to make the best of it. But the increasing desire I felt to get to England, that I might seek out my grandfather, and put him in possession of his diamonds, always prevented this state of things enduring very long. I had obtained from Mrs Reichardt an idea of the value of these stones, and of the importance of their restoration to my relative, and I had often thought of the satisfaction I should enjoy in presenting myself before him, as the restorer of such valuable property, which, no doubt, had long since been given up as lost.

But latterly, I thought less of these things; the chance of leaving the island seemed so remote, and the prospect of ever seeing my grandfather so very distant, that I had ceased to take any interest in the contents of the belt. The diamonds seemed to become as valueless as they were useless; a handful of wheat would have been much more desirable. It was now some time since I had seen the belt, or inquired about it.

Thus we lived without any incident occurring worth relating—when one day the appearance of the atmosphere indicated a storm, and a very violent hurricane, attended with peals of thunder and lurid flashes of lightning, lasted during the whole of the day and evening. The wind tore up the trees by the roots, blew down our outhouses, made terrible havoc in our garden, and threatened to tumble our hut over our heads.

We could not think of going to our beds whilst such a tempest was raging around us, so we sat up, listening to the creaking of the boards, and anticipating every moment that the whole fabric would be blown to pieces. Fortunately, the bark with which I had covered the roof, in a great measure protected us from the rain, which came down in torrents; but every part was not equally impervious, and our discomfort was increased by seeing the water drip through, and form pools on the floor.

The thunder still continued at intervals, and was sometimes so loud as to have a most startling effect upon us. My companion knelt down and said her prayers with great fervour, and I joined in them with scarcely less devotion. Indeed it was an awful night, and our position, though under shelter, was not without danger. The incessant flashes of lightning seemed to play round our edifice, as if determined to set it in a blaze; and the dreadful peals of thunder that followed, rolled over our heads, as if about to burst upon the creaking boards that shut us from its fury.

I fancied once or twice that I heard during the storm bursts of sound quite different in character from the peals of thunder. They were not so loud, and did not reverberate so much; they seemed to come nearer, and then the difference in sound became very perceptible.

"Great God!" exclaimed Mrs Reichardt, starting up from her kneeling posture, "that is a gun from some ship."

The wind seemed less boisterous for a few seconds, and the thunder ceased. We listened breathlessly for the loud boom we had just heard, but it was not repeated. In a moment afterwards our ears were startled by the most terrifying combination of screams, shrieks, cries, and wailings I had ever heard. My blood seemed chilled in my veins.

"A ship has just struck," whispered my companion, scarcely above her breath. "The Lord have mercy on the crew!"

She sank on her knees again in prayer, as if for the poor souls who were struggling in the jaws of death. The wind still howled, and the thunder still roared, but in the fiercest war of the elements, I fancied I could every now and then hear the piercing shrieks sent up to heaven for assistance. I thought once or twice of venturing out, but I remembered the safety of my companion was so completely bound up with my own, that I could not reconcile myself to leaving her; and I was also well aware, that till the terrible fury of the tempest abated, it was impossible for me to be of the slightest service to the people of the wrecked ship, even could I remain unharmed exposed to the violence of the weather.

I however awaited with much impatience and intense anxiety till the storm had in some measure spent itself; but this did not occur till sunrise the next morning. The wind fell, the thunder and lightning ceased, the rain was evidently diminishing, and the brightness of the coming day began to burst through the darkest night that had ever visited the island.

Mrs Reichardt would not be left behind; it was possible she might be useful, and taking with her a small basket of such things as she imagined might be required, she accompanied me to the rocks nearest the sea.

On arriving there, the most extraordinary scene presented itself. The sea was strewed with spars, masts, chests, boats stove in or otherwise injured, casks, empty hen-coops, and innumerable pieces of floating wreck that were continually dashed against the rocks, or were washed ashore, wherever an opening for the sea presented itself. At a little distance lay the remains of a fine ship, her masts gone by the board, her decks open, in fact a complete wreck, over which the sea had but lately been making a clean sweep, carrying overboard everything that could not resist its fury.

I could see nothing resembling a human being, though both myself and my companion looked carefully round in the hope of discovering some poor creature, that might need assistance. It appeared, however, as if the people of the ship had taken to their boats, which had been swamped, and most probably all who had ventured into them had been devoured by the sharks.

Had the crew remained on board, they would in all probability have been saved; as the vessel had been thrown almost high and dry.

As soon as we had satisfied ourselves that no sharks were in the neighbourhood, I launched my little boat, and each taking an oar, we pulled in the direction of the wreck, which we reached in a few minutes.

She had heeled over after striking, and the water was quite smooth under her lee. I contrived to climb into the main chains, and from thence on board, and was soon afterwards diligently exploring the ship. I penetrated every place into which I could effect an entrance, marvelling much at the variety of things I beheld. There seemed such an abundance of everything, and of things too quite new to me, that I was bewildered by their novelty and variety.

Having discovered a coil of new rope, I hauled it on deck, and soon made fast my little boat to the ship. Then I made a hasty rope ladder which I threw over, and Mrs Reichardt was in a very few minutes standing by my side. Her knowledge was necessary to inform me of the uses of the several strange things I saw, and to select for our own use what was most desirable. She being well acquainted with the interior of a ship, and having explained to me its numerous conveniences, I could not but admire the ingenuity of man, in creating such stupendous machines.

The ship having much water in the hold, I was forced to dive into the armoury. It was the first time I had seen such things, and I handled the muskets and pistols with a vast deal of curiosity; as my companion explained to me how they were loaded and fired, I at once saw their advantage over the bow and arrow, and was selecting two or three to carry away, when I hesitated on being assured they would be perfectly useless without ammunition. I might have remained content with my own savage weapons that had already served me so well, had not Mrs Reichardt, in the course of our survey, discovered several tin canisters of powder perfectly uninjured, with abundance of shot and bullets, of which I quickly took possession.

From other parts of the vessel we selected bags of grain, barrels of flour, and provisions of various kinds; wearing apparel, boxes of tools, with numerous bottles and jars, with the contents of which I was perfectly unacquainted, though their discovery gave great gratification to my companion. What most excited my wonder, were various kinds of agricultural implements that we found in the hold, and in a short time I was made aware of the proper employment of spades, harrows, ploughs, thrashing-machines, and many other things, of the existence of which I had never before dreamt.

We found also quantities of various kinds of seeds and roots, and some sort of twigs growing in pots, which Mrs Reichardt particularly begged me not to leave behind, as they would be of the greatest use to us; and she added that, from various signs, she believed that the ship had been an emigrant vessel going out with settlers, but to what place she could not say.

We made no ceremony in breaking open lockers and chests, and every where discovered a variety of things, which, could we transfer to our island, would add greatly to our comfort; but how they were to be got ashore, was a puzzle which neither of us seemed capable of solving. Our little boat would only contain a few of the lighter articles; and as many of these as we could conveniently put together were shortly stowed in her.

With this cargo we were about returning, when my companion called my attention to a noise that seemed to come from a distant corner of the vessel, and she laughed and exhibited so much satisfaction that I believed we were close upon some discovery far more important than any we had yet hit upon.

We continued to make our way to what seemed to me a very out of the way part of the vessel, led in a great measure by the noises that proceeded from thence. It was so dark here, that we were obliged to get a light, and my companion having procured a ship's lantern, and lighted it by means of a tinderbox, led me to a place where I could discern several animals, most of which were evidently dead. She however ascertained that there were two young calves, three or four sheep, and as many young pigs, still giving very noisy evidence of their existence. She searched about and found some food for them, which they ate with great avidity. The larger animals she told me were cows and horses; but they had fallen down, and gave no signs of life.

My companion and myself then entered into a long debate as to how we were to remove the living animals from the dead; and she dwelt very eloquently upon the great advantages that would accrue to us, if we could succeed in transporting to the island the survivors.

After giving them a good feed, seeing we could not remove them at present, we descended safely to our boat and gained the shore without any accident. Then having housed our treasures, we were for putting together a raft of the various planks and barrels that were knocking against the rocks, but as I knew this would take a good deal of time, I thought I would inspect the ship's boats, which, bottom upwards, were drifting about within a few yards of us.

To our great satisfaction, one I ascertained to be but little injured, and having forced her ashore, with our united exertions we turned her over. In an hour we had made her water-tight, had picked up her oars, and were pulling merrily for the wreck.

CHAPTER XLIII

Had the cows or horses been alive, they must have been left behind, for we could not have removed them, but the smaller animals were with comparatively little difficulty got on deck, and they descended with me into the boat. We added a few things that lay handy, and in a few minutes were laughingly driving our four-footed treasures on shore, to the extreme astonishment of the gannets, which seemed as though they would never cease to flap their wings, as their new associates were driven by them.

In the same way we removed the most portable of the agricultural implements, bed and bedding, cots, and hammocks, furniture, the framework of a house, preserved provisions of all kinds, a medicine chest, boxes of books, crates of china and glass, all sorts of useful tools, and domestic utensils; in short, in the course of the next two or three weeks, by repeated journeys, we filled every available place we could find with what we had managed to rescue.

Then came another terrible storm that lasted two days, after which the wreck having been broken up, was scattered in every direction. I however managed to secure the drift wood, tubs, spars, and chests, which were all got on shore, and proved of the greatest service to me some time afterwards.

Numerous as our acquisitions had been in this way, both of us had been infinitely better pleased had we been able to rescue some of the ill-fated crew, to whom they had once belonged. But not one of them could have escaped, and only one body was cast on shore, which was that of a young woman, who lay with her face to the ground, and her wet clothes clinging round her. We turned her carefully over, and I beheld a face that seemed to me wonderfully fair and beautiful. She had escaped the sharks, and had been dead several hours—most probably she had been cast on shore by the waves soon after the ship struck, for she had escaped also the rocks, which, had she been dashed against, would have left fearful signs of their contact on her delicate frame.

The sight of her corpse gave me many melancholy thoughts. I thought of the delight she might have caused both of us, had she been saved. What a pleasant companion she might have proved! Indeed, as I looked on her pale cold features, I fancied that she might have reconciled me to ending my existence on the island— ay, even to the abandonment of my favourite scheme of seeking my grandfather to give him back his diamonds.

We took her up with as much pity and affection as if she were our nearest and dearest relative, and carried her home and placed her on Mrs Reichardt's bed; and then I laid some planks together, in the shape of what Mrs Reichardt called a coffin—and I dug her a deep grave in the guano.

And all the while I found myself crying as I had never cried before, and my heart seemed weary and faint. In solemn silence we carried her to her grave, and read over her the funeral service out of the Prayer-book, kneeling and praying for this nameless creature, whom we had never seen alive, as though she had been our companion for many years; both of us shedding tears for her hapless fate as if we had lost a beloved sister. And when we had filled up her grave and departed, we went home, and passed the most miserable day we had ever had to endure since we had first been cast upon the island.

I had now numerous occupations that kept me actively employed. Still I could not for a long time help recalling to mind that pale face that looked so piteously upon me when I first beheld it; and then I would leave off my work, and give myself up to my melancholy thoughts till my attention was called off by some appeal from my companion. I made a kind of monument over the place where she was buried, and planted there the finest flowers we had; and I never passed the spot without a prayer, as if I were approaching holy ground.

I must not forget to add, that a few days after the wreck we were agreeably surprised by visitors that, though unexpected, were extremely welcome. I had noticed strange birds wandering about in various parts of the island. On their coming under the notice of my companion, they were immediately recognised as fowls and ducks that had no doubt escaped from the ship.

We might now, therefore, constitute ourselves a little colony, of which Mrs Reichardt and myself were the immediate governors, the settlers being a mingled community of calves, sheep, pigs, and poultry, that lived on excellent terms with each other; the quadrupeds having permission to roam where they pleased, and the bipeds being kept within a certain distance of the government house.

The old hut had suffered so much from the storm that I determined on building another in a better position, and had recourse to the framework of the house I had taken from the wreck. I had some difficulty in putting the several parts together, but at last succeeded, and a small, but most commodious dwelling was the result. Near it I laid out a new garden, wherein I planted all the orange-trees we had reared, as well as many of the seeds and roots we had brought from the wreck. A little beyond I enclosed a paddock, wherein I planted the twigs we had found in pots, which proved to be fruit trees.

When I had done this, I thought of my agricultural implements, and very much desired to make use of a handy plough that was amongst them, when I learned the advantages that might arise from it. At first, I yoked myself to the plough, and Mrs Reichardt held it: this proved such hard and awkward work that I kept projecting all sorts of plans for lessening the labour—the best was that of yoking our calves, and making them pull instead of myself. This was more easily thought of than done. The animals did not prove very apt pupils, but in course of time, with a good deal of patience, and some manoeuvring, I succeeded in making them perform the work they were expected to do.

Thus, in building, gardening, planting, and farming, the time flew by quickly, and in the course of the next year the aspect of the place had become quite changed. The guano that enriched the soil made every kind of vegetation thrive with an almost marvellous rapidity and luxuriance. We had a comfortable house, up which a vine was creeping in one place, and a young pear-tree in another. We were supplied with the choicest oranges, and had apples of several kinds. We had abundance of furniture, and an inexhaustible stock of provisions. We had a most gorgeous show of flowers of many different species; our new kitchen garden was full of useful vegetables—young fruit trees were yielding their produce wherever they had been planted—the poultry had more than doubled their number—the calves were taking upon themselves the full dignity of the state of cow and bull—the ewes had numerous lambs—and the pigs had not only grown into excellent pork, but had already produced more than one litter that would be found equally desirable when provisions ran scarce. We had two growing crops, of different kinds of grain, and a large pasture-field fenced round.

The Little Savage, at seventeen, had been transformed into a farmer, and the cultivation of the farm and the care of the live stock soon left him no time for indulging in vain longings to leave the island, or useless regrets for the fair creature who, even in death, I had regarded as its greatest ornament.

Two years later, still greater improvements, and still greater additions became visible. We were establishing a dairy farm on a small scale, and as our herds and flocks, as well as the pigs and poultry, increased rapidly, we promised in a few years to be the most thriving farmers that had ever lived in that part of the world by the cultivation of the land.

CHAPTER XLIV

Although my first experimental voyage had proved so hazardous, now that I was better provided for meeting its perils, I became anxious to make another attempt to circumnavigate the island. The boat that had belonged to the wrecked ship, from the frequent trips I had made in her to and from the shore, I could manage as well as if I had been rowing boats all my life.

With the assistance of Mrs Reichardt, who pulled an oar almost as well as myself, we could get her along in very good style, even when heavily laden, and our labours together had taken from her all that timidity which had deterred her from trusting herself with me, when I first ventured from the island.

I was, however, very differently circumstanced now, to what I was then. Instead of a frail cockle-shell, that threatened to be capsized by every billow that approached it, and that would scarcely hold two persons comfortably, I was master of a well-built ship's-boat, that would hold half a dozen with ease, and except in very rough weather, was as safe as any place ashore.

I had repaired the slight damage its timbers had received, and had made an awning to protect us when rowing from the heat of the sun; I had also raised a sail, which would relieve us of a good deal of labour. When everything was prepared, I urged Mrs Reichardt to accompany me in a voyage round the island; an excursion I hoped would turn out equally pleasant and profitable.

I found her very averse to trusting herself farther from shore than was absolutely necessary. She raised all kinds of objections— prominent among which were my want of seamanship for managing a boat in the open sea; the danger that might arise from a sudden squall coming on; her fear of our getting amongst a shoal of sharks, and the risk we ran of driving against a projecting rock; but I overruled them all.

I showed her, by taking little trips out to sea, that I could manage the boat either with the sail or the oars, and assured her that by keeping close to the island, we could run ashore before danger could reach us; and that nothing could be easier than our keeping out of the reach of both rocks and sharks.

I do not think I quite convinced her that her fears were groundless, but my repeated entreaties, the fineness of the weather, and her dislike to be again left on the island, whilst I was risking my life at sea, prevailed, and she promised to join me in this second experiment.

Her forethought, however, was here as fully demonstrated as on other occasions, for she did not suffer the boat to leave the shore till she had provided for any accident that might prevent our return in the anticipated time.

A finer day for such a voyage we could not have selected. The sky was without a cloud, and there was just wind enough for the purpose I wanted, without any apprehensions of this being increased. I got up the awning, and spread the sail, and handing Mrs Reichardt to her appointed seat, we bid farewell to our four-footed and two-footed friends ashore, that were gazing at us as if they knew they were parting from their only protectors. I then pushed the boat off, the wind caught the sail, and she glided rapidly through the deep water.

I let her proceed in this way about a quarter of a mile from the island, and then tacked; the boat, obedient to the position of the sail, altered her course, and we proceeded at about the same rate for a considerable distance.

Mrs Reichardt, notwithstanding her previous fears, could not help feeling the exhilarating effect of this adventurous voyage. We were floating, safely and gracefully, upon the billows, with nothing but sea and sky in every direction but one, where the rugged shores of our island home gave a bold, yet menacing feature to the view.

My heart seemed to expand with the majestic prospect before me. Never had mariner, when discovering some prodigious continent, felt a greater degree of exultation than I experienced, when directing my little vessel over the immense wilderness of waters that spread out before me, till it joined the line of the horizon.

I sat down by the side of Mrs Reichardt, and allowed the boat to proceed on its course, either as if it required no directing hand, or that its present direction was so agreeable, I felt no inclination to alter it.

"I can easily imagine," said I, "the enthusiasm of such men as Columbus, whose discovery of America you were relating to me the other day. The vocation of these early navigators was a glorious one, and, when they had tracked their way over so many thousand miles of pathless water, and found themselves in strange seas, expecting the appearance of land, hitherto unknown to the civilised world, they must have felt the importance of their mission as discoverers."

"No doubt, Frank," she replied. "And probably it was this that supported the great man you have just named, in the severe trials he was obliged to endure, on the very eve of the discovery that was to render his name famous to all generations. He had endured intolerable hardships, the ship had been so long without sight of land, that no one thought it worth while to look out for it, and he expected that his crew would mutiny, and insist on returning. At this critical period of his existence, first one indication of land, and then another made itself manifest; the curiosity of the disheartened sailors became excited; hope revived in the breast of their immortal captain; a man was now induced to ascend the main-top, and his joyful cry of land woke up the slumbering spirit of the crew. In this way, a new world was first presented to the attention of the inhabitants of the old."

"It appears to me very unjust," I observed, "that so important a discovery should have become known to us, not by the name of its original discoverer, but by that of a subsequent visitor to its shores."

"Undoubtedly," said Mrs Reichardt, "it is apparently unfair that Americus Vespucius should obtain an honour which Christopher Columbus alone had deserved. But of the fame which is the natural right of him whose courage and enterprise procured this unrivalled acquisition, no one can deprive him. His gigantic discovery may always be known as America, but the world acknowledges its obligation to Columbus, and knows little beyond the name of his rival."

"Were the immediate results of so large an addition to geographical knowledge, as beneficial to the entire human race as they ought to have been?"

"I do not think they were. The vast continent then thrown open to the advance of civilisation, may be divided into two portions, the south and the north. The former was inhabited by a harmless effeminate race, who enjoyed many of the refinements of civilisation; their knowledge of the arts, for instance, as shewn to us in the ruins of their cities, was considerable; they possessed extensive buildings in a bold and ornate style of architecture; they made a lavish use of the precious metals, of which the land was extremely rich, and they wore dresses which shewed a certain perfection in the manufacture of textile fabrics, and no slight degree of taste and art in their formation.

"The Spaniards, who were led to this part of the continent by a desire to enrich themselves with the gold which the earliest discoverers had found in the new country in considerable quantities, invaded the territories of this peaceful people, and, by their superior knowledge of warlike weapons, and the ignorance of the intentions of their invaders that prevailed amongst the natives of all ranks, by a series of massacres, they were enabled, though comparatively but a small force, to obtain possession of the vast empire that had been established there from time immemorial, and turn it into a Spanish colony.

"The blood of this harmless race flowed like water; their great Incas or Emperors were deposed and murdered, their splendid temples plundered of their riches, their nobles and priests tortured to make them change their faith, and the great mass of the people became slaves to their more warlike conquerors. It was in this way the gold of Mexico and Peru enriched the treasury of Spain; but every ingot had the curse of blood upon it, and from that time the Spanish power, then at its height, began to decline in Europe, till it sunk in the scale of nations among the least important. The colonies revolted from the mother country, and became independent states; but the curse that followed the infamous appropriation of the country, seems to cling to the descendants of the first criminals, and neither government nor people prospers; and it is evident that all these independent states must in time be absorbed by a great republic, that has sprung up by peaceable means, as it were at their side, whilst they were content to be colonies."

"To what republic do you allude?"

"You may remember that I told you that the entire continent was divided into south and north."

"Exactly."

"The history of the southern portion I have rapidly sketched for you, that of the northern you will find of a totally different character."

"Pray let me hear it."

"When North America was first discovered, it was found to be inhabited by a race of savages, divided into several tribes. They had no manufactures; they had no knowledge of art or science; they lived in the impenetrable woods in huts, having no pretension to architecture; they went almost entirely naked, were extremely warlike, and fond of hunting, and were known to devour the enemies they killed in battle.

"To this barbarous race came a few adventurous men across the stormy Atlantic, from the distant island of England—"

"Ah, England!" I exclaimed, "that is the country of my parents—that is the home of my grandfather; let me hear anything you have to say about England."

Mrs Reichardt smiled at my animation, but proceeded without making any comment upon what I had said.

"England possessed at this period many adventurous spirits, who were ready to dare every danger to obtain for their country a share in the honours which other lands had assumed through the enterprise of their navigators. By such men different portions of the northern continent of America were discovered; the fame of these new lands, their wonderful productiveness and admirable climate, soon spread amongst their countrymen, and from time to time various ships left the English ports with small bands of adventurers, who made what were termed settlements in the country of these savages—not by mercilessly massacring them as the Spaniards had done in the south, and then plundering them of all they possessed, but by purchasing certain districts or pieces of land from the original occupants, which they peacefully cultivated; as their numbers increased, they multiplied their habitations, and obtained by barter of the savages fresh accessions of territory."

"The English showed themselves a much more humane people than the Spaniards," I observed. "But did they never come into collision with the wild natives of the country?"

"Frequently," Mrs Reichardt replied, "but in some measure this was unavoidable. As new settlers from England landed in the country, they required more land; but the savages were now not inclined to barter; they had become jealous of the strangers, and were desirous of driving them back to their ships before they became too numerous. Acts of hostility were committed by the savages upon the settlers, which were often marked by great brutality: this exasperated the latter, who joined in a warlike association, and notwithstanding their numbers and daring, drove them further and further from their neighbourhood, till either by conquest, treaties, or purchase, the Englishmen or their descendants obtained the greater portion of North America."

"Do they still hold possession of it?" I asked.

"Up to a recent date, the whole of this vast acquisition was a colony in obedience to the government of England; but a dispute having arisen between the mother country and the colony, a struggle took place, which ended in the latter throwing off all subjection to the laws of England. The extensive provinces joined together in a union of equal privileges and powers, which has since gone by the name of the Government of the United States of North America. This is the great republic to which I just now alluded, that is gradually absorbing the minor Southern States into its—union, and threatens at no very distant date to spread the English language and the English race over the whole continent of America."

"Has England then completely lost the country she colonised?" I inquired, feeling more and more interested in the subject.

"No, a great portion still remains in her possession," she replied. "The people preserved their allegiance when their neighbours thought proper to rise in revolt, and are now in a state of great prosperity, governed by the laws of England, and supported by her power. The English possessions in North America form an extensive district. It is, however, but an inconsiderable fraction of the vast countries still remaining under the dominion of England. Her territories lie in every quarter of the globe; indeed the sun never sets upon this immense empire—an empire with which the conquests of Alexander, and of Caesar, or the most formidable state that existed in ancient times, cannot for a moment be compared; and when we bear in mind that in all these various climates, and in all these far-distant shores, the flag of our country affords the same protection to the colonist as he would enjoy in his own land, we may entertain some idea of the vast power that government possesses which can make itself respected at so many opposite points from the source whence it emanates."

I was so much interested in this description, that I had neglected to notice the rate at which the boat was driving through the water. I now rose with great alacrity to shift the sail, as we had got several miles from the island, and if I did not take care we might be blown out of sight of land. I lost no time in putting her on another tack, but we had not proceeded far in this direction when I found the wind lull, and presently the sail drooped to the mast, and there was a dead calm.

It became necessary now to take to our oars, and we were presently pulling with all our strength in the direction of land. This went on for some time till we were both tired, and I was surprised at the little progress we had made. We lay on our oars and took some refreshment, and then pulled with additional vigour; but I began to suspect that we were receding from the land instead of approaching it, and called Mrs Reichardt's attention to the fact of the island diminishing in size notwithstanding the length of time we had been pulling towards it.

"Ah, Frank," she said, in a melancholy tone of voice, "I have for some time entertained suspicions that all our strength was being expended in vain. It is very clear that we have got into a current that is every moment taking us farther out to sea, and if a breeze does not soon spring up, we shall lose sight of the island, and then, heaven only knows what will become of us."

I shook out the sail, in hopes of its catching sufficient wind to lead us out of the current, but not a breath of air was stirring. We did not possess such a thing as a compass; our provisions were only calculated for a pleasure trip—we had only one small jar of water, and a flask of spirit, a few biscuits, two large cakes, a chicken, and some dried fish. The land was rapidly receding; I could only mark its position with respect to the sun that now was pouring its burning rays upon our little bark. If it had not been for the awning we could not have endured it; the heat was so oppressive.

We had been obliged to give over rowing, as much from the fatigue it occasioned, as from the hopelessness of our labour.

We now sat with sinking hearts watching the fast retreating land. It had become a point—it diminished to a speck, and as it disappeared from our anxious sight, the sun set in all his glory, and we were drifting at the mercy of the current we knew not where, with nothing but sky and sea all around us.

CHAPTER XLV

Vainly I stretched my eyes around the illimitable field of ocean, in hope of discerning some indication of that power whose ships I had been told traversed every sea; but nothing like a vessel was in sight—the mighty waters stretched out like an endless desert on every side. There was no sign of man in all this vast space, except our little boat; and in comparison with this space, how insignificant were the two helpless human beings who sat silent and motionless in that boat awaiting their destiny.

The stars came out with marvellous brilliancy. I fancied that I had never seen them appear so bright; but probably the gloominess of my thoughts made them look brighter by contrast. I seemed the centre of a glorious system of worlds revolving above me with a calm and tranquil beauty, that appeared to reproach me for giving way to despair in a scene so lovely.

The great mass of water, scarcely moved by a ripple, now appeared lit up with countless fires, and a purplish haze, like a low flame, was visible in every direction. I directed the attention of my companion to this strange appearance. Notwithstanding the intensity of her anxiety, she immediately entered into an explanation of the phenomenon, and attributed it to a peculiarly phosphoric state of the sea, caused by myriads of creatures which possess the quality of the glow-worm, and rising to the surface of the water, made the latter seem as though enveloped in flame.

I sat a long time watching the singular appearances that presented themselves whenever I dashed down the oar. It looked as though I was beating fire instead of water, and flame seemed to come from the oar with the drops that fell from it into the sea.

In this way hours passed by: we were still floating with the current; the moon and stars were now coldly shining over our heads; the ocean around us was still gleaming with phosphoric fires, when

Mrs Reichardt advised me to take some nourishment, and then endeavour to go to sleep, saying she would keep watch and apprise me if anything happened of which it might be advantageous to avail ourselves.

The only thing I desired was the appearance of a vessel, or the setting in of a breeze, of which at present not a sign existed. I felt disinclined either to eat or to drink: but I proposed that my companion should make a meal and then go to sleep, as it was much more proper that I should keep watch than herself. The fact was, we were both anxious that the other should be the first to diminish our little stock of food; but as neither would be induced to do this, it was decided that our provisions should be divided into certain portions, which were only to be taken at sunrise and sunset, and that we should during the night relieve each other every three hours in keeping watch, that if we saw land, or a ship, or the wind should spring up, we might consult immediately as to our course.

I only succeeded in inducing her to lie down at the bottom of the boat, to obtain a little sleep, previously to her taking my place that I might so rest myself. She first said her usual prayers for the evening, in which I joined, and in a few minutes I was glad to hear by her regular breathing, that she was obtaining that repose of which I was certain she stood greatly in need.

I was now the sole observer of the stupendous spectacle that spread out around and above me the most sublime feature in this imposing scene appeared to be the silence which reigned supreme over all. The heavens were as mute as the sea. It looked as if the earth had been engulfed by a second deluge, and all living nature had perished utterly from the face of it.

I felt a deep feeling of melancholy stealing over me: and could not forbear reproaching myself for embarking in this hazardous enterprise, and risking a life that I was bound to preserve. What could become of us both I knew not—but I was sensible that if we were not speedily picked up, or made some friendly shore, there existed but little hopes of our surviving many days.

I made up my mind that the island we should never see again, and though I had been so anxious for so many years to quit it, now that fate had separated us for ever, I could not console myself for the loss of a home endeared to me by so many recollections. But my great grief was the loss of my grandfather's diamonds. He had now no chance of having them restored to him. If they were found they would become the property of the discoverer; and he would never know how his daughter perished on a rock, and how his grandson was swallowed up by the waters of the great deep.

And then I thought of that glorious England I had so long hoped to see, and my heart sunk within me as I gazed out upon the boundless prospect. There was not a voice to murmur consolation, not a hand to offer me assistance. Was I never to see those white cliffs which had been so often described to me, that I could call them to mind as clearly as if they stood in all their pride and beauty before my eyes?

How often had I dreamed of approaching the hallowed shores of England—how often had I heard the cheerful voices of her people welcoming the Little Savage to his natural home—how often had I been embraced by my aged grandfather, and received into the happy circle of his friends, with the respect and affection due to his heir. I had dreamed happy dreams, and seen blissful visions; and the result was starvation in an open boat on the illimitable ocean.

Mrs Reichardt still slept, and I would not wake her. As long as she was insensible to the dangers of her position she must exist in comparative happiness; to disturb her was to bring her back to a sense of danger and misery, and the recollection that my folly had brought her to this hopeless state.

I noticed that a small cloud was making its appearance in the horizon, and almost at the same instant I observed it, I felt a breeze that was just sufficient to flap the sail against the mast. In a few minutes the cloud had greatly increased, and the wind filled the sail. I fancied it blew in a direction contrary to the current; and in the belief that it did so I soon got the boat round, and to my great joy she was presently scudding before the wind at a rate that was sensibly increasing.

But the cloud presently began to envelop the heavens, and a thick darkness spread itself like a veil in every direction. The wind blew very fresh, and strained the mast to which the sail had been fixed; and now I began to entertain a new fear: some sudden gust might take the sail and capsize us, or tear it from its fastenings. I would gladly have taken in the sail, but I considered it as rather a hazardous experiment. Mrs Reichardt lay in a position that prevented my getting at it without disturbing her, or running the risk of tipping the boat over, when it would be sure to fill immediately, and sink with us both. Though we could both swim, I felt assured that if we were once in the water, there would remain very little chance of our protracting our lives beyond a few hours.

The boat, therefore, continued to run before the wind at a rapid rate, the slight mast creaking, and the sail stretching so tight, I expected every minute that we should be upset. At this moment Mrs Reichardt awoke, and her quick eye immediately took in the full extent of her danger.

"We shall be lost," she said hurriedly, "if we do not take in that sail!"

I was fully aware of this, but she had seen more of a sailor's perils than I had, and knew better how to meet them. She offered to assist me in taking in the sail, and directing me to be very careful, we proceeded, with the assistance of the awning, to the mast, and after a good deal of labour, and at some risk of being blown into the sea, we succeeded in furling the sail, and unshipping the mast.

We were now in quite as much danger from another cause—the surface of the sea, which had been so smooth during the calm, was now so violently agitated by the wind, that the boat kept ascending one great billow only to descend into the trough of another. We often went down almost perpendicularly, and the height seemed every moment increasing; and every time we went thus plunging headlong into the boiling waters, I thought we should be engulfed never to rise; nevertheless, the next minute, up we ascended on the crest of some more fearful wave than any we had hitherto encountered, and down again we plunged in the dark unfathomable abyss that, walled in by foaming mountains of water, appeared yawning to close over us for ever.

It was almost entirely dark; we could see only the white foam of the wave over which we were about to pass; save this, it was black below and black above, and impenetrable darkness all around.

Mrs Reichardt sat close to me with her hand in mine—she uttered no exclamations of feminine terror—she was more awe-struck than frightened. I believe that she was fully satisfied her last hour had come, for I could hear her murmuring a prayer in which she commended her soul to her Creator.

I cannot say that I was in any great degree alarmed—the rapid up and down motion of the boat gave me a sensation of pleasure

I had never before experienced. To say the truth, I should have greatly enjoyed being thus at the mercy of the winds and waves, in the midst of a black and stormy night on the trackless ocean, had it not been for my constant thoughts of my companion, and my bitter self-reproaches for having led her into so terrible a danger.

I was now, however, called from these reflections, by the necessity of active employment. The boat I found shipped water at every plunge, and if speedy means were not taken to keep the water under, there was little doubt that she would soon fill and go down. I therefore seized the iron kettle we had brought with us to cook our dinner, and began rapidly bailing out the water, which was already over our ankles. We continued to ship water, sometimes more and sometimes less; and Mrs Reichardt, actuated no doubt by the same motives as myself, with a tin pan now assisted me in getting rid of the treacherous element.

By our united exertions we kept the water under, and hoped to be able to get rid of the whole of it. About this time it began to rain very heavily, and although the awning protected our heads, so much fell into the boat, that notwithstanding our labours we continued to sit in a pool.

We were, however, glad to find that as the rain fell the wind abated, and as the latter subsided, the sea became less violent, and we shipped less water. I was now able by my own exertions to keep the boat tolerably dry, and Mrs Reichardt, ever provident, spread out all the empty vessels she had brought with her to catch the rain, for as she said, we did not know how valuable that water might become in a short time.

The rain continued to pour down in a perfect torrent for several hours; at the end of which the sky gradually cleared. The sea, though still rough, presented none of those mountainous waves that a short time before had threatened to annihilate us at every descent, and there was just sufficient breeze to waft us along at a brisk rate with the assistance of our sail.

Mrs Reichardt helped me in putting up the mast, and directly we began to feel the breeze, she insisted on my taking some refreshment. It was vitally necessary to both, for our labours had been heavy for several hours. We therefore ate sparingly of our provisions, and washed down our meal with a pannikin of water mingled with a little spirit.

CHAPTER XLVI

The morning dawned upon a boundless expanse of sea. The first object that presented itself to my sight was an enormous whale spouting water about a quarter of a mile distant from me; then I observed another, then a third, and subsequently, several more; they presented a singular and picturesque appearance, as one or other of these vast animals was continually throwing up a column of water that caught the rays of the sun, and looked very beautiful in the distance.

I looked in vain for land; I looked equally in vain for a ship; there was nothing visible but this shoal of whales, and Mrs Reichardt endeavoured to cheer me by describing the importance of the whale fishery to England, and the perils which the men meet with who pursue the fish for the purpose of wounding them with an iron instrument called a harpoon.

I felt much interest in these details; and my companion went into the whole history of a whaling expedition, describing the first discovery of the huge fish from the ship; the pursuit in the boats, and the harpooning of the whale; its struggles after having been wounded; its being towed to the ship's side; the subsequent manufacture of oil from the blubber of the animal, and the preparation of whalebone.

In attending to this discourse, I completely forgot that I was being tossed about in the open sea, I knew not where; and where I might be in a short time it would be proved I was equally ignorant: perhaps I should be a corpse floating on the surface of the ocean waiting for a tomb till a shark came that way; perhaps I should be suffering the torments of hunger and thirst; perhaps cast lifeless upon a rock, where my bleached bones would remain the only monument which would then declare that there once existed in these latitudes such a being as the Little Savage.

Where now could be the island I, though long so anxious to quit, now was a thousand times more desirous of beholding? I felt that nothing could be more agreeable to me than a glimpse of that wild rocky coast that had so often appeared to me the walls of an intolerable prison.

I strained my eyes in vain in every direction; the line of the horizon stretched out uninterrupted by a single break of any kind all around. Where could we be? I often asked myself; but except that we were on the wide ocean, neither myself nor my companion had the slightest idea of our geographical position. We must have been blown a considerable distance during the storm: much farther than the current had taken us from the island.

I calculated that we must have passed it by many a mile if we had continued the same course; but the wind had shifted several times, and it might be that we were not so very long a sail from it, could we gain the slightest knowledge of the direction in which it was to be found. But this was hopeless. I felt assured that we must abandon all idea of seeing it again.

In the midst of these painful reflections, my companion directed my attention to an object at a very considerable distance, and intimated her impression that it was a ship. Luckily, I had brought my glass with me, and soon was anxiously directing it to the required point. It was a ship: but at so great a distance that it was impossible, as Mrs Reichardt said, for any person on board to distinguish our boat. I would have sailed in that direction, but the wind was contrary: I had, therefore, no alternative but to wait till the ship should approach near enough to make us out; and I passed several hours of the deepest anxiety in watching the course of the distant vessel.

She increased in size, so that I could observe that she was a large ship by the unassisted eye; but as we were running before the wind in a totally different direction, there seemed very little chance of our communicating, unless she altered her course.

Mrs Reichardt mentioned that signals were made by vessels at a distance to attract each other's attention, and described the various ways in which they communicated the wishes of their respective captains. The only signal I had been in the habit of making was burning quantities of wood on the shore and pouring water on it to make it smoke—this was impossible in our boat.

My companion at last suggested that I should tie a table-cloth to the mast; its peculiar whiteness might attract attention. The sail was presently taken in, and the table-cloth spread in its place; but, unfortunately, it soon afterwards came on a dead calm—the breeze died away, and the cloth hung in long folds against the mast.

No notice whatever was taken of us. We now took to our oars and pulled in the direction of the ship; but after several hours' hard rowing, our strength had so suffered from our previous fatigues, that we seemed to have made very little distance.

In a short time the sun set, and we watched the object of all our hopes with most anxious eyes, till night set in and hid her from our sight. Shortly afterwards a light breeze again sprung up; with renewed hope we gave our sail to the wind, but it bore us in a contrary direction, and when morning dawned we saw no more of the ship.

The wind had now again shifted, and bore us briskly along. But where? I had fallen asleep during the preceding night, wearied out with labour and anxiety, and I did not wake till long after daybreak. Mrs Reichardt would not disturb me. In sleep I was insensible to the miseries and dangers of my position. She could not bring herself to disturb a repose that was at once so necessary to mind and body; and I fell into a sweet dream of a new home in that dear England I had prayed so often to see; and bright faces smiled upon me, and voices welcomed me, full of tenderness and affection.

I fancied that in one of those faces I recognised my mother, of whose love I had so early been deprived, and that it was paler than all the others, but infinitely more tender and affectionate: then the countenance seemed to grow paler and paler, till it took upon itself the likeness of the fair creature I had buried in the guano, and I thought she embraced me, and her arms were cold as stone, and she pressed her lips to mine, and they gave a chill to my blood that made me shake as with an ague.

Suddenly I beheld Jackson with his sightless orbs groping towards me with a knife in his hand, muttering imprecations, and he caught hold of me, and we had a desperate struggle, and he plunged a long knife into my chest, with a loud laugh of derision and malice; and as I felt the blade enter my flesh, I gave a start and jumped up, and alarmed Mrs Reichardt by the wild cry with which I awoke.

How strongly was that dream impressed upon my mind; and the features of the different persons who figured in it—how distinctly they were brought before me! My poor mother was as fresh in my recollection as though I had seen her but yesterday, and the sweetness of her looks as she approached me—how I now tried to recall them, and feasted on their memory as though it were a lost blessing.

Then the nameless corpse that had been washed from the wreck, how strange it seemed, that after this lapse of time she should appear to me in a dream, as though we had been long attached to each other, and her affections had been through life entirely my own. Poor girl! Perhaps even now some devoted lover mourns her loss; or hopes at no distant date to be able to join her in the new colony, to attain which a cruel destiny had forced her from his arms. Little does he dream of her nameless grave under the guano. Little does he dream that the only colony in which he is likely to join her is that settlement in the great desert of oblivion, over which Death has remained governor from the birth of the world.

But the most unpleasant part of the vision was the appearance of Jackson; and it was a long time before I could bring myself to believe that I had not beheld his well known features—that I had not been stabbed by him, and that I was not suffering from the mortal wound he had inflicted. I however at last shook off the delusion, and to Mrs Reichardt's anxious inquiries replied only that I had had a disagreeable dream.

In a short time I began to doubt whether the waking was more pleasant than the dreaming—the vast ocean still spread itself before me like a mighty winding sheet, the fair sky, beautiful as it appeared in the rays of the morning sun, I could only regard as a pall—and our little bark was the coffin in which two helpless human beings, though still existing, were waiting interment.

"Has God abandoned us?" I asked my companion, "or has He forgotten that two of his creatures are in the deepest peril of their lives, from which He alone can save them?"

"Hush! Frank Henniker," exclaimed Mrs Reichardt solemnly; "this is impious. God never abandons those who are worthy of His protection. He will either save them at His own appointed time—or if He think it more desirable, will snatch them from a scene where so many dangers surround them, and place them where there prevails eternal tranquillity, and everlasting bliss.

"We should rather rejoice," she added, with increasing seriousness, "that we are thought worthy of being so early taken from a world in which we have met with so many troubles."

"But to die in this way," I observed gloomily; "to be left to linger out days of terrible torture, without a hope of relief—I cannot reconcile myself to it."

"We must die sooner or later," she said, "and there are many diseases which are fatal after protracted suffering of the most agonising description. These we have been spared. The wretch who lingers in torment, visited by some loathsome disorder, would envy us, could he see the comparatively easy manner in which we are suffered to leave existence.

"But I do not myself see the hopelessness of our case," she added. "It is not yet impossible that we may be picked up by a ship, or discover some friendly shore whence we might obtain a passage for England."

"I see no prospect of this," said I; "we are apparently out of the track of ships, and if it should be our chance to discover one, the people on board are not likely to observe us. I wish I had never left the island."

Mrs Reichardt never reproached me—never so much as reminded me that it was my own fault. She merely added, "It was the will of God."

We ate and drank our small rations—my companion always blessing the meal, and offering a thanksgiving for being permitted to enjoy it. I noticed what was left. We had been extremely economical, yet there was barely enough for another day. We determined still further to reduce the trifling portion we allowed ourselves, that we might increase our chance of escape.

CHAPTER XLVII

Five days and nights had we been drifting at the mercy of the winds and waves; all our small stock of food had been devoured—though we had hoarded every crumb, as the miser hoards his gold. Even the rain water, as well as the water we had brought with us, we had drained to the last drop.

The weather continually alternated from a dead calm to a light breeze: the wind frequently shifted, but I had no strength left to attend to the sail—the boat was abandoned to its own guidance, or rather to that of the wind. When becalmed we lay still—when the breeze sprang up we pursued our course till the sail no longer felt its influence.

Five long days and nights—days of intolerable suffering, nights of inexpressible horror. From sunrise to sunset I strained my eyes along the line of the horizon, but nothing but sky and wave ever met my gaze. When it became dark, excited by the deep anxiety I had endured throughout the day, I could not sleep. I fancied I beheld through the darkness monstrous forms mocking and gibbering, and high above them all was reared the head of the enormous python I had combated in the Happy Valley. And he opened his tremendous jaws, as though to swallow me, and displayed fold upon fold of his immense form as if to involve and crush the boat in its mighty involutions.

I was always glad when the day dawned, or if the night happened to be fair and starlight; for the spectres vanished when the sun shone, and the tranquil beauty of the stars calmed my soul.

I was famishing for want of food—but I suffered most from want of water, for the heat during the day was tremendous, and I became so frantic from thirst, that nothing but the exhortations of Mrs Reichardt would have prevented me from dashing myself into the sea, and drinking my fill of the salt water that looked so tempting and refreshing.

My companion sought to encourage me to hope, long after all hope had vanished—then she preached resignation to the Divine Will, and in her own nature gave a practical commentary on her text.

I perceived that her voice was getting more and more faint—and that she was becoming hourly more feeble. She was not able to move from her seat, and at last asked me to assist her to lie down at the bottom of the boat. Then I noticed that she prayed fervently, and I could often distinguish my name in these petitions to the throne of Grace.

I felt a strange sensation in my head, and my tongue became in my mouth as a dry stick—from this I was relieved by chewing the sleeve of my shirt; but my head grew worse. My eyes too were affected in a strange manner. I continually fancied that I saw ships sailing about at a little distance from me, and I strove to attract their attention by calling to them. My voice was weak and I could create only a kind of half stifled cry. Then I thought I beheld land: fair forests and green pastures spread before me—bright flowers and refreshing fruits grew all around—and I called to my companion to make haste for we were running ashore and should presently be pulling the clustering grapes and should lay ourselves down among the odorous flowers.

Mrs Reichardt opened her eyes and gazed at me with a more painful interest. She knew I was haunted by the chimeras created by famine and thirst; but she seemed to have lost all power of speech. She motioned me to join her in prayer; I, however, was too much occupied with the prospect of landing, and paid no attention to her signs.

Presently the bright landscape faded away, and I beheld nothing but the wide expanse of water, the circle of which appeared to expand and spread into the sky, and the sky seemed lost and broken up in the water, and for a few minutes they were mixed together in the wildest and strangest confusion. Subsequently to this I must have dropt asleep, for after a while I found myself huddled up in a corner of the boat, and must have fallen there from my seat. I stared about me for some time, unconscious where I was. The bright sun still shone over my head; the everlasting sea still rolled beneath my feet.

I looked to the bottom of the boat, and met the upturned gaze of my fellow voyager—the pale face had grown paler, and the expression of the painful eye had become less intelligent. I thought she was as I had seen her in my dream, when she changed from her own likeness to that of the poor drowned girl we buried in the guano.

I turned away my gaze—the sight was too painful to look upon. I felt assured that she was dying, and that in a very short space of time, that faithful and affectionate nature I must part from forever.

I thought I would make a last effort. Though faint and trembling, burning with fever, and feeling deadly sick, I managed by the support of the awning to crawl to the mast, and embracing it with one arm I raised the glass with the other hand, and looked carefully about. My hand was very unsteady and my eyes seemed dim. I could discern nothing but water.

I should have sunk in despair to the bottom of the boat, had I not been attracted at the moment by a singular appearance in the sky. A cloud was approaching of a shape and appearance I had never observed before. I raised the glass again, and after observing this cloud for some time with great attention, I felt assured that what I considered to be long lines of vapour was an immense flock of birds.

This discovery interested me—I forgot the intensity of my sufferings in observing the motions of this apparently endless flock. As the first file approached, I looked again, to see if I could make out what they were. God of heaven! They were gannets.

I crawled back to my companion as rapidly as my feeble limbs would allow, to inform her of the discovery I had made. Alas! I found that I was unheeded. I could not believe that her fine spirit had fled; no, she moved her hand; but the dull spiritless gaze seemed to warn me that her dissolution was fast approaching. I looked for the spirit flask, and found a few drops were still left there; I poured these into her mouth, and watched the result with the deepest anxiety I had ever known since the day of my birth.

In a few minutes I found that she breathed more regularly and distinctly—presently her eyes lost that fixedness which had made them so painful to look upon. Then she recognised me, and took hold of my hand, regarding me with the sweet smile with which I was so familiar.

As soon as I found that consciousness had returned, I told her of the great flock of gannets that were evidently wending their way to their customary resting place, and the hope I entertained that if they could be kept in sight, and the wind remained in the same quarter, the boat might be led by them to the place where they laid their eggs.

She listened to me with attention, and evidently understood what I said. Her lips moved, and I thought she was returning thanks to God—accepting the flight of the birds as a manifest proof that He was still watching over us. In a few minutes she seemed so much better that she could sit up. I noticed her for some time watching the gannets that now approached in one vast cloud that threatened to shut us out from the sky—she then turned her gaze in an opposite direction, and with a smile of exultation that lit up her wan face as with a glory, stretched her arm out, pointing her hand to a distant portion of the sea. My gaze quickly followed hers, and I fancied I discovered a break in the line of the horizon; but it did not look like a ship. I pointed the glass in that direction, and felt the joyful assurance that we were within sight of land.

This additional discovery gave me increased strength: or rather hope now dawning upon us, gave me an impulse I had not felt before. I in my turn became the consoler. I encouraged Mrs Reichardt, with all the arguments of which I was master, to think that we should soon be in safety. She smiled, and something like animation again appeared in her pale features.

If I could save her, I felt I should be blessed beyond measure. Such an object was worth striving for; and I did strive. I know not how it was that I gained strength to do what I did on that day; but I felt that I was supported from On High, and as the speck of land that she had first discovered gradually enlarged itself as we approached it, my exertions to secure a speedy rescue for my companion from the jaws of death, continued to increase.

The breeze remained fair and we scudded along at a spanking rate, the gannets keeping us company all the way—evidently bound to the same shore. I kept talking to Mrs Reichardt, and endeavouring to raise her spirits with the most cheering description of what we should do when we got ashore, for God would be sure to direct us to some place where we might without difficulty recover our strength.

Hitherto she had not spoken, but as soon as we began to distinguish the features of the shore we were approaching she unclosed her lips, and again the same triumphant smile played around them.

"Frank Henniker, do you know that rock?"

"No!—yes!—can it be possible? O what a gracious Providence has been watching over us!"

It was a rock of a remarkable shape that stood a short distance from the fishing-pool. It could not be otherwise, the gannets had led us to their old haunts. We were approaching our island. I looked at my companion—she was praying. I immediately joined with her in thanks-giving for the signal mercy that had been vouchsafed to us, and in little more than an hour had the priceless satisfaction of carrying her from the shore to the cottage, and then we carefully nursed ourselves till we recovered the effects of this dreadful cruise.

CHAPTER XLVIII

My numerous pursuits, as I stated in a preceding chapter obliging me to constant occupation, kept me from useless repining about my destiny, in being obliged to live so many years on this far-distant corner of the earth, I had long ceased to look for passing ships—I scarcely ever thought about them, and had given up all speculations about my grandfather's reception of me. I rarely went out to sea, except to fish, and never cared to trouble myself about anything beyond the limited space which had become my inheritance.

The reader, then, may judge of my surprise when, one sultry day, I had been busily engaged for several hours cutting down a field of wheat, Mrs Reichardt came running to me with the astounding news that there was a ship off the island, and a boat full of people had just left her, and were rowing towards the rocks. I hastily took the glass she had brought with her, and as soon as I could get to a convenient position, threw myself on the ground on the rock, and reconnoitred through the glass the appearance of the new comers.

I soon noticed that a part were well armed, which was not the case with the rest, for they were pinioned in such a manner that they could scarcely move hand or foot. We concealed ourselves by lying our lengths on the grass. As the boat approached, I could discern that the unarmed party belonged to a superior class of men, while many of the others had countenances that did not prepossess me at all in their favour.

We lay hid in the long grass, from which we could command a view of our approaching visitors.

"I think I understand this," whispered Mrs Reichardt. "There is mischief here."

"Had I not better run home and get arms?" I asked.

"No," she replied, "you had better not. If we are able to do any good, we must do it by stratagem. Let us watch their movements, and act with great caution."

My companion's advice was, I saw, the wisest that could be pursued; and therefore we remained in our hiding places, narrowly observing our visitors as they approached. They entered the fishing-pool, and I could then distinctly not only see but hear them. To my extreme surprise, one of the first men who jumped out of the boat was John Gough, who had brought Mrs Reichardt to the island. He looked older, but I recognised him in a moment, and so did my companion. Her admonitory "Hush!" kept me from betraying the place of our concealment—so great was my astonishment—having long believed him and all his lawless associates to have been lost at sea.

He was well armed, and evidently possessed some authority; nevertheless, I thought I could detect an air of concern in his features, as he offered to help one of the captives out of the boat. The latter, however, regarded him with an air of disdain, and, though his hands were tied behind him, leaped ashore without assistance. He was a man of commanding stature, with a well bronzed face, and a look of great energy of character. He wore a band of gold lace round his cap, and had on duck trousers, and a blue jacket and waistcoat.

"Come, captain!" exclaimed John Gough, "I bear you no malice. Though you have been rather hard upon us, we won't leave you to starve."

"He's a deuced deal better off than he desarves to be," cried a man from the boat, whom I at once recognised as the fellow on whom I had drawn my knife for hurting Nero. "If we had made him walk the plank, as I proposed, I'm blowed if it wouldn't have been much more to the purpose than putting him on this here island, with lots o' prog, and everything calkilated to make him and his domineering officers comfortable for the rest of their days."

"Hold your tongue, you mutineering rascal," exclaimed the captain angrily. "A rope's end at the yard-arm will be your deserts before long."

"Thank ye kindly, captain," replied the fellow, touching his hat in mockery. "But you must be pleased to remember I ain't caught yet; and we means to have many a jolly cruise in your ship, and get no end o' treasure, before I shall think o' my latter end; and then I means to die like a Christian, and repent o' my sins, and make a much more edifying example than I should exhibit dangling at the end of a rope."

The men laughed, the captain muttered something about "pirates and mutineers," but the rest of the officers wisely held their tongues.

I now noticed an elderly man of very respectable appearance, who was not pinioned like the rest. His hair was quite white, his complexion very pale, and he looked like one oppressed with deep sorrow and anxiety. He rose from his seat in the boat, and was assisted out by John Gough.

"I'm very sorry that we are obliged to leave you here, Mr Evelyn," said Gough, "but you see, sir, we have no alternative. We couldn't keep you with us, for many reasons; and therefore we have been obliged to make you a sharer in the fate of our officers."

"And werry painful this is to our feelings, sir, you may believe," said another of the mutineers mockingly. "I'm quite moloncholy as I thinks on it."

The men again laughed; but the person so addressed walked to the side of the captain without making any observation. The other captives also left the boat in silence. They were eight in all, but four of them were evidently common seamen by their dress—the others were officers. All were well-made, strong men.

"What a precious pretty colony you'll make, my hearties!" exclaimed one of the mutineers, jeeringly, as he helped to land a cask, and some other packages, that they had brought with them. "It's a thousand pities you ain't got no female associates, that you might marry, and settle, and bring up respectable families."

"Talking of women," cried the one who had first spoken, "I wonder what became of the one we left here so cleverly when we was wrecked at this here place six years ago."

John Gough looked uneasy at this inquiry, as if the recollection was not agreeable to him.

"And the Little Savage," continued the fellow, "what was agoing to send his knife into my ribs for summat or other—I forget what. They must have died long ago, I ain't no doubt, as we unfortnitely left 'em nothin' to live upon."

"No doubt they died hand in hand, like the Babes in the Wood," said another.

I still observed John Gough; he seemed distressed at the turn the conversation had taken.

"Now, mates," he said hurriedly, "let us return to the ship. We have done what we came to do."

"I votes as we shall go and see arter the Missionary's woman and the Little Savage," cried the fourth. "I should like, somehow, to see whether they be living or not, and a stroll ashore won't do any on us any harm."

"I shall remain here till you return," said John Gough; and he threw himself on the grass with his back towards me, and only a few yards from the place in which we were concealed. The rest, after making fast the boat, started off on an exploring expedition, in the direction of the old hut.

CHAPTER XLIX

The captives were grouped together, some sitting, and some standing. Not one of them looked dejected at his fate; though I could see by their movements that they were impatient of the bonds that tied them. My attention was most frequently directed to the old gentleman who had been addressed as Mr Evelyn. Notwithstanding the grief expressed in his countenance, it possessed an air of benevolence and kindness of heart that even his settled melancholy did not conceal. I could not understand why, but I felt a deeper interest for this person than for any of the others—a sort of yearning towards him, mingled with a desire to protect him from the malice of his enemies.

Almost as soon as they were gone, John Gough beckoned to Mr Evelyn to sit down by his side. Possibly this was done to prevent his assisting his companions to regain their liberty, as he, not being pinioned like the rest, might easily have done, and they might have overpowered their guard before his companions could come to his assistance. But Gough was well armed, and the rest being without weapons of any kind, it was scarcely probable that they would have risked their lives in so desperate an attempt.

Mr Evelyn came and quietly sat himself down in the place indicated. I observed him with increasing interest, and singular to relate, the more I gazed on his venerable face, the more strongly I felt assured that I had seen it before. This of course was impossible, nevertheless, the fancy took possession of me, and I experienced a strange sensation of pleasure as I watched the changes his features underwent.

"John Gough, I am sorry to see you mixed up in this miserable business," said he, mildly addressing his companion. The other did not answer, and as his back was turned towards me I could not observe the effect the observation had upon him.

"The men who have left us I know to be bad men," continued the speaker; "I expect nothing but wickedness from them. But you I am aware have been better brought up. Your responsibility therefore becomes the greater in assisting them in their villainy."

"You had better not let them hear you, Mr Evelyn," replied Gough, at last, in something like a surly tone; "I would not answer for the consequences."

"Those I do not fear," the other answered. "The results of this transaction can make very little difference to a man on the verge of the grave, who has outlived all his relatives, and has nothing left to fall back upon but the memory of his misfortunes: but to one in the prime of life like yourself, who can boast of friends and relatives who feel an interest in your good name, these results must be serious indeed. What must be the feelings of your respectable father when he learns that you have joined a gang of pirates; how intense must be the grief of your amiable mother when she hears that you have paid the penalty that must sooner or later overtake you for embracing so lawless a life."

"Come, Mr Evelyn," exclaimed Gough, though with a tremulousness in his voice that betrayed the state of his feelings, "you have no right to preach to me. I have done as much as I could for you all. The men would have made short work with you, if I had not interposed, and pointed out to them this uninhabited island."

"Where it seems you left a poor woman to be starved to death," continued Mr Evelyn.

"It was no fault of mine," replied the man; "I did all I could to prevent it."

"It would have been more manly if you had remained with her on this rock, and left your cowardly associates to take their selfish course. But you are weak and irresolute, John Gough; too easily persuaded into evil, too slow to follow the impulses of good. The murder of that poor woman is as much your deed as if you had blown her brains out before you abandoned her. Indeed I do not know but what the latter would have been the less criminal."

John Gough made no answer. I do not think, however, his mind was quite easy under this accusation, for he seemed restless, and kept playing with his pistols, with his eyes cast down.

"Your complicity in this mutiny, too, John Gough, is equally inexcusable," continued Mr Evelyn. "It was your duty to have stood by Captain Manvers and his officers, by which you would have earned their eternal gratitude, and a handsome provision from the owners of the vessel."

"It's no use talking of these things now, Mr Evelyn," said Gough, hurriedly. "I have taken my course. It is too late to turn back. Would to God," he added, dashing his hand violently against his brow, "I had had nothing to do with it."

"It is never too late, John Gough, to do good," here cried out Mrs Reichardt, as she rose from her place of concealment, as much to my surprise as that of all who could observe her. But nothing could equal the astonishment of Gough when he first caught sight of her features;—he sprang to his feet, leaving his pistols on the ground, and clasping his hands together, exclaimed, "Thank God, she is safe!"

"Yes," she replied, approaching him and taking his hand kindly. "By an interposition of Providence, you are saved from the guilt of one murder. In the name of that God who has so signally preserved you against yourself, I command you to abandon your present wicked designs."

The man hesitated, but it seemed as if he could not take his gaze from her face, and it was evident that her presence exerted an extraordinary influence over him. In the meantime I had made my appearance on the scene, not less to the astonishment of the lookers-on; and my first act was to take possession of the pair of pistols that Gough had left on the ground; my next to hurry to the group of captives, who had been regarding us, in a state as it were of perfect bewilderment, and with my American knife to cut their bonds.

"I will do whatever you think proper," said John Gough. "Believe me I have been reluctantly led into this, and joined the mutiny knowing that I should have been murdered if I did not."

"You must endeavour to make what amends are in your power," continued Mrs Reichardt, "by assisting your officers in recovering possession of the ship."

"I will gladly assist in whatever they may think feasible," said the man. "But we must first secure the desperate fellows who have just left us, and as we are but poorly provided with weapons, that of itself will be a service of no slight danger. To get possession of the ship I am afraid will be still more hazardous; but you shall find me in the front of every danger."

Here Captain Manvers and the others came up to where John Gough and Mrs Reichardt were conversing; he heard Gough's last speech, and he was going to say something, when I interposed by stating that there was no time now for explanations, for in a few minutes the fellows who had gone to the hut would return, and the only way to prepare for them was for the whole party to go to our house, to which Mrs Reichardt would lead them, where they would find plenty of arms and ammunition. In the meantime I would keep watch, and observe their motions, and by firing one of the pistols would signal to them if I was in any danger. Lastly, I recommended that the oars should be removed from the boat, to prevent the mutineers making their escape to the ship.

My appearance and discourse attracted general attention. I particularly noticed that Mr Evelyn started as soon as he caught sight of me, and appeared to observe me with singular carefulness; but that, no doubt, arose from my unexpected address, and the strange way in which I had presented myself before him.

The Captain approving of my proposal, the whole party, after taking away the boat's oars, moved off rapidly in the direction of the house. I again concealed myself in the grass, and waited the return of the mutineers. They did not remain away long. I could hear them approaching, for they laughed and shouted as they went along loud enough to be heard at a considerable distance. When they began to descend the rocks, they passed so close to me, that I could hear every word that was spoken.

"Well, flesh is grass, as the parson says," said Jack; "they must have died sooner or later, if we hadn't parted company with so little ceremony. But, hallo! my eyes and limbs! Where's John Gough? Where's the captain? Where's all on 'em?"

It is impossible to express the astonishment of the men on reaching the spot where they had so lately left their prisoners, and discovering that not a trace of them was to be seen. At first they imagined that they had escaped in the boat, but as soon as they saw that the boat was safe, they gave up that idea. Then they fancied John Gough had taken the prisoners to stroll a little distance inland, and they began to shout as loud as their lungs would permit them. Receiving no response, they uttered many strange ejaculations, which I could not then understand, but which I have since learned were profane oaths; and seemed at a loss what to do, whether to wander about the island in search of them, or return to their ship.

Only one chanced to be for the former, and the others overruled him, not thinking it was worth their while to take so much trouble as to go rambling about in a strange place. They seemed bent on taking to the boat, when one of them suggested they might get into a scrape if they returned without their companion. They finally resolved on sitting down and waiting his return.

Presently, one complained he was very sleepy, as he had been too busy mutineering to turn into his hammock the previous night, and the others acknowledged they also felt an equal want of rest from the same cause. Each began to yawn. They laid themselves at their full length along the grass, and in a short time I could hear by their snoring, as Jackson used to do, that they were asleep.

I now crept stealthily towards them on my hands and knees, and they were in such a profound sleep, that I had no difficulty whatever in removing the pistols from their belts. I had just succeeded in this, when I beheld the captain, and John Gough, and Mr Evelyn, and all the rest of them, well armed with guns and pistols, approaching the place where we were.

In a few minutes afterwards the mutineers were made prisoners, without their having an opportunity of making the slightest resistance. I was much complimented by the captain for the dexterity with which I had disarmed them; but while I was in conversation with him, it is impossible to express the surprise I felt, on seeing Mr Evelyn suddenly rush towards me from the side of Mrs Reichardt, with whom he had been talking, and, embracing me with the most moving demonstrations of affection, claim me as his grandson.

The mystery was soon explained. Mr Evelyn had met so many losses in business as a merchant, that he took the opportunity of a son of his old clerk—who had become a captain of a fine ship, employed in the South American trade—being about to proceed on a trading voyage to that part of the world, to sail in his vessel with a consignment of goods for the South American market. He had also another object, which was to inquire after the fate of his long-lost daughter and son-in-law, of whom he had received no certain intelligence, since the latter took ship with the diamonds he had purchased to return home. The vessel in which they sailed had never been heard of since; and Mr Evelyn had long given up all hopes of seeing either of them again, or the valuable property with which they had been entrusted.

On their going to the house, he had asked Mrs Reichardt my name, stating that I so strongly resembled a very dear friend of his, he believed had perished many years ago, that he felt quite an interest in me. The answer he received led to a series of the most earnest inquiries, and Mrs Reichardt satisfied him on every point, showed him all the property that had formerly been in the possession of Mrs Henniker and her husband: related Jackson's story, and convinced him, that though he had lost the daughter for whom he had mourned so long, her representative existed in the Little Savage, who was saving him from the fate for which he had been preserved by the mutineers.

I have only to add, that I had the happiness of restoring to my grandfather the diamonds I had obtained from Jackson, which were no doubt very welcome to him, for they not only restored him to affluence, but made him one of the richest merchants upon Change.

I was also instrumental in obtaining for the captain the command of his ship, and of restoring discipline amongst the crew. The ringleaders of the mutiny were thrown into irons, and taken home for trial; this resulted in one or two of them being hanged by way of example, and these happened to be the men who so barbarously deserted Mrs Reichardt. She accompanied me to England in Captain Manvers's vessel, for when he heard of the obligations I owed her, my grandfather decided that she should remain with us as long as she lived. We however did not leave the island until we had shown my grandfather, the captain, and his officers, what we had effected during our stay, and every one was surprised that we could have produced a flourishing farm upon a barren rock. I did not fail to show the places where I had had my fight with the python, and where I had been pursued by the sharks, and my narrative of both incidents seemed to astonish my hearers exceedingly.

I must not forget to add, that the day before our departure, John Gough came to me privately, and requested my good offices with the captain, that he might be left on the island. He had become a very different character to what he had previously been; and as there could be no question that the repentance he assumed was sincere, I said all I could for him. My recommendation was successful, and I transferred to John Gough all my farm, farming stock, and agricultural implements; moreover, promised to send him whatever he might further require to make his position comfortable. He expressed great gratitude, but desired nothing; only that his family might know that he was well off, and was not likely to return.

Perhaps John Gough did not like the risk he ran of being tried for mutiny, or was averse to sailing with his former comrades; but whatever was the cause of his resolution, it is certain that he remained behind when the ship left the island, and may be there to this hour for all I know to the contrary.

We made a quick voyage to England, and as my readers will no doubt be glad to hear, the Little Savage landed safely at Plymouth, and was soon cordially welcomed to his grandfather's house in London.

THE END.